"Arend writes gripping, emotional, heart-filled [romances] that grab you by the heart and don't let go until the very last page."
—Jaci Burton, *New York Times* bestselling author

"All the passion, thrills, and excitement any reader can ask for! Vivian Arend takes you on a wild ride of unforgettable emotion, sizzling sensuality, and breathtaking action."
—Maya Banks, *New York Times* bestselling author

"A pulse-pounding romance . . . There are many things that set this book apart from what's out on the market today . . . [It] fuses together passion, danger, and excitement in what promises to be a highly unique series!"   —*Fresh Fiction*

"I found myself holding my breath and sitting on the edge of my seat."   —*Night Owl Reviews*

"This is definitely a series I will follow."   —*Smexy Books*

"[It] kicks ass! This is the best romance I've read this year!"
—*Joyfully Reviewed*

"An impressive romance that lives up to its series name . . . a thrill ride from start to finish and [it] perfectly combines romance, sexiness, and adventure . . . Don't miss this one. I highly recommend it."   —*Romance Novel News*

"Arend's characters are complex, charismatic, and realistic, while the frequent and increasingly daring sex scenes threaten to scorch the pages."   —*Publishers Weekly*

Churchill County Library
553 S. Maine Street
Fallon, Nevada 89406
(775) 423-7581

continued . . .

"Arend provides a stellar mix of searing sex and emotional exploration that will keep you glued to the page! Sizzletastic!"
—*RT Book Reviews*

Praise for the novels of
New York Times bestselling author Vivian Arend

"An adrenaline rush of fiery, all-consuming passion and breathtaking romance."
—Jaci Burton, *New York Times* bestselling author

"The bitter cold of Alberta, Canada, is made toasty warm by the super-sexy Coleman brothers of Six Pack Ranch . . . skillfully written erotic passion." —*Publishers Weekly*

"Vivian Arend pours intense passion into her novels."
—*Library Journal*

"Arend once again proves that no matter what the genre, she's a master." —Lauren Dane, *New York Times* bestselling author

"This is a new favorite cowboy series, and a must read!"
—*The Book Pushers*

"[A] rare combination of romance, adventure, humor, and screaming hot sex, all in one." —*Long and Short Reviews*

"Arend instills humor and heart into a story."
—*Book Lovers Inc.*

"I have fallen in love with this paranormal werewolf shifter series by Vivian Arend. With her humorous writing style, the off-the-chart chemistry and love scenes, and the endearing and wonderful characters, this series has become auto-buy." —*Pearl's World of Romance*

Berkley titles by Vivian Arend

HIGH RISK
HIGH PASSION
HIGH SEDUCTION

HIGH
SEDUCTION

VIVIAN AREND

BERKLEY BOOKS, NEW YORK

THE BERKLEY PUBLISHING GROUP
Published by the Penguin Group
Penguin Group (USA) LLC
375 Hudson Street, New York, New York 10014

USA • Canada • UK • Ireland • Australia • New Zealand • India • South Africa • China

penguin.com

A Penguin Random House Company

HIGH SEDUCTION

A Berkley Book / published by arrangement with the author

Copyright © 2014 by Vivian Arend.
Penguin supports copyright. Copyright fuels creativity, encourages diverse voices,
promotes free speech, and creates a vibrant culture. Thank you for buying an authorized
edition of this book and for complying with copyright laws by not reproducing, scanning,
or distributing any part of it in any form without permission. You are supporting writers
and allowing Penguin to continue to publish books for every reader.

BERKLEY® is a registered trademark of Penguin Group (USA) LLC.
The "B" design is a trademark of Penguin Group (USA) LLC.

For information, address: The Berkley Publishing Group,
a division of Penguin Group (USA) LLC,
375 Hudson Street, New York, New York 10014.

ISBN: 978-0-425-26335-8

PUBLISHING HISTORY
Berkley mass-market edition / February 2014

PRINTED IN THE UNITED STATES OF AMERICA

10 9 8 7 6 5 4 3 2 1

Cover art by Gene Mollica.
Cover design by Lesley Worrell.
Interior text design by Laura K. Corless.

This is a work of fiction. Names, characters, places, and incidents either are the product
of the author's imagination or are used fictitiously, and any resemblance to actual persons,
living or dead, business establishments, events, or locales is entirely coincidental.

If you purchased this book without a cover, you should be aware that this book is
stolen property. It was reported as "unsold and destroyed" to the publisher, and neither
the author nor the publisher has received any payment for this "stripped book."

For those who were told it couldn't be done,
and did it anyway

CHAPTER 1

,,,,,,,,,,,,,,,,,,,,,,,,,,,,

A low buzz of propellers settled in his ears, then inched down his spine like an eerie warning. Timothy Dextor planted his feet a little more firmly on the gravel. He leaned on his truck door and stared upward, waiting for the first glimpse of the chopper to break through the low December cloud cover.

The deep-toned buzz in the distance increased in volume briefly before stuttering. The noise smoothed momentarily, then choked again, leaving a far quieter pulse accompanied by the thin whistle of the north wind.

His heartbeat skipped, then changed to a rapid pulse as the bright red body of a chopper burst from the clouds. A red top, twirling as it fell, the side-to-side motion barely balanced by the spin.

The rapid descent could mean disaster within the next thirty seconds. That is, if someone other than who he expected was flying.

Sure enough, the next move was not a continued free fall

toward certain death, but the reignition of the tail rotor. With
a smooth swoop toward the clearing on the north, the helicopter leveled then hovered over the treetops with scant
meters to spare.

Tim grinned. Good to know some things hadn't changed.
The entire time it took for the chopper to circle then land
neatly beside the large industrial-looking building, he was
busy thinking about the things that had changed. Like him.
Like his priorities.

Changes that meant the meeting that was now inevitable
would be fiery and exciting and, hopefully, far more satisfying than the last time they'd been involved. Him and Erin.

The passenger door on the chopper opened. A slim man
eased himself to the ground, pausing to rest his hands on
his knees. His head hung low, and his body language
screamed his discomfort as he fought to stay vertical. By
the time the main propellers slowed their rotation, the man
had finally found his feet and made his way none too steadily
toward the building.

Such a typical Erin tactic.

Tim was too far away to see details, but he could picture
her perfectly. The thick mass of hair she kept drawn back
into a ponytail most of the time. Her smooth dark skin, soft
under his fingers. Her long, lean body, firm under his
demanding touch. Her dark eyes that would glitter at him
in amusement. In passion. Flash all too often in anger.

All those images were crystal clear in his memory.

It was definitely Erin who exited the pilot's door a minute
later. Confident body position, head held high. Damn near
cocky in her circle around the chopper and subsequent strut
to headquarters.

Yeah, that was something that hadn't changed one bit,
and Tim was glad. Of course, it also meant his chances of
getting kicked in the nuts sometime in the next hour were
at an all-time high.

The thought of the coming storm shouldn't have made him grin so hard.

It had taken five minutes longer than Erin Tate expected to break the most recent applicant. Five minutes, and a spiraling descent wild enough that if she'd been a passenger and not behind the controls of the chopper, even she might have questioned their chances of survival.

Only she was the one handling the stick and adjusting controls, and that made all the difference. It was why she'd avoided the fate of the newest member wannabe to the Lifeline team who was in the change room attempting to pull himself together after his abrupt and explosive episode of nausea.

She squared her shoulders, stared at the wall, and determinedly hid the smirk that wanted to escape.

Across the room, her boss tossed her a dirty look. "You realize I'm on to you, right?"

"Of course, you are. Sir."

Marcus Landers snorted his disbelief. "And don't try to hand me that ultra-polite *sir* shit. Not now. Not after you've convinced all the candidates I'd shortlisted that they'd rather be stationed on Kodiak Island than join the insane crew based in Banff. What are we supposed to do on the next call-out? Go without a paramedic?"

"I have no objection to a competent search-and-rescuer joining the team," Erin insisted.

"Sure looks that way to me." Marcus tossed five files onto his desk, the papers spreading like fall leaves tossed in the wind. "All qualified, all eager to move here, and the longest any of them lasted is three weeks. I deserve an explanation. What is your goddamn problem?"

Erin eased back on her flippant mind-set a notch. It wasn't Marcus's fault, but he needed to understand she wasn't deliberately being a troublemaker. "I didn't like their attitudes," she shared honestly.

"Their attitudes?" Marcus's brows were near the ceiling. "This from the woman who tells me to fuck off on a regular basis, and you had a problem with their *attitudes*?"

Erin twisted to face him.

Marcus had established their elite search-and-rescue team years ago with the reputation of hiring only the best. They went into remote areas and hauled people out of danger at the risk of their own lives. Climbers, avalanche specialists—people not only skilled in what they did, but who craved the adrenaline rush that came from staring death in the face and snatching people from the edge of disaster.

He leaned back in his chair and waited expectantly, and a frustrated sigh escaped her. Marcus supported their team through thick and thin. His experience in the field before he'd lost his arm and been grounded meant he knew what they were up against.

Trouble was, he occasionally focused too hard on the job skills rather than the weakest link in the people themselves. Erin almost hated to do it, but her boss needed to be schooled in one harsh reality. "I've never suggested you drop to your knees and service me, though, have I?"

Instant shock registered on his face. "You've got to be kidding."

"The one who lasted three weeks finally cornered me in the change room to suggest he'd waited long enough for a taste of brown sugar."

"Crap." Marcus took a deep breath. "Erin, I'm damn sorry."

She shrugged. "Not your fault the members of the old-boys' club are threatened by a female in a position of authority. You aren't the one with the problem." Erin stiffened her spine again. "Only I won't work with the asses."

"Which means it is my problem. We need a full team in place before the winter holiday season gets under way."

Marcus rested his one good hand on the desk, his amputated left arm tight to his body as he stood. "The medics from the hospital—they're good on a temporary basis?"

"Never had an issue with any of them."

He nodded, then made a face. "I'll arrange for more loaners while I extend the search for new members, but in the meantime?"

Erin waited as he strode to her side to poke his finger directly in her face.

"Next time there's bullshit happening, tell me instead of taking matters into your own hands. I don't doubt your skills or your ability to make a point. This is a team, however, and you're a vital part of it. Anyone who can't respect that doesn't deserve to be a part of Lifeline."

"Dealing with them is so much fun, though," she deadpanned.

He rolled his eyes. "Ten-million-dollar chopper, and you're using it to teach respect. How about we do it my way in the future, all right?"

Erin grinned. "I'll think about it."

She scooted out of Lifeline HQ before the next round of fireworks started. Marcus was right. While she was more than capable of taking care of herself, there was a warm glow inside knowing someone else was about to feel the wrath for their idiotic behavior.

The parking lot held one more vehicle than expected, and she paused. Her bit of showboating must have attracted tourist attention. Better to nip this in the bud and make nice—a little one-on-one conversation could hush up any potential rumours.

A tall man stood outside his truck, staring into the distance with his profile toward her. Jet-black hair just long enough to curl slightly at his neckline topped what was a lovely-looking masculine build. It was a warm enough December afternoon that she'd grabbed a light coat, forgoing the thick winter parka needed on more inclement days. This fellow wore a much-faded leather jacket, collar flipped up against the wind. A scruff of beard shadowed a firm jawline, lips that were firm and slightly parted in a cocky smile.

Hmm, under the right conditions she liked a little ungroomed cockiness.

"Can I help you?"

The stranger turned from examining the airfield to face her. A pair of brilliant blue eyes caught her full on. There were lines at the corners of his eyes, his skin deeply tanned from exposure to the sun. A vast amount of time spent outdoors was clearly written into his skin. She stepped a couple of paces closer before her eyes and brain connected.

Her stranger was all too familiar.

"Tim?"

The slightly cocky smile bloomed into a full-out grin, teeth flashing white against his skin. "Hello, love. Good to see you up to your old tricks."

The roundhouse kick that burst free was instinctive. It was wrong, perhaps, to lash out physically at someone she hadn't seen in years, but the response was as involuntary as breathing.

Her heel failed to make contact with his gut as planned, however. Instead she found her foot trapped in a strong grip, and before she could adjust her attack he'd flipped her around, catching her against his body with her arms pinned behind her back.

"Kitten, pull in your claws," he warned.

His voice stroked nerve endings even as her blood boiled. She struggled briefly to assess his hold, but unless she truly wanted to hurt him, he had her locked in position. "I'm not your kitten, and you can goddamn let me go before I call the cops."

"Just protecting myself," he said.

After all the time that had passed since they'd been together, the flash of anger that hit was far too strong. She ground the word out through clenched teeth. "Spider."

She hadn't expected to be instantly set free. Had thought maybe he'd forgotten what the word meant. Or that maybe he would simply ignore her.

Yet a second later only the icy wind surrounded her.

Tim not only let her go, he retreated far enough away that they were in no danger of any further accidental physical contact. "That wasn't nice," he growled.

"Neither was . . ." She shook her head. This wasn't the time or place for the discussion, especially since she wasn't even sure if she wanted to bring up their disastrous past. "Forget it. What are you doing here?"

He raised a brow. "Isn't it obvious?"

Erin opened her mouth to lambast him for being an obnoxious jerk when it hit. Hard. "You've come to apply for the position on Lifeline."

"Right in one, love." He tilted his head toward the chopper. "Don't think you can scare me off with your circus tricks, either."

Dammit if he wasn't right. What's more, Lifeline was important to her, and the skills Tim possessed were exactly what the team needed. She wasn't going to chase off the best candidate out of some egotistical revenge. The knot in her stomach didn't make it any easier to deal with the potential issues involved in having the man around again, though. "You have an interview?"

He shook his head. "Figured I'd do a cold drop-in. Unless you want to put in a good word for me?"

Jeez. Bossy bastard had her over the coals, and he knew it. Was gloating over it.

She directed a warning glare in his direction. "Push me too far, and I swear I'll find a way to fix you. As in how they fix animals. Got it?"

She didn't wait for an answer, but simply twirled on her heel and returned to HQ. The candidate she'd shaken up earlier dodged aside and all but ran for his car as she passed. One solid tug jerked the main door open, and she was back in the staff area, the familiar displays on the walls and the relaxed and yet efficient setting calming her nerves even as Tim's body only half a pace behind set her off balance.

Marcus glanced up from where he was working behind his desk, his gaze leaping off her to the man stepping into sight on her right. "What's up, Erin?"

She took a deep breath. "Marcus, this is Tim Dextor. He's a SAR-trained paramedic. The best I've ever been with." She didn't wait for Marcus to respond, just turned to Tim and poked him in the chest, staring him down, longing for a reason to smack him a good one. "Don't fuck with me again."

She ignored the question in Marcus's eyes. Avoided looking into Tim's face for fear of what she might see there.

Most of all, though, she ignored the ache in her belly that said far too strongly that working with the man was going to be incredible and horrid for all sorts of reasons.

The best I've ever been with.

As her words echoed in her brain she had to admit the comment applied to far more than his skills as a SAR.

CHAPTER 2

Erin left the room, her footsteps echoing off the walls. She didn't exactly stomp, but there was no doubt in Tim's mind that she was staking out her territory. Showing that this was where she belonged, and no matter that she'd vouched for him, he had a lot of work to do.

Fine by him. It was only what he'd expected. She was out the front door and vanished from sight before he faced Marcus.

He held out his hand. "Good to meet you."

Marcus rose to accept his greeting, his gaze traveling quickly over Tim. Assessing. Judging. "That's quite the compliment Erin gave you."

"And a fine verbal kick in the ass, as well," Tim admitted readily. "I suppose you'd like to hear a little more about both?"

He was gestured toward a chair as Marcus resumed his position behind the desk. "If you're here for more than a tour, yes. Background résumé would be a great starting point."

Tim pulled out the information he'd prepped, placing the envelope on the desk. "Fifteen years' experience as a paramedic. I've been in Newfoundland and Labrador for most of it, the last five doing time on the Hibernia oil platform."

"Ah, the connection to Erin becomes clearer." Marcus laid the papers in front of him, glancing through them quickly. "She flew transport there for a few years, didn't she?"

"We worked together, yes." Tim laughed. "Her skills as a pilot seem to have gotten stronger since I was a regular passenger, but she's still playing the same tricks."

Marcus made a rude noise. "You caught her spinning-top imitation, did you?"

Tim shrugged. "Not a bad way to eliminate weaker candidates, actually. If they can't take a bit of a whirl in a controlled setting, they'll never deal with it during an emergency."

"You saying you wouldn't have an issue with Erin shaking you up?" Marcus raised a brow. "You got nerves of steel?"

"Plus a stomach of iron," Tim quipped, smiling as Marcus laughed. "Seriously, after the time I've spent on the platform in all kinds of weather conditions, a spinout is a kid's ride at the fair. If you don't have to lash yourself in place while doing a rescue, it's not enough to get the blood pumping."

"Can you do more than lash yourself down?" Marcus asked. "We use winch and cable in a lot of situations, but with the territory we patrol, we get call-outs with a lot of variety. We've got some of the best climbers around on the team, and we use them when we can, but all the team members are versatile. Skiing, snowshoeing—if you've been on a platform for five years, how up to date are you with winter rescues and avalanche situations?"

Tim gave a rundown of his recent updates while Marcus shuffled through the papers. Not only his training but the things Tim did for entertainment. The mention of BASE jumping made Marcus blink once or twice, but pretty much he kept his opinion to himself. They shared a few stories regarding the head of the SAR based in St. John's, a man whom Marcus knew somewhat from his previous missions.

Comfortable conversation. Tim enjoyed the discussion, at ease with the man he'd heard so much about over the years. The search-and-rescue community was small at times, names and stories shared. Outstanding rescues were discussed as inspiration and studied for training. What Marcus had accomplished with his team in the west had been noticed and admired across the country. Their work as an elite team in an area where the government resources were simply unable to handle the emergencies that arose was a godsend to the community.

Becoming a part of Lifeline would be a huge compliment, of that Tim was certain. The fact that it would allow him to get close to Erin was the icing on the cake.

Or maybe it was the other way around, in that he'd have an interesting job while he accomplished what had really brought him to Banff.

"Your certifications and skills are up to date." Marcus nodded, then leaned forward with a stern expression. "Now tell me what you did that got Erin's back up. Because while I'm interested in having you test with Lifeline, I admit to being stumped."

"Because she recommended me while she also stopped short of offering to castrate me?"

Marcus chuckled. "I know Erin. If she were pissed enough she wouldn't offer to do the deed, she'd reach out and use her bare hands. Does she have a reason for that attitude?"

Tim shrugged. "Maybe, or it might have been a misunderstanding. It was about seven years ago. We were a lot younger, and I, at least, was a lot stupider."

Marcus didn't say anything for a while, just looked thoughtful. He nodded slowly. "Yeah, we all had those days. So, if you end up on Lifeline, is this misunderstanding going to become an issue in terms of working as a team?"

"Not as far as I'm concerned, and I can't imagine Erin being anything but professional."

"You're right there." Marcus pulled a face. "Except for her language becoming more than a little colourful at times."

Tim laughed. "That hasn't changed, either, then. No, Marcus, I'm very interested in being considered for the position. I've got strengths you can use, and I'm a strong team player. You can trust me to deal with Erin."

Marcus rose to his feet. "Let me make a couple calls to your references, then I'll be in touch."

They shook hands again, Tim pausing at the door of the office. He turned back. "You don't have any rules about no fraternizing between teammates, do you?"

Marcus shook his head. "I'd have a revolt on my hands if I did. My lead climber is engaged to one of the team. And my girlfriend subs in at times." He gave Tim a harder look. "You looking for a job, or using Lifeline as a dating service?"

"The job is key, but a balanced life involves more than hauling people out of trouble," Tim said.

"Can't argue with you on that one when I've been raked over the coals too many times lately by my brother, and my partner." Marcus grinned. "With the little display of attitude I spotted earlier, if you persuade Erin to change her mind, then you're a better man than most."

"We'll see what I can do."

Tim tipped an imaginary hat, then left the Lifeline headquarters with a bounce to his step that hadn't been there for a long time.

New job possibility, fresh start. And a second chance at making both Erin and himself very happy.

It was a good goal. It was time for the changes.

Erin held herself back as the door opened and Alisha's surprised face appeared.

"Hi. What's—?"

That was all Alisha got out before Erin pushed past her into the house. "I need to talk to you," she snapped.

Alisha rocked on her heels and blinked hard. "Okay. Did I do something wrong?"

Dammit. Erin shook her head, pacing farther into the room as she ditched her boots and yanked off her coat. "No, not you, it's that damn son of a bitch—"

Devon, one of the other Lifeline team members, rose from where he'd been sitting on the couch, a twist to his smile as he examined Erin too knowingly. "Which guy pissed you off this time?" he asked.

Erin jerked to a stop. "I thought you weren't here."

"I'm back." He glanced between the two women, and comprehension flashed. "But . . . I was just leaving. Nice to have you drop in, Erin. Stay as long as you'd like. I'll go . . ."

He waved his hands helplessly for a moment, obviously searching for some excuse to hightail it out of his own house.

His willingness to make himself scarce relaxed her enough to see the humour in the situation. "Okay, I was a little rude there. I didn't mean to chase you away."

"But you'd like to talk in private with Alisha?"

She nodded.

He bowed slightly. "Then I can give you privacy. Not a problem."

Devon slipped on a pair of boots and the coat Alisha handed him, dropping a kiss on her cheek and heading out the door. "I'll grab something for supper. Any requests?"

Alisha clutched her hands together dramatically. "My turn to choose. Sushi. Lots of wasabi."

Devon sighed heavily. "When are you going to admit that stuff isn't real food? But fine, I'll be back in a while. You joining us, Erin?"

She shook her head. "I have other plans for tonight, but thanks."

Alisha waited patiently until Devon vanished behind the

door, the solid wood closing out the cold air that poured in. She crawled onto the couch and looked up expectantly. "Not that I mind you coming over, and I'm glad you're here, but what gives? You look as if you've seen a ghost."

Erin blinked in surprise. "Damn near did."

"Really?" Alisha sputtered.

"A ghost from my past," Erin corrected. "Before you picture floating white sheets and scary moans." She sat across from Alisha and considered how much she wanted to share. "Remember I told you there was someone I'd been with that was pretty serious?"

Alisha nodded. "But it didn't work out."

"I left," Erin confessed.

"Because it didn't work out. That's what I just said." Alisha shook her head. "I'm confused. You're going to have to bite the bullet and explain this one, Erin."

Erin stared at the ceiling, the tension in her limbs leaching out as she mentally forced herself to simply tell the story. "I left him. As in, we were living together, and something happened that made me uncomfortable, so I went home and packed."

A soft curse floated from Alisha, and in spite of the situation, Erin smirked. Getting the little blonde to swear was an accomplishment.

Alisha was no longer curled up on the couch like a kid with a teddy bear. She stood over Erin, fists on her hips. "Wait. You packed and left. Does that mean you never talked to him about what he'd done wrong? Was it that terrible?" She frowned harder, the expression somehow wrong on her petite features. "Did he hurt you?" she demanded.

Fire flashed in Alisha's eyes as the questions continued, and Erin held up a hand, wondering where her confidence had vanished to. This wasn't her—this hesitant and confused woman.

The fact that she'd turned into a jellyfish the moment Tim

showed up set her teeth on edge. That was total and complete bullshit, and she wasn't having any of it.

She sat upright and met Alisha's gaze. "Tim knew what he'd done wrong before we even talked about it, but yes, we did talk." Partial truth. They'd talked about what had happened that night at the party, but not her real reasons for leaving. "We talked rather loudly and vigorously, if I remember correctly."

Alisha grimaced. "Also known as shouting at each other?"

Erin nodded. "We might both have a touch of a temper."

"You?" Alisha rolled her eyes. "Say it ain't so."

"I know, really, right?" Even the lighthearted teasing couldn't settle her concerns. Erin's fears hovered like a bird on a windy day. "The fighting I could handle, and he did admit he'd been wrong, but I still had to leave."

Alisha paced away, thinking it through. She twisted back, her blonde hair shining in the beam of afternoon sun pouring in the window. "You don't have to explain why you left. If you felt you had to, good for you. But you saw him? Where?"

Erin wanted to kick herself for feeling excitement along with the fear. "At Lifeline HQ. He's applying for the position of paramedic with the team."

"Oh, shoot." Alisha's eyes got wide. "Could you work with him if he got the job? Is he good enough?"

"Recommended him to Marcus myself." Erin shook her head. "He'd be a great addition to the team. He's smart, and brave, and the man could talk the angels out of the heavens in terms of dealing with civilians during rescues."

"What's the problem, then?" Alisha asked.

"Don't let me make a fool of myself with him," Erin begged.

Her friend's confusion was clear. "And is that something that's likely to happen? I mean, Erin, face it. You're on my list of 'least likely to act the fool,' if I've never told you that before."

Erin paced the length of the room and back, nervous energy pouring out of her like she'd sprung a leak. "If anyone could do it, it's him."

"Wow, that's some kind of endorsement." Alisha raised a brow. "I can't wait to meet this master of men."

The phrase made Erin cringe. More than that, though, there was something very wrong with the little voice in her head that was pleased that Alisha was already involved with Devon, and thus couldn't be targeted by Tim.

Jealousy was another emotion she rarely felt, and she didn't enjoy experiencing it now any more than when she had years ago. "It's up to Marcus, I suppose. If he gives Tim a shot."

"I guess. But yes, I promise to kick some sense into you if I see you acting stupid around him." Alisha eyed her curiously. "Unless you decide stupid is something that you want."

"Right." Erin drawled.

Alisha folded her arms. "Don't snap to any final decisions. I mean, Devon makes me crazy at times, but I love the guy, and in the end that's the part that counts. Maybe this Tim of yours screwed up, but it was years ago. People change. Sometimes for the better."

Erin couldn't argue with logic, but the idea that Tim had changed alarmed her even more. If she'd found it difficult to resist him then, how would she stop herself now?

She chatted with Alisha for a while longer, then found a reason to leave before Devon returned. She couldn't handle any more of the two of them and their perfect, sweet relationship. No matter how vigorous their sex lives, it was still sweet, and Erin needed a dose of *not sweet*.

Good thing she already had plans to deal with that itch.

CHAPTER 3

,,,,,,,,,,,,,,,,,,,,,,,,,,,,

The rooms he'd rented were large enough Tim should have been unpacking and relaxing, but restlessness dragged him down like the barometer falling before a nor'wester. Seeing Erin had ripped through his hard-fought-for calm more than he'd thought possible, and he took the time to settle himself. To go through his agenda and get back on track.

Working with Marcus's team at Lifeline was only one option. If he got the job, great. If not, his plans still required him to stay in Banff, so he pulled out his phone and started through his contact list.

Jobs were always available if you had the skills and knew where to look.

He left messages with a few people and lined up an interview for the following day. A name went past on his phone as he scrolled through and he paused, wondering if he should bother.

The temptation to track down his old friend was too strong to resist. He put through the call and waited for a response.

"Phillip here."

"Phillip. Timothy Dextor from St. John's calling. First Street Fire Division. How are you?"

A low laugh carried over the phone. "Timothy. I'm doing well. I haven't seen you in years. Are you in town?"

"I am."

No hesitation. "If you're free, drop in for a visit. Have you seen the club?"

"Not yet, although I've heard good things." While Tim didn't plan on being a regular there, curiosity was one thing he rarely resisted. "I would love to join you. What time is good?"

"Come by about eight. I'll leave your name with the doorman." Phillip paused. "You want to play or watch?"

Tim had no intention to play sexual games with anyone in Banff except Erin. "You can show me around, but I'll be observing."

"That's fine. Looking forward to seeing you."

From outside his window a series of coloured flashes shone in and lit the walls. Tim paced over to discover a police cruiser driving slowly past. The blue-and-red lights on the roof reflected off the windows of the second- and third-storey apartments and the ground-level restaurants and shops. People wandered the sidewalks, traces of dirty snow piled to the side along the street edges and stacked waist deep over the grass in the park kitty-corner to his upper-floor suite.

Quiet for a tourist town. It was off-peak season still, and he'd selected a street away from the action, but how peaceful the location was surprised him in a good way. The kind of excitement he was looking for wasn't found in crowded bars. Not anymore.

Time for the next move.

He showered and dressed, tempted to call Erin. Drop by her house and get the next awkward conversation over with. The shock in her eyes upon seeing him had been real, but then so had the desire. There'd been a split second when she'd been unable to hide her body's response, melting into his when he'd pinned her against him.

He would offer his apologies and they would go forward. She was stubborn, but he was, too. She had to fight him and her inner cravings.

That shifted the odds in his favour.

Erin adjusted her corset one final time and straightened her skirt before heading back into the bar area. The flash of admiration in the familiar bouncer's eyes as she stepped out of the ladies' room settled over her like a soft blanket.

Soothing and comforting. Safe, because she knew he wouldn't attempt to touch her. The sweet taste of power slipped up her spine at the thought, but today instead of continuing to buzz in her veins, unease washed her. Something was off, but she couldn't see a reason why—

Timothy.

Damn him anyway. She eased a hip onto a tall bar stool and smiled across at the owner of the bar-slash-club known as The Wild. "You're pouring drinks, Phillip? Not often I see you back there."

"It's a special night. I have a guest coming in later, and I want to see his face when he walks in the door." Phillip moved easily behind the counter, pulling a bottle from the shelf and adding ice to glasses. The gentle clink as they bumped together merged into the soft music playing in the background.

Nothing rowdy or wild here, no matter what the bar's name. Erin liked the place more than the Rose and Crown, where the rest of the Lifeline team tended to hang out on nights off.

It gave her a place of her own. Something different from spending her time working and playing with the team. Because while she admired them and trusted them in the field, this part of her life was her own and she didn't want them mixed in it.

Which made the idea of Tim joining Lifeline all the more dangerous to consider.

Phillip slid a drink toward her, and she accepted it readily. He would give her the usual. Not much alcohol—just enough for the taste—and the rest mix. Not only did she have to keep her wits about her in case she got an emergency call-out, but a place like The Wild was no place to get sloppy.

Drunk was far too uncivilized, and Phillip was all about being proper. About maintaining control, a sentiment she agreed with one hundred percent.

A pair of strangers took the bar stools to her left. The nearest man stared unabashedly down the front of her corset before smiling at her. Erin returned the smile, careful to stay on the edge of inviting. She didn't want to encourage him, but there was no fun snuffing a guy's hopes before he'd even gotten started.

She turned to her host. "A guest who's important enough to make you hit the counter. You have guests all the time. What makes this one special, or do I not want to know?"

Probably something to do with the upper rooms, an area she'd put off limits for herself for so many reasons. Didn't mean Phillip didn't keep trying.

Sure enough, Phillip eyed her closer. "You have a standing invitation to explore."

Erin tilted her head to the side. "You trying to talk me into walking on the Wild side again, Phil? I do love your determination." She lifted her glass in salute and turned her back, facing into the room to observe what was happening.

The gathering this evening was smaller than it would be later in the holiday season, but enough people strolled the bar to make watching interesting. Dancing, flirting, mischief—a little of everything.

More than a few eyes turned her direction, gazes lingering on her legs, her breasts. She would readily admit she enjoyed being admired, but there was nothing else to entice her tonight to do more than observe the crowd.

The man to her right leaned in closer. "Can I buy you a drink?"

She indicated her glass. "Already have one, thanks."

He held his beer bottle in the air to match hers. "Then, bottoms up."

The guy was so darn earnest Erin wanted to laugh, at least until he snuck a hand around her uninvited, talking loudly as he introduced himself.

Erin glanced wordlessly at Phillip.

Phillip motioned with his head, and a moment later a bouncer was there, gently guiding her next-door drinker and his buddy to a private table. The offer of preferential treatment distracted them even as they were conducted away.

Erin leaned on the bar, amused by the interaction. "Am I causing problems, Phillip?" she asked.

He shrugged. "You would enjoy yourself a lot more upstairs than down here pushing my patrons' buttons for whatever small edge it knocks off your itch."

The judgmental assessment was unexpected. She twisted on her stool and took him in, his unreadable eyes examining her silently until she had to look away. "My body, my choice."

There was nothing she could say more powerful—that they'd established the first time he'd proposed she might like to join the private section of his club. She knew what went on upstairs. Knew it too well, and had rejected it thoroughly.

Timothy.

The fact that she'd chosen to come here tonight of all nights suddenly disgusted her. Another example of her having lost her spine the instant the man stepped into her territory.

This had been a bad idea from the start. She picked up her purse. "Thanks for the drink. I think I'll call it a night."

Phillip's classic control wavered. "But you just—" He

glanced over her shoulder, and his expression broke into a smile. "—must meet someone before you go."

Out of nowhere a sense of complete dread struck. What were the odds? How was it possible? But she was nearly positive before she'd seen the proof.

Her bar stool was slowly rotated until she looked into the deepest of sky-blue eyes matched by the sexiest smile.

"Of all the gin joints, right?" Tim drawled. "You're looking lovely, kitten."

A shiver rolled up her arm as he took her hand and delicately lifted it to his lips. When he paused, waiting for permission, she knew what she had to say. What she had to do.

Get the hell out of there. Run. Hide. Do anything but dip her chin slightly and give the man permission.

She should have known he couldn't simply arrive and throw her world into a whirlwind. The dark blue dress shirt he wore lay open at the collar, the colour complementing his deep tan. The scruff that had covered his chin earlier in the day was shaved clean, so clean she wanted to rub against his skin to test the satiny smoothness. His hair was slightly unruly as if he'd recently dragged a hand through it, or crawled out of bed after hours of sweaty sex . . .

. . . and this was not where she wanted her brain to go. Not really. Tim didn't help her stick to platonic thoughts, though, as he slowly rotated her hand until her palm lay upward. Then he gently kissed the inside of her wrist.

There was no way anyone could have missed her reaction. The entire damn bar might have shaken along with her body.

"I take it you two know each other?" Phillip didn't try to hide his amusement.

Tim didn't let her go, but simply answered the question without taking his gaze from where it was fixed on Erin's face. "We've met a time or two."

"I was just inviting Erin to come upstairs for a visit." It was clear Phillip was delighted by the turn of events. "Perhaps you can entice her to join us."

Erin reached deep and broke the spell Timothy was weaving. She shifted until she slid off the stool, her high-heeled boots landing on either side of his leg. The bare skin of her inner thighs brushed roughly against the stiff fabric of his dark black jeans.

"Thanks, but you'll have to take Tim for a tour on your own." She stepped around him, ignoring the urge to rub wantonly. There was only one solution to the situation. Diversion and distraction. "I have someone waiting for me."

Tim twisted to watch as she worked her way across the floor to where a couple of men were seated in a private booth.

"Well done," Phillip goaded him. "I've never seen anyone get her feathers ruffled in that short a time before."

Tim ignored the rebuke and focused on the priorities. "Does she know them?"

"No."

Great. He'd pushed her into someone else's arms for the night. He fought the grumble of possessiveness that suggested he storm across the room and relocate the man's nose up his ass. Erin slipped onto the seat next to one stranger and cozied in tight.

Tim deliberately faced Phillip. "Erin's a regular, then. Does she ever play?"

The other man shook his head. "Told me she wasn't interested in anything more than people watching and enjoying what she could safely get down here. I enjoy having her around, and the locals like her. She's smart and sassy, and doesn't take shit from anyone."

"But she never goes upstairs, and she never goes home with anyone," Tim guessed.

"You're good," Phillip admitted. "No. Most locals come for the views and the drinks, not the entertainment offered upstairs."

A sense of something he could have called happiness hit

Tim hard at the news that Erin wasn't a regular among The Wild's more specific clientele. "I'll take a pass on the tour tonight."

Phillip smiled shrewdly. "You staying in town, then?"

"I'll be around. Don't know if I'll be doing more than stopping for a drink."

His friend's gaze surveyed the main bar again, lingering where Erin was located. "If you're planning on getting involved with her, I can see your sense of danger hasn't diminished over the years."

Tim tipped his head slightly. "It's not about the risk, Phillip. She's the one that got away, and I intend to fix my mistakes, for both our sakes."

"Good luck with that." Phillip gestured toward the room. "Your mark is leaving."

Tim slipped a business card over the counter toward his friend. "Get in touch. We'll have dinner and get caught up for real. Excuse me while I run."

Phillip took the card with a laugh. "You're not going to be simply running, my friend. I hope you're ready for an all-out sprint."

By the time Tim twisted toward where he'd last seen Erin, she'd made it to the door. One of the men from the table had an arm tucked around her as he attempted to help her one-handed with her wrap.

The first ideas that rushed Tim weren't pretty, until he looked a little closer and noticed that though the guy was touching her, Erin's body remained stiff, maintaining air space between them even as she smiled and teased. And when she glanced toward Tim and their eyes met briefly, it strengthened his conviction that her little flirtation was a ploy.

He sauntered toward the door, not wanting to spook her all over into making a decision she'd regret. If she wanted to go home with some stranger, that was her choice. Having her go home with the ass just to make a point to Tim would be wrong.

Only, on the other side of the door his assumptions were justified. The guy who'd escorted Erin stood against the wall, frustration on his face.

There was no sign of Erin.

Tim leaned next to the guy, offering a lighter when the man fumbled in his pockets, a cigarette dangling from his lips. "Troubles?" Tim asked.

The guy lit the smoke gratefully before pointing down the street. "My evening's entertainment took a phone call, then disappeared," he grumbled. "She's a doctor, can you believe it? Had to run to the hospital for some kind of emergency."

"Bummer," Tim answered in agreement, which was better than smacking the guy a hard one for considering any woman, not just Erin, his "evening's entertainment." "The night is young, though."

The man nodded. "Yeah."

Tim left him holding up the building and paced the sidewalk, turning his collar up against the strong wind that had risen since he'd entered the bar. A Chinook was brewing, the strong winds from the west that could change the temperatures from below freezing to summertime heat in only hours. Ice crystals stung his skin as the wind howled past.

Erin was nowhere to be seen, but instead of tracking her he headed to his new home. The hunt had only begun, and there weren't many places she could hide. Not when she really wanted to be found.

Now he had to convince her of that.

CHAPTER 4

'''''''''''''''''''''''''''''''''

She'd slept horribly after ditching her "date" outside the bar. Not only were her dreams filled with heated and sweaty memories involving her and a certain blue-eyed devil, but in the sleepless moments between fitful tossing and turning, Erin felt guilty for deceiving the nameless guy from the bar into thinking she was interested in him.

She couldn't even blame that on Tim, even though she wanted to, badly. It was her own fault because *he* hadn't forced her to act the fool—and there was that word again.

Maybe she'd better get Alisha a pager so she could provide instant responses for help, like an AA sponsor. "Hi, my name is Erin, and I'm addicted to a guy who's no good for me. I've stayed clean for nearly seven years."

The midday call-out for a rescue was a welcome diversion in spite of the tiredness in her body.

All around Lifeline headquarters the team hurried to gather gear. Devon and Alisha worked in the storage room as Tripp shouted a list of supplies at them. Erin shrugged on a warmer jacket and gloves before dodging around their winch man, Anders.

"It's too early in the season for an accident at the ski hill," Anders complained. "There's been no time for the snowpack to build for avalanche conditions."

Marcus shook his head. "Details coming once you're in the air—but it's not an avalanche. The gondola lift is out, and has been for the last three hours."

People had been stuck on the gondola for three hours? Not good.

"I'm going to warm her up," Erin shouted over her shoulder a second before sliding through the doors into the icy-cold air.

Over the past twenty-four hours the Alberta weather had lived up to its volatile reputation, changeable to the extreme. Erin was grateful the Chinook winds that had blasted through last night were over. They'd shaken the town up, rushing past and dragging temperatures up.

But this morning a low-pressure ridge had turned everything around. It was cold, but calm enough that she could fly. The frigid temperatures meant other concerns, and she began checklist procedures for liftoff, contacting the local airfield with the word that they'd need clearance soon.

Marcus stuck his head in the door as she worked through systems. "No need to stop at the hospital to pick up a paramedic," he announced.

She finished three more adjustments before glancing his way, horrified suspicion growing. "Why not?"

"There's more than enough in place already. They have a full SAR contingent on the hill, only they're having issues getting at the gondolas suspended over the extreme slopes. That's where you come in."

Relief that he hadn't called Tim in was far too strong. She really needed to get over herself. "Got it. Now let me do my job."

"Break a leg," Marcus shouted, closing her in and letting her concentrate.

In a short time the team was in place and Erin lifted off, the low buzz of her headset speakers familiar and calming. Her physical response was always like this in the early moments of a mission. Having to start flying immediately ensured there was no time for the butterflies to get rolling before she had to be on the job and focused.

Tripp turned on the general speakers so he could talk to everyone on the chopper. He'd taken the passenger seat at her side, the rest of them belted into the back where they had jumper seats and stretcher space if needed.

"Everyone comfy?" Tripp asked. He got a chorus of affirmation from the crew before heading into the details. "Ski patrol and search-and-rescue trainees have been working since ten A.M. That storm that blew through last night did a hell of a job on the hill."

"Did you say the gondola is stuck?" Alisha asked. "Why don't they use the emergency generator to get it emptied?"

Erin wondered that as well. She glanced over the passing snowfields. The surface was partially covered by the recent heavy snowfall, but more spots than usual were exposed to the tree line by the strong winds they'd experienced.

"It's too dangerous. Two of the towers supporting the aerial cables have lost structural integrity, and they're afraid to move anything past them."

"Damn, that kind of breakdown seems impossible," Devon said. "I'd assume they do all sorts of testing before opening for the season."

"It's not a disaster they could have planned for," Tripp explained. "They had a power outage about an hour after the gondola was already ferrying passengers up to the hill. Nothing too unusual—figured some water from last night's storm got into one of the electrical lines and shorted the system. That they could deal with fairly simply. They switched to emergency power, like you suggested, Alisha, and had started to empty out the passengers when one of the gondola operators hit the panic button and shut the whole thing down again. He was watching a cabin rise toward him over the steepest section when the entire tower and gondola listed sharply to the right."

"Scary." Alisha looked out the window. "So they turned everything off and . . . what? Have been evacuating the old-fashioned way ever since?"

"The extremely wet fall we had, in combination with last night's Chinook winds, weakened the support base of a couple strategic towers. Too much water got worked into cracks in the rocks from the softened snow. Trees shifting in the wind, that kind of thing. Add in the sharp cold snap— conditions were primed to break a section of the cliff away. There were two small landslides this morning when temperatures dropped. Unfortunately, they happened after the lift was already full, so yeah. All the cabins need to be emptied."

"Any trees on the gondola support lines?"

"Nothing, just the danger caused by the posts. Trees on lines they can deal with, but one tower has lost the base under a full foot and the top is threatening to break away. They can't run the backup generator and do an orderly evacuation, not with that potential disaster."

"Damn, and the temperature keeps dropping, doesn't it?" Devon asked.

Erin shivered even as she stayed en route for the hill. Three hours was a long time to have no heat, or a way to move to stay warm.

"The ski patrol have been evacuating all the people they could on the sections that are low enough, but they don't want to attempt the areas over the ravines."

"Those drops are steep." Anders cut in. "Are we winching them down?"

"If the wind stays low so Erin can put you in place, yes. We'll go in pairs, partnering up with some of their people as

well. The hill has all the backup ground support in place—
we just need to get the people out of the gondolas they've
been trapped in for the last three hours."

Erin joined the conversation. "I can handle the flying,
only let me know if we're extracting them or dropping them
to bugout positions."

"Time to arrival?" Tripp asked.

"Fifteen minutes."

Erin ignored the rest of the conversation that buzzed in
her ears, even though she kept the speaker open, not only
to stay in touch but to get into the swing of the rescue. The
energy the team put out invigorated her. Calmed her, in a
way. Made her attention narrow to the here and now, which
was all she needed to focus on.

As they crested the hill and spotted the parking lot, it
was obvious not everything was business as usual. The local
SAR had set up tented areas, steam rising from them—
places for rest and recovery as they checked the people rescued from their trapped positions for frostbite and reactions.
Getting stuck on a lift for an extended period of time wasn't
something that happened often, but all the hills were prepared for it. Erin nodded at the obvious competence shown,
everything from the heated recovery areas to the orderly
evacuation of the parking area for those who had chosen to
ski out.

The ski patrol had cleared the helipad, and she dropped
onto the center easily, one member guiding her while keeping the crew who would be joining them behind the safety
line.

Tripp gave the order. "Alisha, Devon, you guys and I will
buddy up with one of their members and access one gondola
each. I'll make the call as we get there which cabin's passengers will be flown out, and which lowered to the ground."

"Can do," Devon responded.

Picking up three additional members wasn't a chore since
the chopper was rated for more. Tripp watched over his

shoulder as the SAR climbed on board before giving Erin the thumbs-up.

Additional voices cut in as the new riders slipped on headsets so they could hear over the loud rotor noises.

"Dan reporting in. Tell us where you want us."

Tripp turned to the back. "Welcome aboard. You have any preferences for belaying up or down?"

"No—we're trained in both."

Erin breathed a sigh of relief. It was one thing to take on other rescuers—their job at the ski hill meant they should have some skills. She just hoped they had enough.

Five minutes later, icy-cold wind blasted through the chopper as she hovered over the first inaccessible gondola, the first between towers connecting an extremely steep cliff.

Erin pointed to the side. "Access road. You want to see if we can lower them to there?"

"Get Alisha and her partner in place." Tripp held up a hand. "I'll contact base."

This part was when she got to play games. Very little wind, nothing but keeping level as a goal. It was all about Anders's skill with the winch, and the ability of the team member who was being lowered to deal with any spin.

Erin eyed the horizon and kept them steady as Anders counted out distance. Alisha shouted, and there was a slight bounce as the winch adjusted to keep Alisha level with the gondola door.

"Lovely," Alisha complained over the portable microphone she wore. "The locking gate on the door is frozen shut. Excuse me, cold and frightened people, while I bang loudly on the handle and freak you out even more."

Tripp cut in. "Erin, the access road is a possibility. They've got Ski-Doos on the way. Alisha, you and Dan belt them in for a transfer. There's SAR on the ground waiting to take off the harnesses."

"Roger. I'm in."

The small camera mounted on the undercarriage of the

chopper allowed Erin to watch Alisha disappear into the gondola, the heavy globelike carrier swaying as the weight redistributed.

It was one moment after another of waiting during the next thirty minutes as she maintained the chopper at level and dropped off three teams. Only once was she required to take civilians from point A to point B, moving carefully as Tripp stared out the window to offer additional guidance.

Perfect visibility, easy weather conditions. It felt good to work without her heart pounding through her throat.

They'd finished transporting the last of the gondola passengers Alisha was evacuating when Erin got a message.

"Uphill. Medical emergency—someone's having a heart attack."

"Dammit." And they had no paramedic onboard. Guilt struck at tossing the last candidate around. "Do we have someone to pick up?"

"Yes. Head to the village."

Erin lifted higher with Anders and Alisha the only other Lifeline members back on board. "How are you guys doing?" she asked.

"Drop me in the hot springs when we're done, okay?" Alisha's teeth rattled as she spoke. "God, those poor people. That was brutally cold, and I was only out in it for a short while."

"Only a little longer," Erin encouraged her. "Shove your hands under Anders's arms, he doesn't mind."

"Ha. Thanks."

Moments of lightness in the middle of the serious. Erin once again was thankful that she'd picked a job so full of rewards.

Tim's hands were numb, but he wasn't about to stop. "Where's the next fire to put out?" he asked.

The SAR next to him pointed. "You are a glutton for punishment. I thought you came out to ski for the day."

"What, and miss all the excitement?" Tim grabbed a fresh first-aid kit and ran for the landing circle that had been cleared.

His interview with the head of the SAR had been cut short when the call for help came in. And whether he worked the hill or not, he was trained. As the most experienced paramedic around, he was recruited on the spot.

Mitchell glanced up as Tim approached. "Can you take this one? My team called in a possible heart attack, but it's on the worst section of the trapped cars. We were trying to leave that gondola until the end for fear of dislodging it, but it looks as if that option is out."

Great. "No problem. Stabilize the victim or stabilize the car first?"

"You focus on the victim. The team coming in will deal with the rest of the civilians and the carriage."

Tim nodded. Then smiled wryly as the bright red body of a familiar chopper came over the ridge. So, he was getting to work with Lifeline today after all.

He waited until the chopper was nearly down, then crouched low and ran toward the open side door. Erin glanced out the window but probably failed to recognize him, as he was covered head to toe in borrowed rescue gear. Strong hands pulled him onboard, and he settled into a seat, the chopper lifting off before he'd strapped in.

He ignored the belts and snatched up a headset instead. "Critical-care paramedic reporting. You can toss me anyway you want—I'm experienced."

Not even a flicker on the chopper as Erin maintained perfect control. "Tim?"

"Right in one, love. Give me a yo-yo ride like a good girl, and we'll get this rescue finished so we can all go have a hot shower."

A masculine laugh carried over the line as the solidly built man across from him passed over a small ear set and microphone. "Anders here. I'll be the one dropping the string for you, and I promise no yo-yos. Only don't distract me with talk about hot showers right now. I think my ass is frozen to the chair."

Conversation paused as Tim switched to the battery-operated headset that would make it much easier to stay in contact during the rescue.

"I'll go first to open the door," Alisha offered.

"Let's drop together," Tim suggested. "Saves the time, and I'm sure Erin is more than capable of keeping us level. If you're up for it, Anders?"

"Erin, what do you think?"

"In these conditions—no problem."

They were tied together, harnesses checked even as they'd discussed it. Anders lowered them smoothly, and they were outside the gondola, worried faces staring at them through the fogged-up glass.

Alisha cranked open the door and Tim grabbed the sturdy metal frame, using one arm around her to help as they carefully pulled themselves aboard.

"Stay very still," Alisha cautioned the eight people clustered in the tight carriage quarters. "I'm going to get you down, and while we do that Tim will take care of your friend there."

Concerned faces shone back from all the occupants. A couple of teens and a group of older skiers—looked like a family out for the day.

The older man sitting on the floor was pale and breathing uneasily, and Tim went straight to work. He talked soothingly as he took heart rate and pulled out supplies. Glimpses of Alisha behind him were impressive. She had the rest of the family slowly putting on shoulder harnesses while she worked to buckle the hip and waist sections securely.

A sudden jolt went through the carriage, and one of the women shrieked.

"Ah, love. It's only the cables giving a bit of a stretch." Tim moved faster, stabilizing his patient and easing a harness around his shoulders before slowly rising to meet Alisha's eyes. "I can help you double up your lifts, if you'd like."

"Belaying them down would be faster," she suggested.

Around them worried faces grew even tighter. "What are you doing about my father?" one of them asked.

"We're going to get you all down," Tim promised. "Alisha, rig a harness for three. You can belay from the ground. I'll harness them from here."

Talking in code around the people they had to rescue, moving as quickly as possible without moving much at all. It was enough to get his blood pumping for the first time that day.

"Tim, channel three," Alisha ordered.

He flipped channels for his earphone even as he did up the last of the buckles on the heart attack patient. "Yes?"

"Erin says she can stay in place, and Anders will help with the belays. If you can rig your patient for winching up, she'll take you and him straight to the hospital once we're all down.

An ominous creak sounded from above as the cables ground through the metal clasp supporting the cabin. "If we can do it fast, yes. Tell her to drop you far to the side. If the gondola falls, you don't want to be under the path—you or the civilians."

Alisha reached out the door and pulled the cable in, hooking it rapidly to the other two people. She stepped back to back with them. "Ready in three, two, one."

Tim nudged them off the platform, and everyone still around him stiffened with worry as the cabin swung hard. "Next set, get ready. Alisha will be helping you down like riding an elevator. All you have to do is hold on to the rope by your chest."

Anders already had a new line outside the open doors, and Tim grabbed it, slipping the hooks into place, double-checking buckles. He placed the woman's hands on the cable and covered them briefly with his own. "Like that. Perfect. You're ready to go."

Her eyes were wide with fear.

"Not a worry, love," he insisted. "That's my lady on the other end of the rope. She's the best there is. Just give me your hand and I'll help you step out."

"You can do it," the gentleman on the floor whispered, barely audible over the noise of the props.

"Take care of my dad," the woman said, staring at Tim.

"As soon as you're gone, he's the next one I'm taking flying."

He eased her out the door, the cable from above stretching taut as she swung away from them, and once again the gondola rocked.

In his ear Anders spoke rapidly. "Tim, how many more?"

"Two and my case. I'm getting them in position right now."

"Roger. Work fast, man, you're running of time."

The world fell three feet, and the man across from him shouted in surprise. His arms stayed steady around his father, though, and Tim nodded encouragingly.

"We'll be out of here in less than two minutes."

Another horrid noise, and another jerk.

"Tim, rush it. I can see the tower up the hill and it's swaying."

Dammit. "Toss me all the lines you can," he ordered. "Now."

He'd put a harness on his patient, and the other two had slipped on the ones they'd been handed. Tim gestured them forward, hands flying over the buckles to lock them in place.

"Keep sitting on the floor. Your ride is here. One second and I'll get you out the door. You'll be bunched together, but hold on tight and let the team get you to safety. There's no time to hesitate, understand?"

They nodded, and Tim hooked a carabiner to the harness on the older man then pushed the others into the clear.

Ignoring the shuddering metal around them, he twirled,

grabbed the line, and yanked the man out the door with him, trusting that Anders had control of the other end.

They'd barely hit free air when a screech of metal fatiguing screamed out. Up the hillside above them, the tower that had been leaning ominously folded with a sudden jerk. The bottom leaned toward them while the top third bent, and the cabin fell away, dropping toward the snow-covered rocks too many feet below them.

Tim breathed a sigh of relief to be out of what would have been a death trap. Or at least he was relieved until he glanced over his shoulder to check Alisha and the other passengers. A thick strand of the support cable had snapped apart, the loose end writhing upward like a cobra about to strike.

The deadly projectile was being pulled down the hill by the runaway cabin, and the loose end reared again, now headed straight in his direction.

CHAPTER 5

,,,,,,,,,,,,,,,,,,,,,,,,,,,,,,

The shouting in her ears was hard to sort out—all of the team were going at it at once. With multiple cables dangling under the carriage of the chopper, the last thing Erin wanted was to make any sudden moves.

But having Alisha, Anders, and Tim all making noise was a clue something huge was off. And the only clear word in the midst of the chaos was a deep-toned order to "lift" repeated again and again.

The urge to respond instantly to Tim's command shouldn't have hit so hard. There was no better reaction anyway, not with the trees close on either side and the deep drop under them. She hated to take the civilians any higher but figured there was a good reason for the order. She adjusted height instantly, rising straight up. "Everyone, quiet. Anders—give me the all clear."

She eyed the screen showing the undercarriage camera view, shocked to see a thick line reaching toward them like an octopus tentacle. It snapped to a halt only a few feet away from Tim and his group as she pulled them skyward.

The order came from Anders, a breathless, relieved tone clear in his voice. "You're good. Stop rising. Holy *shit*, that was close. You okay, Tim?"

"I might need to change my underwear, but other than that, no worries."

His dry comment dragged a moment of laughter from Anders. "Okay, then. Let's head to the emergency base."

Erin wasn't sure exactly what had happened. "What the heck was that?"

Tim came back on the line. "A loose end, but it's all tied up now. You did good, pilot lady. Lifted us sweetly out of trouble. My thanks."

"You're welcome." She'd get the full details when they weren't still in the middle of an op. "Alisha, what about you?" Erin asked.

"We're good. There's another group of Ski-Doos approaching. The patrol will take us down, and I'll meet you at base."

"Tim, how is your party doing?" Anders asked. "We'll have you at ground level in under five minutes."

"We're good, but ready to get acquainted with the ground again."

"Roger that." A very calm response for hanging under the chopper, but she didn't expect anything else from Tim.

Erin focused on her task, following Anders's verbal cues as he helped guide her toward the landing pad. He winched up two lines simultaneously, and in the end he had their passengers in the perfect position as she hovered and allowed time for the ski hill SAR team members on the ground to unhook the civilians and clear her path.

The quiet in her ears as she shut down the rotors seemed too loud.

She stepped from the cockpit, cursing herself as she instantly looked around for Tim.

A red-coated SAR ran up. "You good to transport a couple people back to Banff who need to hit the hospital ASAP?"

"Anytime. Let me check in with the rest of my team, and we'll be good to go."

Erin flipped open her mic and put out a call for information. "What's your location, and who's ready to come home with me?"

"Alisha here. Devon and I are staying to help with some ground recovery. Don't worry about us—we'll get a ride back with some locals."

"Tripp is with a couple of the people you need to transport," Anders shared. "We'll take his group plus the paramedic and his heart-condition patient with us. Can we leave in five?"

"No problem." Erin headed back to get ready. "Everyone else okay?"

"No worries."

The return flight to Banff was quiet. Erin turned down her headset as the guys in the back were busy looking after the five passengers they'd brought with them for the hospital.

Now that the rescue was over, the rush of all the other emotions she wanted to avoid loomed far too large. Already she was dreading having to talk to Tim.

It was crazy, the knots she'd been tangled in. He was only a man. One she had a past with, yes, but that didn't make any difference now.

She was a professional and so was he, and if he got assigned to the team, they could work together. They'd just proved that.

An inkling of an idea struck. Maybe she needed a dose of him to get him out of her system. It had been so long ago, and they'd been young. Perhaps all the nervous energy growing from lingering over her memories was more from her imagination than reality. She'd built up their issues in her head until they'd become a disaster, and a dose of real life would knock some sense into her.

Or maybe she was deceiving herself and getting together with him was a really bad idea.

Tempting beyond belief, though.

The hospital staff met them at the helipad, taking charge of the people needing medical attention. Tim handed over his patient, then returned to the chopper to flash his deadly smile her way.

"Very nice, Erin. Fine bit of flying."

Erin smiled grudgingly. "Thanks. What I want to know is how you managed to end up in the middle of trouble."

"Like usual? Isn't that what you want to say?" His eyes glittered brightly a second before he shivered, tugging his coat closer around himself. "You know me—trouble calls my name like a sweet siren, and I'm helpless to resist her."

There were all kinds of innuendo in that sentence, and temptation poked Erin again.

Would getting him out of her system work as an inoculation? Or would it give her a full dose of the fever?

She was saved from having to decide as Tripp patted her on the back. "Great job, but I'm nearly frozen. Take us back to HQ, then I'll treat you all to a trip to the hot springs."

Oh lord, yes. "You are a gentleman and a prince."

Anders turned to Tim. "You coming with us?"

She had to give him credit. He didn't check her reaction. Ignored the potential danger—brave man—and answered Anders. "I'd love to."

Marcus eyed Tim as he paced into HQ with the rest of the team. "You again. Did I hire you in my sleep, or something?"

"That would be a first." Tim grinned. "Nah, I was out at the hill for an interview and to take in a little skiing, but it seemed the fates had other plans."

"He did great," Anders commented. "He, Alisha, and Erin stayed very cool under pressure. Very impressive, actually."

"Credit where it's due," Tim offered. "Erin did her job, and Anders knows his stuff. Makes it easier to step off into the unknown when the support team is strong."

Marcus looked volumes at the mutual back-patting going on, then let them off without a long debrief. "We'll talk about the rescue tomorrow, once Alisha and Devon return. You guys look like human icicles. Go get warmed up," he ordered.

They ended up at the Banff Hot Springs, Tim getting a ride over with Tripp. Erin distracted herself from thinking too hard by examining Banff with new eyes, trying to see it as a newcomer would. The decorative river rock covering all the buildings. Old-fashioned light posts lining Main Street. The mountains rising around town as a backdrop to the historic manors and castlelike hotels. It was beautiful and unique. A kind of medieval oasis mixed with rustic wilderness, the two meeting within inches of civilization.

Even the pool entrance featured thick rockwork on the walls, steam rising invitingly from the water's surface beyond the observation deck. It truly was a fascinating and beautiful location.

By the time Erin had changed and persuaded herself to get her ass in the water, the three guys were already gathered in the deepest section of the pool, hanging on the wall and chatting. The curved surface in the northwest corner formed a semicircle for them to see each other's faces while they floated.

She stepped in slowly, the heat making her toes tingle as the cold in her extremities leached away. The icy-cold air was pleasant now that there was hot water surrounding her.

Anders spotted her and gestured her forward, and she paced through the chest-deep water, relaxation wrapping around her physically and easing a little of the mental tension as well. It was hard to stay uptight when her body was melting.

"So we've already got the line in place to drop the kid, but he's suddenly all panicked." Tripp paused his storytelling to move aside to make room for Erin at the wall.

"We put you in the cabin with the shortest drop." Anders frowned. "Was he that afraid of heights?"

Tripp shook his head. "We had them harnessed up, but we'd told them to leave their backpacks in the corner to be recovered later. His reaction only got worse when I told him he could reclaim his bag from the base camp, and that the RCMP would be around to make sure nothing got stolen. I thought he was going to pass out right then and there. I had to promise to send it down when I could."

"Uh-oh. I see where this is going." Anders rolled his eyes. "What was in the bag that he didn't want found?"

A grin escaped Tripp. "Some of BC's finest-grown pot. He didn't have that much—he wasn't dealing, but yeah, if the kid had smoked that much pot all by himself he could have flown down from the gondola car without being rescued."

"Crazy kids." Anders rested his head on the lip of the pool, nearly submerging himself. "What the hell do they need drugs for when they're in the middle of that kind of terrain?"

"Who knows? Maybe the adrenaline rush of stepping off a vertical cliff with a snowboard strapped to their feet isn't enough." Tim slipped off the wall and stood in the open space in front of them, working his fingers over his shoulder muscles.

Erin couldn't look away.

"Like I said, crazy kids." Anders chuckled. He cracked open one eye. "You put something out during the rescue today?"

"Just tight. Been a while since I did that many buckles and lifts in a row."

"Move over here," Tripp offered. "If you're not squeamish about a guy giving you a rubdown."

Tim slipped in front of the other man. "Hell, no. I'm not an idiot."

The hot water had already taken the edge off the dreaded cold that had settled in Erin's veins during the time they'd

spent in the air. The changing expressions Tim offered as
Tripp dug his thumbs into tight muscle spots, the occasional
groan of affirmation as Tripp hit tender spots—

Erin wiggled in one spot and tried to put a name to what
was rolling inside. It wasn't that she wanted to be the one
squeezing Tim's biceps. She didn't want to be easing a thumb
along his neck muscle as he tipped his head to one side and
Tripp traced the long, strong line.

Liar.

Jealousy? Of Tripp touching Tim?

She joined in the conversation as it continued, but what
she wanted was to face away instead of being tormented as
the realization sank in that yes, she was feeling a little of the
green-eyed monster.

Turning away, though, was impossible. There was something mesmerizing as strong masculine fingers drifted over
the sculpted curves of Tim's upper body. He moved in obedi-
ence to Tripp's tugs and direction, muscles flexing smoothly,
bulging and elongating in a finely choreographed dance.
The slick of water clinging to his skin only highlighted the
shadows, making the cuts deeper, harder, his lean body
showcased like some exotic production.

"What do you think, Erin?"

She blinked herself alert only to discover his gaze fixed
on hers, laughing blue eyes catching hold and freezing her
in position. She had no idea what the guys had been talking
about.

Was it too much to hope she hadn't been noticeably
drooling?

To cover her tracks she deliberately yawned, stretching
her arms overhead. "Sorry, I was snoozing on my feet. What
are we discussing?"

Tim's gaze dropped from her face to trickle over her body
as she stretched, and once more the urge to get up close and
personal with the man rode her hard. He wasn't hiding his
admiration even as he pressed into the massaging hands on

his shoulders. "You're a miracle worker, Tripp," he breathed. "Thank you."

They separated, floating into more distant positions as Tripp shrugged. "Years of cross training—I bet we're all pretty good with our hands."

Tim's hands are fabulous in all sorts of ways. Erin caught the flash of fire in his eyes as his lips twisted into a secretive grin. As if he'd heard her private thoughts.

"We were talking about Tim joining the Lifeline team," Anders offered.

"She already put in a good word for me." Tim pushed himself up on the deck edge, water streaming off his torso and tight abdominal muscles. "I'll wait to see what Marcus thinks."

Tripp nodded. "Well, you get my vote of confidence, if you can face other rescue call-outs as well as you did today. That was a scary situation that developed out of the blue with that snapping cable, and you got out just fine."

"Thanks to Erin and Anders." Tim gestured toward them. "I call it like I see it. Nice to know I could drop in and instantly feel the confidence I did working with you. You should be proud of that."

There was such magic in the man's charisma. There was no denying its strength as both Tripp and Anders beamed. Erin enjoyed a good pat on the back as much as the next girl, but Tim's comments were made even better because they were sincerely meant.

What a mixed-up conundrum she faced. Torn between fresh emotions and a fearful mix of old ones.

She didn't know which way to turn, and the literally steaming-hot man sitting on the pool edge seemed determined to give her far too many options that led to only one destination.

Tripp headed out with a comment about picking his partner up from work. Anders left the pool soon after, covering a yawn and offering to get together soon, no matter what Marcus decided about Tim joining the Lifeline team.

Erin . . . hovered. As if she wanted to go home, and wanted to stay, and both desires were so evenly balanced she'd gotten stuck in limbo.

They moved into the cooler section of the pool, thoroughly heated by the past hour. The colder water around them was still a perfect contrast to the air temperature, and they found a place on the gentle slope of the concrete beach where they could enjoy both the water and air.

He rolled to his side and let himself admire her all over again, the one-piece swimsuit she wore clinging just right and offering a more seductive view than if she'd been naked. Nearly.

Erin lifted her head off her arms and damn near growled. "Do you have to do that?" she whispered.

"Do what?" He stroked her with the words, tempted to stroke her with his fingertips as well, but knowing it was too early.

She narrowed her gaze. "Don't play coy, it doesn't suit you."

"What does suit me, kitten?" he asked. "Or shall I tell you what I'd like to be doing instead of simply admiring you?"

She opened her mouth, anger or frustration rising once again.

He spoke quickly to finish his thoughts before she could lambast him. "Your flying is the best I've ever seen, and you've sculpted your body into a strong tool for your job. You've done well over the years. I'm happy to see it."

His final words took the wind out of her blustering sails, her lips twitching into a smile. "You haven't changed much yourself. Still able to charm the savage breast, and win all people to your side." She grinned hard for a moment. "Tripp has a boyfriend, by the way. So don't get your hopes up."

Minx. "He told me on the drive over to the pool. I wasn't

planning on seducing him, just enjoying the man's skilled touch. That is possible without wanting to become lovers."

She pulled in a ragged breath, her dark eyes glittering as she fought to match his gaze. "Pleasure without emotional attachment."

"Oh, I'm very emotionally attached already," Tim insisted, knowing that they weren't talking about the man at all anymore. "Physical and mental and emotional connections are always mixed up, kitten. You can't have one without the others, or it's like masturbation. Even the best private session is missing something vital."

Another crack appeared in her untouchable façade as a smile escaped. "What is it with you and talking about jerking off? I remember you doing that at the worst possible times, as if you were trying to see who you could freak out."

"And if I remember correctly, you always laughed. Said you didn't mind if a few uptight eavesdropping cranks got a bit of the stuffing knocked out of them."

She nodded slowly, glancing to see who was near this time, but the closest person was out of earshot. Erin rolled to her side, her lean body only inches away.

When she spoke it was in a low, husky voice that scraped his spine as if she'd applied her fingernails to his skin. "And are you trying to knock some stuffing around?"

"Just saying that emotion doesn't have to be all or nothing. I got to see Tripp in action today. I talked to people who admire him, and I've formed an opinion, which is I like the man. I don't want to fuck him, but I'd go out of my way to make him smile."

His blandly spoken honesty drew out a snort of laughter. "Like I said, you haven't changed."

He made an instant decision and shifted closer, connecting their bodies at the hip and shoulder, daring her to move away. There was nothing intrinsically intimate about the gentle brushing of bare skin.

Far, far too intimate at the same time.

"That's where you're wrong. I have changed, a hell of a lot. I'm here to prove that to you."

She took a quick breath in, a pulse beat visible at the base of her throat. "I thought you were here for a job."

It might be too soon, but part of having grown up meant he was not going to lie, not even by omission. "That as well, but I'm really here for you. I want you back, Erin, and I'm willing to work for it."

Between them the water rippled as a family swam past, the small waves cresting over her skin and his where they lay side by side. A minor tremour, miles apart from the tsunami of passion that could flood over them soon if he had his way.

Erin lifted her gaze to meet his. Stared silently for a good sixty seconds. Nothing but the gurgle of the pool gutters and low voices.

His breathing.

Hers.

She rolled toward him, increasing the contact points between them. His arm rested between her breasts, her knee slightly over his thigh, and he tensed. She was solid muscle and soft skin. A combination of strength and feminine beauty that he could hardly wait to experience all over again.

"You're awfully confident. What if I don't want you back? What if I told you that while you're a part of my past, I don't want you in my future?"

"Not even as a co-worker?"

She trickled her fingers over his chest and he held his breath, fascinated by this new side of her. Bolder, more determined. He loved it, and wondered how long she'd hold that stance.

Erin tilted her head as she dribbled water over his skin. "I could work with you. You are talented, and the team could use you."

"I have talents in other areas as well," he teased.

"So do Devon and Alisha, but I don't sleep with them."

"Touché." He crossed his arms under his head, tightening his abdomen as she continued to drive him mad. "So you won't sleep with me. I can handle that. Until you ask."

She snapped her fingertips against his stomach, the tiny blow stinging on the wet, bare skin. "You're such an ass."

"You just earned a spanking," he warned.

A low laugh escaped her. "See? There's that old Timothy I knew so well. The new Tim, if he's changed, wouldn't try to dole out punishments I haven't agreed I want to earn."

He set his teeth to stop from growling as those damn fingers went lower, teasing the top line of his swim trunks. He bent a knee to hide his rising erection because her touch was setting him on fire.

"So, let me get this straight." Erin leaned all the way over, folding her hands on his chest and resting her chin on top. "You think you've changed enough that you'd agree to fool around with me at my speed, within my limits. You won't attempt to steer us toward something stupid like what happened years ago."

"I apologized for that at the time," Tim pointed out. "While it was wrong, it was also a misunderstanding, and I knew it as soon as it happened. We both did."

"And now?"

He walked that fine line between the complete truth and what she needed to hear for them to move forward. "I will go at your pace," he promised.

Nothing mentioned regarding how far they would eventually go, or what type of pleasures, because while he'd allow her to dictate how fast they moved forward, they both knew they weren't talking about chaste kisses and handholding.

She stared into space as she considered his offer.

Did she have any idea she was still stroking him? The repetitive brushing of her fingertips sent flickers of electric desire over his skin, offering a taste of the heat to come.

Erin sat up suddenly, shivering for a moment in the icy air. "If this thing between us gets . . . awkward, I want you to leave."

He blinked in surprise. "What?"

"I have a good thing here, Tim. With Lifeline. With my friends, and my home. I'm happily established. If things don't work out, I'm not the one going wheels up this time."

"You're playing hardball."

"Damn right, I am. I think I deserve that assurance after the crap you pulled years ago." Erin adjusted herself until her shoulders were submerged again, her chin raised high. Determination in her expression.

Tim loved it. He didn't want a woman who would cave in and let him run roughshod over her, no matter what she'd mistakenly thought before. "You have yourself a deal."

It didn't matter that she was back in the heated water, Erin's shoulders still shook briefly. He liked knowing he affected her that hard.

"I have a request of my own," Tim added.

She raised a brow, the exquisite arch making her look positively edible. "And that would be?"

Tim flipped on the charm to flash his brightest smile. Turned up the accent and gave her a dose of his best Irish-slash-Newfoundland drawl. "Now, kitten, I'd be needing a ride home, if you would."

She laughed, then impulsively swooped in and gave him a hug. Tight. Friendly. As nonsexual as the earlier pat on the back he'd received from Tripp. "You are one of a kind, Tim. One of a kind."

CHAPTER 6

She took her time getting dressed, partly to mess with him, partly to consider exactly what she'd agreed to.

This was not a situation to go into without a game plan or she'd end up fucked, and not in the good way.

It was tempting to phone Alisha and beg for an intervention, but she refused to allow herself to lose control like that. She had been the one to accept his challenge. She could do this.

If their relationship stayed on the surface, there was no reason she couldn't slowly work them toward some hot, satisfying sex. The man used to play her like a Stradivarius violin. She could imagine he'd only gotten more talented in the years they'd been apart.

And frankly, she wanted to know if he was on the level. If he was going to ignore her wishes, whip out his dick and start shaking it like some mighty he-man ruler of them all, she wanted that to show up early in the game.

Before her heart got involved.

He was waiting for her outside the pool looking as if he belonged there. Leaning on a railing, his towel under an arm. Legs crossed at the ankle as he stared at the gondola tower on Sulfur Mountain and the mountain valley beyond. He'd tucked most of his dark hair under a knit ski cap, but the ends sticking out had already frozen in the cold temperatures.

She resisted touching one of the white frosted tufts, pointing instead toward the parking lot. "This way."

"It's a beautiful place, Banff." Tim took a deep breath as he paced by her side. "I miss the scent of the ocean, but that wind fresh from running over the glaciers is just this side of heaven."

"I'm in love with the location," Erin admitted. "The winters are clear and cold, but no matter how brutally frigid it gets, the crystal blue skies are enough of a reward to make me never want to give up living here."

Tim settled into the car beside her. "Ever think about traveling the world like we'd talked about when we were young?"

Erin laughed briefly. "I'd forgotten that. No, I love traveling through Canada. A few places in the U.S. I still want to see, like the Grand Canyon and Joshua Tree, but there's so much here to explore. I can't imagine running out of places to play anytime soon."

He hummed softly, staring out the window at the cliff face of Mount Rundle as they descended into town.

Things turned awkward for a moment on her part as she realized she'd used the phrase *places to play*. Those were not the memories she wanted to be resurrecting. She adjusted the car heaters to cover her gaffe before asking, "Where are you living?"

"Bear and Caribou."

Erin whistled. "Sweet. Who'd you kill to get into one of those apartments?"

"Oh, did I end up in a coveted location?" He laughed. "I

guess I was lucky, then. When I called, they said there was an opening, so I took advantage of it."

"I'm in the fourteen hundred block. Less night life, more family houses."

"I look forward to seeing your place sometime."

His response was so ultra-polite Erin nearly laughed in his face. "Don't play too hard. I want to be in charge of how fast and how far we go, but I'm not looking for a pushover."

"I'll be anything but," Tim insisted. She pulled down the side street in front of his place, and he faced her. "I will listen to you, Erin. I promise."

She swallowed hard, that final brush of fear throbbing like a warning signal before she slammed it aside and decided to take a chance. "Then show me your apartment."

It was only a short walk from the car through the security doors of the complex. Erin avoided looking directly at Tim as they entered the elevator, the pristine gold and glass doors closing with a gentle *whoosh*.

The ride up was silent but for the loud beating of her heart.

He held out an elbow as the elevator opened, and she instinctively tucked her fingers around his biceps. The move was familiar and calming even after years apart. She needed a little calm after discovering he'd scored not only a unit in the best apartment complex in town, but one of the penthouse suites.

"The view isn't anything spectacular, not since Banff building code forbids anything higher than three storeys, but I like it," Tim admitted, unlocking the door and gesturing her in.

The room sparkled, final afternoon sunshine streaming in the tall bank of windows on the western wall.

"How do you manage these things?" she asked Tim, pacing in to run her fingers over the back of the luxurious leather couch.

He dropped his gear by the hall closet, pausing in the middle of hanging up his jacket. "Manage what?"

Erin gestured around her. "You make a call and end up with a gorgeous suite, fully furnished as well, right?"

He nodded.

"You go for an interview at the ski hill and just happen to end up right where you need to be to become involved with Lifeline, impressing all my co-workers. It's as if you've got horseshoes up your ass."

Tim stood before her, slipping her coat off her shoulders, his hands lingering on her arms. "I most certainly do not have anything of the sort up my . . . anywhere."

So close. He stood so close that heat from his body brushed hers as they gazed at each other. His pupils were wide black circles in the blue, as if they were black suns set against the Alberta sky. He lifted a hand slowly until his knuckles caressed her cheek, a single, tantalizing stroke that was followed by him tucking a strand of hair behind her ear.

He stepped away and Erin sucked for air, fighting to keep from gasping. He didn't need to know how quickly he could affect her. Although he was probably already aware.

Tim had moved to the kitchen, pulling out glasses and pouring them drinks as he spoke. "It was easier renting a furnished place than transporting my things all the way across Canada. I didn't have much in the first place, not since I've been working on the oil platform."

All around them was glass and chrome. Bold wood features and soft expensive leather. The entire place screamed money. "It's beautiful."

Tim offered her a glass. "It's comfortable, which is more important. Go ahead, look around if you'd like. I have a phone call to make."

He left her, seating himself on the couch and pulling out his cell phone. Erin watched him for a moment, then took him at his word.

Earth-toned tiles underfoot gave way to deep brown

wood planks in the first room off the hall. The neatly arranged office was followed by a guest bedroom. Sparse but tidy, it looked comfortable and completely generic, like most rental places. Nothing there to make it into a home.

The next room, however . . .

Erin stood in the doorway of the master bedroom and debated the wisdom of going in. The four-poster bed with its sturdy log pillars at the corners was visible from where she stood, and that sight alone was enough to set her heart pounding. A thick quilt in a deep crimson lay on its surface, pillows at the head of the mattress.

Curiosity overtook her, and even though it was wrong, she did it anyway—crossed the room to stand beside the massive king-sized mattress. She trickled her fingers over the soft quilt, the material cool to the touch—the kind of fabric that would heat perfectly against naked skin.

She wrapped a hand around the nearest post, her fingers unable to meet around the thick support. Her breathing picked up as she squatted, ran a hand down the wood, and grasped the edge of the quilt. She lifted it out of the way to reveal large metal circles discreetly attached to the lower part of the corner posts, barely visible under the edge of the hanging quilt.

Her rapid heart rate skipped a beat. This room was definitely more set up for Tim's tastes than the guest room.

She ignored the warning signals going off in her brain and chose to walk to the window. Here on the opposite side of the house she'd expected to see the back alley below, or the windows of the opposite apartment house. Instead she discovered a small courtyard, glowing lights in strategic positions to showcase a snow-clad bench and statuary.

Erin moved to the left, away from the bed and into the bathroom, still fascinated by the mysterious parklike area outside on the rooftop. In the summer it probably held flowerbeds, or a fountain. Now in the dead of winter the snow created sculptures of its own by decorating the small fir trees and railings with pillow tops of white. The surfaces transformed into fairy-tale-like structures topped by mushroom-shaped caps.

In the distance, Tim continued to talk—a low buzz that eased her fears of being watched as she explored. She turned to stare into decadence. Soaker tub, double-sized shower. A sink counter long enough to sleep on. More mirrors than was decent—anyone tempted to have sex in the enormous shower would end up reflected multiple times.

Erin escaped the room before her mind provided images of Tim's fairer skin contrasting with her own darker tones, both of them slick and wet and . . .

There was a smaller laundry room and storage space to finish the tour, distracting enough to pull herself from the X-rated thoughts she'd begun to follow. A more serious question struck her.

How could he afford the suite on a paramedic's salary?

Erin returned to the living room just as Tim placed his phone on the coffee table and rose to his feet. The sun had dipped behind the mountain while she'd been gone, and sunset light transformed the place into a mess of red, orange, and gold.

"You like it?" he asked, moving to her side.

"Incredible. It's very comfortable."

Tim dipped his head. "You're welcome any time."

The urge to accept his offer right here and now was far too tempting, which was why she had to take a different route. She avoided his eyes, just in case he managed to side-track her. "Thanks. I should go."

The expectation remained—he would ask her to join him for supper, or for another drink, or something. After pushing so hard to start things up between them, there was no way he'd simply allow her to walk away.

Only he nodded and opened the closet. "I hope I hear something from Marcus in the next couple days, but if not, perhaps I'll see you soon."

He helped her on with her coat, his hands restrained. He didn't touch any more than necessary, not pushing the connection between them, and Erin kicked her own ass for feeling a touch of disappointment.

She'd asked for this. Asked to be in charge. Was she really going to complain when he gave her what she wanted? *Bullshit*.

He accompanied her down the elevator, making small talk about restaurants she suggested. Polite. Generic. They paused at the front door of the apartment house, Erin wavering in what to do next. She'd had this all figured out that morning, but some time in the past twelve hours the world had changed.

Tim smiled, a soft expression with a hint of mischief in it. "Thank you for a most interesting day." He leaned in and kissed her. Lips gentle against hers. Warm body only inches away as his breath caressed her cheek. He pressed a business card into her hand, curling her fingers around it as he pulled back.

The fleeting connection hadn't nearly satisfied her craving. Erin struggled to speak, but nothing came out.

His eyes spoke volumes, as if he were reading her discomfort. "Call me," he said.

And that was it. The brief kiss. A gentle touch to her cheek. Tim opened the main door and let her out. Erin returned to her car in a daze, a tingling ache in her gut, and lower.

Damn the man.

He'd given her exactly what she'd asked for. Why was she so pissed off at him?

His nerves were stretched taut as if balanced on the edge of a knife. Tim paced to the window, but Erin's taillights were long gone. The only thing left was the faint scent of her shampoo lingering on the air, haunting him.

She'd explored the suite thoroughly. He was glad of that,

even though he'd had to damn near nail his ass to the couch to stop from crowding after her, especially when she slipped into his bedroom.

He wandered in there now, full of energy he had no way to release. Or at least not the way he wished. Being around Erin, learning the chance of them coming together again, had driven his need to the breaking point.

Which was why he'd mastered himself. Stepped back and, as promised, really listened.

Not just to her words, but her body. To the things that her gaze said as she examined him when she thought he wasn't looking. Erin had some definite ideas of how she wanted this to go—how they were going to be together.

He didn't want to make assumptions, didn't want to run slipshod over her desires, but there was a sensation of . . . untruth in her words when she said she didn't want him, that she wanted to limit their desires, or go slowly.

Not a deliberate lie, but one she wasn't even aware of telling to him, and to herself. There was something slightly off between her actions and what she'd stated was her goal, and damn if he wasn't eager to help her realize just how much more she wanted.

He could wait, be patient, but in the meantime he was hard and aching, and hell if he was going to stay that way. Having the strength to follow Erin's deliberately slow lead would be impossible if he didn't take the edge off.

Tim turned off the hall lights and entered his bedroom, the slightly rumpled edge of the quilt catching his eye. Another jolt of lust hit at the realization that Erin had noticed the bed was more than it appeared.

Had she paused and remembered? Were the images and memories that flooded him as clear for her? Tim sat on the mattress and leaned back on the heavy post, pressing against his cock with a hand.

They'd been so young, so eager to try new things. Sexual pleasures of all kinds, tested one by one.

She'd enjoyed it when their experimentation had turned to ropes.

Intricate designs woven over her skin, soft white cotton contrasting with her darker skin tone and making beautiful patterns that came alive as sensual art.

Hands secured behind her back as he'd held her in place, pressing her head lower to the mattress so he could ease his cock into her sex from behind. His hardness slipping into soft, wet heat again and again until they were both ready to scream.

Or ropes to control her, to give the illusion of being subdued. Like the current setup with this bed—places to secure her limbs so she'd be completely at his mercy. Not so he could take his pleasure, but so he could give to her.

It was always about giving.

Except now, at this moment. Now his body demanded that he take. The memories taunted him, and Tim stripped off his clothes. Slowly. Once again meticulous and deliberate, no matter how tight his balls had drawn, or how heavy his cock felt as he released it from his briefs.

He paused to picture her, spread-eagle on his bed. Her dark hair loose on his pillow, her arms stretched overhead, wrists secured to the headboard. He could see her exquisite body laid out before him, and he wrapped a hand around his cock and pulled languidly. Prolonging the pleasure. Easing over his fullness, rubbing the escaping moisture over the sensitive head.

He'd done this before while she'd watched. Taken himself in hand and stood beside her to let her enjoy every move, his own pleasure rising because of her responsiveness. Her eyes huge as her tongue snuck out to moisten full pouting lips. As if fascinated by the pressure he used, the speed of the strokes. She'd stared, mesmerized, her body a lush banquet before him. Innately sensual, moving from one position to the next with her bold beauty on display.

His urgent need for release increased.

They'd teased, touching themselves while trying to force the other to the breaking point first. Dirty talk, sexual images. Tim increased the tightness of his grip, increased his speed slightly until pleasure raced up his spine.

Erin would smile, mischief breaking over her face as he'd draw closer to the end. Her fingers stroking her clit, dipping between her soft folds into her core and coming back glistening with her sweet juices.

Tim squeezed his eyes shut and gritted his teeth, attempting to hold off for one more second, to cling to the images of the past for one more moment, but it was too much to ask. Not when he could as good as taste her skin, smell the passion in the room. The desire. Her need and his all wrapped up together. Release exploded from him as sticky wetness poured over his fingers. He gasped, semen jerking from him on every pull as he used his other hand as a cover to contain the mess.

His heart pounded, his breathing uneven. They'd been apart for years, yet he could picture being with her as if it were yesterday. Another shudder rocked him, and he groaned, letting the final bits of tension wash away.

Tim collapsed on the mattress, the edge taken off, his body moderately satisfied, but his mind and soul still longing for her. For the real connection of being with Erin again.

Whatever it took, he would make that a reality.

CHAPTER 7

'''''''''''''''''''''''''''''''

Tim entered Lifeline headquarters with a spring in his step, excitement and pleasure there as Marcus stood to greet him.

"You're prompt." Marcus held out his hand and Tim shook it firmly. "Let's go through a few things before the others get here."

"Love to." Being offered a trial run with Lifeline that morning had been the next step in what needed to happen. "Glad to know my references checked out."

Marcus laughed. "After I'd talked to the first three I wondered if you'd given me a list of hired actors to contact. The glowing reports were a touch overwhelming. Luckily for you my conversation with reference number four was more realistic."

Tim joined Marcus in the boardroom, settling into one of the oversized chairs. "They didn't sing my praises?"

"Oh, he still said you were good." Marcus pushed over paperwork for Tim to sign. "But he mentioned you have troubles with authority, that you're a great team player until you think you know better, and that if he never had to see you again it would be too soon."

"I have an idea who that was," Tim drawled.

"So not everyone thinks you're the golden boy, but they agree you shine in your area of fieldwork." Marcus leaned forward, his elbows resting on the table. "I want both. Your SAR skills, and your ability to work with others. While you're on my team I expect you to check your ego and put it on the line for the others. Going solo doesn't work—not with the situations we get called into."

Tim nodded slowly. "I won't blindly follow where there's a clear danger," he cautioned, "nor will I allow another team member to make a mistake that will cost them or the people we're rescuing."

"I understand. I'm the same way, but this is where trust comes in. Lifeline works together, which means there are times that sharing solutions needs to end. The best person takes charge at the right time. Occasionally more than one option could work, and whoever is leading the mission makes the decision. Second-guessing is dangerous because it takes time, and that's a situation we want to avoid."

"Agreed." Tim passed back the contracts. "I'll focus on providing medical attention first and foremost, which means I expect to be given preference when it comes to saving lives. I don't make suggestions casually."

"That's how it's always worked with the team." Marcus handed over a set of keys and a card with a handwritten five-digit number. "Door is coded for a silent alarm—the entire building actually. If it goes off, the RCMP and I get a call, and someone will be here in under ten minutes. There's an extra key there for the supply locker. Go through and familiarize yourself with our layout. If you need to change things up, be sure you do a session with Tripp so there's no hesitation when it comes to heading out on a call."

"Narcotics stored here at headquarters?" Tim asked.

"Some. We've had a few break-ins with people looking

for drugs, so we keep a minimal supply on hand and double-lock them." Marcus pointed to the second key. "I'll show you where we keep the contact numbers for the hospital when you need refills. Also . . ."

He handed Tim a metal whiskey flask.

Tim raised a brow, unscrewing the lid and sniffing. Marcus's expression didn't give anything away, so Tim took a small shot, sucking for breath as the high-test alcohol cruised past his tonsils.

Marcus grinned. "Medicinal purposes only, of course."

"Now, you'll be one of me best-ever bosses, I'd be thinking." Tim passed over the hooch, drawling out his brogue. "'Tis a sweet dram."

"You know it." Marcus tipped back a hit, coughing momentarily as he returned the flask. "Keep it, it's yours. Welcome to the team—if you make it through probation."

Tim chuckled as he tucked the container into his pocket. "The presents usually come after I've finished hell week."

Marcus rose to his feet, gesturing toward the door. "You might need that whiskey to make it through, but I have a feeling about you, Tim. I think you'll do fine."

Just outside the boardroom doors, Tim jerked to a stop. The entire team stood before him, shoulder to shoulder, arms crossed, expressions set into unreadable neutrality.

"They're your team now." Marcus spoke from behind him, the words quiet but clear. "Everything hangs in the balance depending on how well you work together. Do you trust them?"

Tim examined each member one at a time, from the tall and muscular Tripp to the petite blonde Alisha, who seemed too delicate for the task of rescuing.

Appearances were deceiving. This group had proven themselves many times over the years—he was the unknown, the one who had to fit into the puzzle.

It looked as if that started right now. A test of some sort.

"I trust them with my life," Tim answered.

Anders nodded.

Something about the way they stood gave it away. Tim's smile grew as he spotted the items carelessly discarded on the floor by their feet. It appeared he was in for an adventure.

"Training games?" Tim asked, not bothering to hide his amusement.

"It seemed a good way to get to know us better," Devon smirked. "You ready?"

There was no time to answer. A flash of anticipation lit Erin's eyes a split second before darkness blocked her from view. Tim jolted, every muscle tightening as the fabric bag Marcus dropped over his head left him blind.

"Be gentle with me," Tim teased, his voice echoing into the silence of the room. "I've never done this before."

A broad shoulder pressed into his stomach, and he was lifted into the air. Tripp, he assumed, or Anders perhaps. No voices, no noise. No hints of where he was being taken. A blanket or something heavy settled on him, but the cold air snuck under the edges as he was carried outside.

Tim relaxed, allowing his rescuer to support him more fully. He maintained enough tension to stop from being a dead weight, but not struggling or making things more difficult.

With nothing to see, Tim relied on his other senses more. The cold sharp feel of the wintry air, the dryer-sheet scent clinging to the blanket.

Ahead of them a van door slid open.

Just because the rest of them were staying silent didn't mean he had to, but for some reason it seemed right to wait. To let them take the lead in this strange initiation. Tim settled into the seat where he was placed and waited for the ride to be over.

When they arrived, it was a place with solid concrete underfoot as he was led from the van and guided up a short flight of stairs.

A gymnasium. There was the unmistakable scent plus

the hollow echolike sounds as they entered. Tim was placed in position, his hands pressed to the back of a chair.

"If you expect a lap dance, I'm afraid I'm not very good."

That pulled a snort of laughter from someone in the room.

Small noises tickled his curiosity, but he held back from removing the blindfold. He would play the game all the way to the end.

Anders finally broke the silence. "We're happy to have you join us, but we thought it would be good to run a short training session together. The team follows four guidelines, Tim. You saw them up on the wall at HQ?"

He listed them quickly. "Have patience, move decisively. Trust your team. Give one hundred ten percent."

That earned him a hum of approval. "You're observant. That's part of what we need from you. We hope you're also creative and innovative."

"And at least somewhat amusing," Tripp added, his voice coming from a long distance away. "A sense of humour is key when we're stuck slogging through some mess for hours on end."

Tim grinned. "I'm not good at stand-up comedy, but I've been told I can turn a tale or two."

"Right now you get to show your talents in a different way." All traces of teasing vanished as Anders snapped out the order. "You've got ten minutes to assemble the team, beginning now. Take off your blindfold."

Damn. Okay, they'd managed to surprise him—this wasn't at all what he'd expected. Tim slipped off the head covering and glanced around the room.

Given that he had a deadline, his first impulse was to instantly head toward the first team member he spotted. The mention of the team rules reminded him to pause. Assessing the situation was always the first step. He had to take the time to judge the situation and not simply fly into it blindly.

He'd been right about the location. It was a gymnasium,

probably at a local school. The floor was covered with equipment of all sorts. Gymnastics, climbing frames. Old lockers.

The other members of the team were scattered around the room. Alisha was the easiest to spot where she hung suspended on the wall near the ceiling. Her eyes were covered with a thick swatch of dark material—even though she was safely roped in, she'd have to be directed to the floor.

In the farthest corner Tripp was also blindfolded, an absolute tangle of ropes and clutter standing between him and a clear section of floor in the middle of the room.

That was where Devon was found. He sat on the top of a gymnastics pommel horse. He waved at Tim, in the process showing off that his hands were tied together in front of him, extra lengths of rope leading downward and vanishing down around either side of the heavy structure he sat on.

"Jeez, you guys have a wicked sense of humour yourselves," Tim noted, turning to face Anders, who stood only a few feet behind him. Nothing tied up, nothing holding him back. Had to be something simple and yet terrible. Anders was the heaviest team member, probably two hundred pounds of sheer muscle. "Let me guess. You're not going to walk beside me, are you?"

Anders grinned evilly and batted his lashes. "Afraid not."

Tim took another quick glance but had no luck in spotting the final member of the crew. "Where's Erin?"

No answer. Bloody hell. He had no time to waste.

"Okay, big guy." Tim reached for Anders's hand. "Time to go for a ride."

He pulled Anders forward while bending at the waist, reaching between the other man's legs, and with one smooth motion Anders was draped over his back in a fireman's carry.

Anders chuckled. "Nicely done."

Tim ignored him, twirling toward the wall where Alisha hung and carefully working his way through the obstacles. "Devon, I need you to talk Tripp through the maze. Got it?"

"No problem." Devon twisted, and his clear voice rang out. "You'll need to do some ducking and crawling, Tripp. Quarter turn to your left to start."

Tim eased his burden a little before lifting them both over a bench blocking the way. "Anders, look around for Erin. Do you see her anywhere?"

"Nothing visible, but I'll keep checking."

Devon continued to drone directions in the background. Tim's burden was heavy enough that his legs were shaking slightly by the time he made it to the wall below where Alisha waited.

"I'm lowering you," he warned Anders.

A second after settling the man on the ground, Tim had the belay rope wrapped around himself, a backup loop around his leg. "Alisha, you ready to come down?"

She adjusted her stance and securely grabbed the rope. "Lower."

Hallelujah, he didn't have to talk her down. "Lowering. Walk slowly, you've got a clear path."

He kept one eye on her, glancing momentarily to the side to see how Devon was coming along with "rescuing" Tripp from the maze. The two of them were nearly together.

"Once I've got Alisha down, we're going to head over to Devon," he informed Anders.

"Still no sign of Erin," Anders warned, glancing at his watch.

How long had it been? At least five minutes, maybe more. "You're touching down in three, two, one . . . now."

Alisha bent her knees to absorb the landing as Tim slowed her to a stop. "Nice ride," she complimented him.

He was already working her rope loop free from her climbing belt. "You'll be walking in front of me toward our target. Listen to my vocal cues, and I'll guide you over the debris."

"Got it."

His heart was pounding, but he took a deep breath and did it again. Picked up Anders, put Alisha in front of him, and stepped slowly toward his penultimate target.

Ahead of them one more challenge was nearly accomplished. "Nice going, Devon."

Tripp stepped through the final tangle and into the clear. "Am I there?"

Devon laughed. "Almost. Three paces, toward eleven o'clock, and you'll hit my station."

They met at the same time. Tim lowered Anders to the floor again. Tripp waited expectantly, Alisha as well, both of them with their eyes still covered. "Give me a second, and I'll fill you guys in," Tim offered.

"I'm not going anywhere," Tripp muttered.

Tim eyed the platform Devon sat on in disgust. "Your rope is too short for you to come and help us lift the anchor rope free."

"Sorry." Devon shrugged. "Two-minute warning."

Shit. "Alisha, I assume your balance is good?"

She snorted. "Umm, yeah."

Good. Tim got Tripp and Anders into position before doing anything else. "When I say, I want you to lift straight up," he instructed them.

Alisha waved a hand. "I don't have anything to lift."

Tim chuckled. "Don't be so sure of that. Devon, lean back."

The man's eyes widened in alarm, but he obeyed.

Tim caught him before he fell, easing him safely off one side. "Alisha, you're giving Devon a lift for a couple minutes. Brace your hands on the wood in front of you to help."

Time ticked away as he arranged Devon over Alisha's shoulders, her added height allowing the man's trapped wrists to remain at a safe level.

"Devon, we need to talk about cutting back on trips to the pub," Alisha muttered, and the rest of them snickered.

"In position, and . . . lift," Tim ordered.

The entire wooden box of the pommel horse shifted position, a scant two inches, but that was enough. "Devon, drop your hands, now."

The rope pulled free from under the wood frame, and Devon cheered.

"Put it down, boys."

He had to be cutting it close. Time would be up, and he still had to find Erin. He helped Alisha lower Devon to the floor, unknotting the rope from the man's wrists. Then he pushed himself on top of the horse. Tim twisted slowly, examining the room, the obstacles. There seemed to be nowhere large enough for a person to hide. "Erin's in the room?" he asked.

Anders nodded in confirmation.

Tim collapsed, sprawling on the padded surface of the pommel horse as a sense of deep satisfaction hit. "Then I call time. Mission accomplished."

Alisha and Tripp removed their blindfolds. Devon checked his watch. "Thirty seconds."

"That's our time to spare. Well done, everyone." Tim clapped in approval.

Anders and Tripp exchanged glances. "You're missing one team member," Anders commented.

Tim shook his head. "You said to assemble the team. We're all here."

For one second he worried he'd guessed wrong, then Alisha smiled. "How did you figure it out?"

Tim hopped to the floor. "Bigger than a bread box. It's the only spot in the entire room with enough space to hold her. Also, I've been on too many rescues with kids who hid when they got scared. It was the only thing that made sense."

He motioned for Devon to help him, and together they lifted off the uppermost section only of the pommel horse.

Erin beamed at him as she uncurled herself from inside the wooden box, crawling over the edge and brushing off the dust. "Thank you. It was getting a trifle close in there."

"Glad you're not claustrophobic," Devon teased.

"Do I pass muster?" Tim asked the members who had gathered around him.

"You're quick on your feet," Anders admitted. "I liked how you got Devon to deal with Tripp. Good use of the team there instead of assuming you had to do it all on your own."

"He did assume I needed more help than I did, though," Alisha pointed out. She faced him straight on, chin held high, her attitude one of competence and power. "You could have asked if I was able to start without you."

Tim nodded slowly. "You're right, I didn't think of that. I underestimated your abilities—I won't do it again. You're capable of doing a self-belay, even blindfolded."

She held up a hand and gave him a high five. "You did well."

"Thanks."

"Now the real test," Tripp warned. "Final, most important decision of the afternoon."

Tim lifted a brow. "Yes?"

Tripp grinned. "Teriyaki or buffalo wings?"

CHAPTER 8

''''''''''''''''''''''''''

Easy conversation flowed around the table as everyone on the team got to know Tim better over a relaxing evening at the team's usual watering hole.

The staff at the Rose and Crown pub had greeted them happily before leading them to the area they'd claimed as their own. Comfortable couches slightly away from the rest of the bar and the live music. A place they could sit and relax.

Erin alternated between lazing and madly assessing exactly what needed to happen next.

They shared rescue stories—a bit of one-upmanship with a twist. Sad stories were in the mix as well. The victims who weren't reached in time, the heartbreak of having to bring home not a found loved one, but their body.

Everyone who worked in search and rescue knew it could go either way at any time. The flip of a coin, a moment's chance, and it didn't matter how skilled the rescuers were.

The unexpected could take even the best of them to their

knees without a moment's notice. It was part of the reason that Tim was there in the first place, replacing Lifeline's badly injured paramedic.

"What's the latest word on Xavier? Anyone heard this week?" Anders asked.

Devon waved. "I stopped in the last time I was in Calgary. He's okay. A little depressed, but slowly recovering."

Damn. "Seeing Xavier a little depressed is like seeing a kicked puppy. Anything we can do?"

Devon shook his head. "He needs more time and therapy. He's still got a good chance of walking again." Devon turned to Tim. "Our man who got hurt back a few months ago."

"Tough to see a teammate suffering that hard." Tim nodded slowly. "If there's anything I can do, let me know."

"Will do. Mostly, we keep in touch. Let him know we're thinking of him." Alisha stared at her drink. "Try not to feel too guilty that he's the one who's there, and we're still here."

Devon caught her hand and squeezed her fingers, but the sentiment was there, in all of them.

Sometimes the bad things that happened were inexplicable and wrong, and all you could do was move forward the best you could.

Erin waited and watched, some of her concerns easing as Tim talked about situations where he'd not only accomplished amazing things, but often placed others he'd worked with into the spotlight. The man sitting with the Lifeline team was a different man from the cocky, occasionally arrogant bastard whom she'd lived with years ago.

Working with him wouldn't be a problem. The skills were still there, the additional years of maturity adding a touch of well-deserved confidence to everything he did.

No, there were other areas she needed to focus on. Other questions.

How far should she take things with Tim? How fast? It was now a given that they would be getting involved, but staying in control was important, and unless she planned ahead she was afraid of losing sight of that, even if Tim appeared to be going along with his promise.

Devon broke in with a change of topic. "Heads up for the holiday season. It's likely to get crazy around here starting any day now."

"You've got your calendar screwed up." Anders leaned back on the couch. "It's still two weeks until Christmas."

"Yeah, but the school break is early this year," Devon warned. "My brother who's a teacher mentioned it to me. The layout of the calendar means everyone from Alberta is off starting next week. The good part is that means school's back in on January second, including the university. Expect the disasters to begin soon."

"Lots of additional work over the holiday season?" Tim asked.

Tripp nodded. "The week between Christmas and New Year's is the worst, with people trying out new gear they got as presents and getting in over their heads."

"Reading week is even crazier," Alisha warned. "Mid-February. Everyone from the university who had family commitments in December goes wild for one week. We've had to go haul people out of the strangest places then."

"Sounds exciting." Tim grinned as the team groaned at his enthusiasm. "Oh, come on. Tell me you're not all thinking the same thing."

Devon shrugged. "Fine, work is exciting, and we wouldn't trade it for anything. But come March I propose we put in for a week off and head somewhere hot."

"Hmm, now you're talking." Tripp raised his glass in approval. "To Lifeline and to excitement, whatever form that takes."

The guys took off on another tangent. Plans for kayaking in Belize or something. Alisha leaned closer to Erin to whisper in her ear. "You got plans for tonight?"

Erin shrugged. "Nothing specific. Why?"

There was no mistaking who Alisha's gaze drifted toward. "Oh, no reason in particular."

"Stop that," Erin ordered, resisting peeking at Tim as well.

Alisha's cheeks dimpled as she grinned. "You could watch a movie with me and Devon if you want an excuse for why you're too busy for your nonspecific plans."

"I don't need an excuse."

"You could invite Tim to come along," Alisha offered relentlessly. "If you want a safe place to spend some time with him."

"You're being annoying." Erin glared at the other woman. "I don't like you enough to put up with annoying."

Alisha laughed. "Now I know you've got something on your mind, because you like me plenty."

There was no avoiding Alisha's glaring positive energy. "You take perky pills this morning or something?" Erin snarked.

"It's all the regular sex. You should try it." Another noise of amusement escaped Alisha. "And you should see your face right now."

Erin could imagine it. "Somewhere between envy and exasperation?"

A small shrug of Alisha's shoulders. "You know how to solve the envy bit. I'm pretty sure I'll continue to be exasperating, so you're stuck with that one."

She winked, then turned to answer Devon, who had laid a hand on her arm on her other side.

Loud laughter rang out from another part of the pub, and Erin let her gaze drift over the entire group, not only Tim. She'd worked with most of them for years now, and it had taken time for her to settle into actually liking them outside rescue situations.

Of all the people she'd become friends with over the years, Alisha was a complete surprise. The relationship was real, though, and Erin gave it a deeper examination.

It was about choices. About trust. She'd found the unexpected in Alisha—something beyond the innocent façade that the blonde projected. The naïve woman had turned out to have nerves of steel, not only on the job but when facing down family.

She'd taken control of her life and grabbed the things she wanted, one of whom was Devon.

Erin did envy her a bit, but that envy was not going to be a wasted emotion. It was going to encourage her to move forward and take hold of her own happiness.

She glanced across the table at Tim. His dark hair framed a laughing expression as he bantered with the team. He held a glass of beer in one hand, his tanned fingers wrapped easily around the stein. She wanted to have those talented hands on her body. Teasing her and bringing her pleasure.

He'd been so . . . proper the entire day. Had kept things light. Casual. He didn't give her any extra attention while the team visited, just easy smiles and glances that were no more intimate than the ones he shared with Alisha or Devon.

Out here in the real world she still wasn't sure what she wanted, but in private, she was ready for the next step. Tim had said the timing was her choice to make, and she was making it.

The conversation died around ten. Tripp was the first to rise to his feet. "Jonah will be home by now, and I should be getting back."

Alisha yawned. "I need to call it a night as well."

"Which means I'm done." Devon lifted Alisha's knuckles to his mouth and kissed them lightly. "Come, my lady. Your chariot awaits."

Farewells echoed, coats were gathered. Erin eyed Tim carefully, but he remained a complete gentleman. All the way up to the moment she slipped beside him and rested her hand on his back.

He stiffened for a moment, then shifted position slightly to allow her to touch him more easily.

"Training tomorrow," Anders reminded them. "Unless we get a call-out. Check in at nine."

"See you then," Tim answered, not even twitching as Erin traced a figure eight with her fingertip. He waited until they were nearly alone, a single busboy clearing the table behind them, before turning slowly to face her.

Her fingers lingered on his side before resting on his hip.

"Do you need a ride home?" he offered, the words coming out soft and husky.

His tone triggered an instant response as a shiver raced up her spine. She shook her head. "I have my car. But if you'd like, I'd love to stop in for a nightcap."

Blue eyes flashed with wildfire before he pulled his response back to casual. Nonchalant. "Of course. I'll meet you at the apartment doors."

Anticipation made her clumsy as she hauled her keys from the ignition. She tucked them safely in her pocket, smoothing the front of her coat. Distracting herself from the torrent of ideas pouring through her brain.

Excitement bubbled through her veins as she stepped through the fresh-fallen snow toward Tim's apartment. She left footprints behind her, the temperatures low enough to let the thin layer of powder settle on the walk. Small puffs of light flakes shot upward as she walked, and she smiled at the winter wonderland around her, her breath a puff of white.

He was waiting for her. A tall, lean shadow standing to one side of the main doors. Tim smiled as he let her in, turning her toward the elevators and leaving his hand behind briefly.

Erin wasn't often giddy, and she wasn't often tongue-tied, but it seemed right now she was both. She wanted Tim's hand on her body again with a whole lot of layers gone so she could fully appreciate the contact. She wanted him to look at her with his beautiful blue eyes that could make her tremble with lust.

She just plain *wanted*.

"I enjoyed the training test the team arranged, but did you get to see any of it?" Tim asked.

She stepped into the elevator. "I was watching what I could through the holes in the top section. Mostly I took a break, though. Napped. Relaxed. No use in all of us working all the time."

He chuckled in response.

Erin turned to him and found herself crowded to the back wall. His arms framed either side of her head as he leaned in tight, his smile shifting into something hungrier.

Feral.

Her breath caught in her throat, and she pressed her hands to the wall as the lift mechanism murmured around them. Tim didn't move. Not closer to her to make contact, nor farther away so she could fill her lungs with much-needed oxygen.

It seemed he was going to keep her there until she grew dizzy and collapsed.

Except it was up to her to take this forward—the realization struck like a siren, and she tilted her head slightly. Pressed forward an inch to connect their bodies in a soft, seductive glide as the elevator eased to a halt.

A low rumble of approval escaped Tim's lips. "Finally."

Their lips met as Erin wrapped her arms around his shoulders, leaning in as they made more intimate communication with their mouths than any recent speech. Hot and directly to the point. Tim kissed her passionately, ripping the limited air from her lungs as their tongues clashed. Fought, then retreated.

His body was a wall of muscle she rubbed against, the contact not enough to satisfy but more than enough to fan the flames. Hungrily, they enjoyed each other even as the desire for more rose quickly.

A strange noise interrupted them. The elevator door pinged, and the musical tone broke through her concentration.

That wasn't the first time she'd heard the sound, only it was the first time it had registered for what it was. They'd been necking for far longer than she'd imagined.

Erin fisted her fingers in his hair and tugged until he broke the connection.

He gasped a couple of times before finding his control. Erin didn't mind the wait. She needed the time to get her legs back in working condition. Behind them the doors slid closed again, and she laughed.

Tim glanced over his shoulder and joined in her amusement. He stood and offered her his hand. "As attractive as I find the elevator, could I interest you in moving this to my apartment?"

His fingers were warm around hers as they exited the elevator and headed to his door. She leaned against him as he slipped his key into the lock. "I'm not staying the night," she warned.

"Stay as long as you want," Tim offered. "Only, please don't tell me you want to play chess or something stupid."

"Strip poker sounds better."

He had her inside the apartment, the door closed behind them and her back in his arms, before she'd finished speaking. His gaze burned her with its intensity, his hands working to remove her coat. "Naked. I can do that."

He kissed her while jerking her coat off her shoulders and abandoning it to the floor. She was lifted in the air and settled on the couch. When she went to protest, he ignored her, instead removing her boots, tossing them aside. Her shirt lifted off her torso, the button on her slacks opened without even trying until suddenly she sat in her underwear on the buttery softness of the leather.

Only then did he slow, taking a deep breath and rocking back on his heels to admire her.

Her heart pounded in her throat. "Strip poker usually involves cards."

"I don't have any," Tim retorted, his gaze lingering on

her breasts. "But to make it fair, that's as far as I'm going. You have to take off the final layers."

Erin's head spun. "Give me a second. Going from winter wear to underwear in three seconds is a bit of a change."

Only it wasn't the near nakedness that had rocked her. It was the order for her to take charge of the final steps. For her to be the one to get naked with him.

Tim eased forward, his hand sliding along her thigh. "Take your time. I'm content admiring you. God, Erin. You have no idea what you're doing to me."

If it was anything like what she was experiencing . . . She leaned forward and unzipped his coat. "Let's make the playing field a little more even," she suggested.

Tim shrugged out of his jacket, throwing it in the general direction of the front door. He'd managed to rid himself of his shoes, but he didn't go any further.

Instead he touched her again, both hands running upward from her wrists toward her shoulders. Slowly, his hands opened and wrapped around her limbs as if trying to make contact with as much of her at one time as he possibly could. He paused when he reached the junction of her shoulders and neck, his thumb caressing like a tender kiss over the spot where her heartbeat pulsed.

Erin took a shaky breath as she waited for him to continue.

Tim turned his hand over and stroked down the center of her body, knuckles soft against her skin. His gaze followed along, as if mesmerized by the sight of them touching.

Her body was nothing but a giant aching need. Breasts heavy, nipples taut. She wanted to squeeze her legs together to ease the pounding in her sex, but he knelt between her thighs. Forced her open to his examination. His admiration. His lust, which matched her own.

"So soft, yet so strong," Tim said, continuing to touch her, his fingertips splayed over her belly. "I've always admired the way you don't take the easy way out ever. Not in work, not in play."

He wrapped a hand around her waist, slipping up to her back. He pulled her forward in an arch to meet her lips as he pressed a kiss over her heart.

Erin relished the connection, craving more. Slid her hands over his shoulders, saddened to discover fabric instead of skin. She tightened her fingers in the material. "You need to give me some skin."

"If you want."

He was gone for a brief moment to undo his buttons, then he was back, shirt open so his heated flesh made contact with hers. Their torsos rubbed as their lips met, and it was amazing and sensual and . . .

She wanted more.

Erin forced her hands off his body and pushed past where he was caressing her back. He smiled against her lips as she unhooked her bra and tugged it from between them. She shoved at her panties, letting them fall from her hips to the floor, leaving nothing but intimate connection.

A sigh escaped her as he kissed his way along her neck, one hand cupping a breast as if he couldn't wait.

Every time he moved, another shot of pleasure roared through her system. "Hell, yes. It's been too long."

Tim paused with his mouth against the upper curve of her skin, his whispered words heating her like a torch. "Too damn long."

His lips closed around her nipple and Erin gasped, stars floating in front of her eyes.

The night had just begun, and already she was half drunk on him.

CHAPTER 9

''''''''''''''''''''''''''''

Ecstasy floated through her veins like expensive liquor. It seemed a shot of Tim, straight up, was all it took. Already she couldn't bear to think of the night being over.

She'd wondered how far she would let things go this first time, and she had her answer. Nothing would satisfy her cravings right now short of everything.

Her body, her choice, and tonight what she wanted was him. Judging from his response, she didn't think her decision would cause any troubles.

Erin twisted her fingers into Tim's hair to keep him at her breast. He slowly licked around her nipple, the delicate tease sending shivers over her skin.

He smiled, then switched sides, leaving one aching tip glistening in the dim lights from the couch side lamps.

"I want to taste you everywhere," Tim said, his accent growing thicker as he admired her. "I'm going to kiss your neck. Suck that sensitive spot under your ear. I want to start at the top and work my way down until you can't walk. I'll lick between your legs until you squirm with pleasure, and then, only then, will I take you again."

"Sweet talker." Erin arched on the couch, lifting her torso toward him. "What if I want to play with you as well? Touch you, and drive you mad. *Oh . . .*"

Tim leaned back from where he'd sucked her earlobe into his mouth. "Tonight is not about me, but you. About me showing how much I've missed you."

Erin gasped as he continued to tease her. "I can handle that."

Maybe. If she didn't pass out first.

Tim caught her gaze. "It's not only how long it's been. A week is too long to be apart from you when I want you so damn bad."

He drifted a single fingertip down her torso. Over her belly. Between her legs. Erin jerked as Tim unerringly settled over her clitoris and slowly rubbed.

His blue eyes trapped her, the dark circles of his pupils widening as he stared, his talented finger tracing unending circles with just the right pressure to build the pleasure.

"I want to watch you break," Tim said. "Want to hear you come apart for the first time in forever. I need to know it's me that's taken you there."

Erin opened her mouth to answer, but all that came out was a long, low moan as Tim slipped two fingers into her core. Stretching and teasing as he stroked deeper. Never looking away, never pausing as he played with her. He tucked the heel of his palm against her mound and every time his fingers plunged into her core, her clit was stroked as well.

Her eyelids fell shut.

Tim laughed softly. "Oh no, kitten. Open your eyes and let me see. Show me your passion. Show me what this"—he curled his fingers inside her, and she gasped—"does to you. That's right. Gorgeous. Beautiful woman, so strong and powerful."

He thrust again, and again, and there was no way to stop the rising tide of pleasure from breaking over her as thoroughly as if she'd been immersed in the ocean. Erin shook as her sex constricted around his fingers, clenching tight. Seeking more.

Her gaze stayed fast on his, sheer delight clear in his expression as he forced her orgasm to drag on and on.

"Tim." A warning? A plea? Although she wasn't sure if it was for him to stop, or for him to go on.

He distracted her with a kiss, slowing his touch, but softly forcing her to ride the final pulses until she quivered under him.

"Hmm, nicely done." Tim pulled his fingers from her, wetness lingering on her labia, and she ached, suddenly empty.

Erin clutched at him, reaching past his open shirt for his belt, but he avoided her and lifted her into his arms.

"You object to moving to the bedroom?" Tim nuzzled under her ear, already in motion down the hallway.

She wrapped her arms around his neck and sighed contentedly. "I'm going to complain bitterly that you're taking me to a firm, flat surface to continue to ravish me." Erin lifted her head and smiled as they entered his bedroom. "You are planning on ravishing me more, aren't you?"

"Definitely. There's not been nearly enough piratelike activity around here for my tastes."

He lowered her to the soft quilt she'd admired the other day, his gaze burning her with its intensity. She preened under his attention for a moment, then noticed the curtains were still wide open.

Tim caught the direction of her glance. He faced her, and somehow she knew even before he spoke that a challenge was about to be issued. "You want me to close the curtains?"

"You plan on putting on a show for the neighbours?" she asked.

"There's no one on this level but us." Tim sat next to her, stroking a hand from her hip toward her ankle. "I could close them, but it's a waste of time."

She leaned on one elbow, wondering why there was a slight sense of disappointment coursing through her. "Forget the windows, and take off your clothes."

His eyes lit up and he followed her directions. Sort of.

Under her, the silky sheets caressed her skin, and she was tempted to roll on their surface like a puppy, wallowing in the sensual pleasure. While she moved back to settle against the pillows, Tim undid the buttons on his cuffs. The tails hung out, and the open shirtfront showcased his chest, offering teasing glimpses of muscular abdomen, but he still wore just as much as before.

Erin moved quickly to the edge of the mattress. Forget lazing about like an Egyptian ruler. "You seem a little hard of hearing right now," she scolded.

She caught his open shirtfront and tugged up and back, dropping the material from his shoulders and leaving bare lots of lovely, firm body. Tim shrugged his shirt off the rest of the way as she got distracted, slipping an open palm over his chest to caress the light layer of hair swirled over the surface. Two hands were needed for this kind of exploration, and she leaned in to plant a kiss inches over a nipple.

Tim wrapped his fingers around her wrists and stopped her from reaching her next goal. "This is about you, remember?"

"I am remembering. This is all about me, and what I want right now is to play." She tugged on his grip, raising a brow until he let her go.

Only she didn't get to help him out of his pants. Tim crawled over her, crowding her against the mattress, and those talented lips were at her throat and she wasn't going to complain.

She used her fingers to trace his shoulder muscles. To enjoy rubbing her thumbs along strands of muscle that tempted her. To run her fingers through his hair, and listen to the sounds of admiration escaping him.

He kissed her belly button and sighed happily. She laughed when he did it a second time, then gasped as he dropped lower and covered her sex without further warning.

"Tim, enough."

He wasn't budging, and this time she wasn't willing to let him get away with it.

Erin wrapped her legs around his head and trapped him. Anyone else would have paused in what they were doing, but Tim simply lifted her hips and stroked her intimately again, his tongue dipping deep inside. Her body lay at an angle, shoulders resting on the mattress, senses being played, pleasure rising.

"*Tim*. Damn you."

His voice vibrated against her. "You want me to stop?"

At this point, no. "Don't you dare," she warned.

He took her up to the point of climax and then, damn the man, he did exactly what she'd told him not to. He dropped her hips and moved away.

Erin was ready for him, though. Ripped open his zipper and pulled his cock free. She slipped on the condom she'd found under the pillow, and he laughed.

She pushed him over, needing her full weight to do it, but he was on his back, cock rising vertically as she straddled him. She found the center where they met. Rubbed over him until it was very clear he was ready for the next stage.

Erin planted both hands on his naked chest as she rocked. "Now are you ready to listen?"

"I always listen," Tim insisted. He settled his hands on her hips and helped her move over him, increasing the intensity tenfold as friction shot skyward.

She straightened, clutching his hands. Pausing the motion. A slight lift of her hips and the broad head of his cock touched her wet core.

"Oh love, yes." Tim's head tilted back in pleasure as she sank onto him. The thickness of his shaft pressed in all the right spots as she worked herself down. She was wet, but between the condom and his girth, it still wasn't easy.

She undulated a few times, loving how they connected so right. How riding him like this rubbed her clit against his body and gave her an extra edge. Even that wasn't enough because he smiled and slipped one hand between her legs, running his fingertips along the seam where they joined. Pulling up moisture to ease his touch.

The tempo increased. Need increased. Erin lifted and lowered more rapidly, savoring the slick, edgy pleasure riding her spine. The tension gathering in her core like a firework about to go off.

"That's it, love. God, you should see what I see." Tim didn't skip a stroke, but his other hand was in motion over her torso. Cupping her breast, fingertips splayed over her belly, curling around her back.

Her breasts swayed as she rode him, gasping breaths escaping them both. Fire flashed in her veins and triggered another climax, and Erin rocked in place, torso shaking as the orgasm gripped her tightly.

Then Tim took over, lifting her hips slightly off him so he had room to move. To thrust upward and drive his cock deep into her core. Her sheath squeezed around him, tightening as he forced the pleasure on and on. She moaned, somewhere between wanting it to never end and needing to collapse in the next second.

Then he shouted, slamming them together and arching up to join her, his body shaking as he released control and took his pleasure.

Erin rested her head on his shoulder and unashamedly let him support her. "I give up," she admitted. "You've fucked me boneless."

"Hmm." He kissed her temple, running his hands over her hair and her shoulders, her butt resting on his strong thighs, his cock still inside her. "We need to work on your stamina."

"I think you're kind of done as well," Erin teased. She

took a deep breath and relaxed further. "At least, you're done for now."

"For a few minutes, yes," Tim teased. "I'm not twenty anymore, but I do recover eventually."

Sleep beckoned. It was too tempting to stay where she was. To roll to the mattress and close her eyes and stay with him, but she couldn't. Didn't want to give up that much power this early in the relationship.

The sex had been amazing, but . . .

Erin rolled her shoulders back and stretched, enjoying how Tim's gaze instantly dropped to her torso, admiration in his every move. Still, it had to be done. She rose, ignoring the loss of him from her body as she shifted to a sitting position, then off the mattress.

Tim reached for her, but she avoided his touch. Matter-of-factly she found her feet and, under the pretense of stretching, got further into a safe zone.

He watched her, a far-too-knowing look in his eyes.

Erin bluffed. "That was great, but I need to be going."

"Okay."

She padded from the room in search of her clothes before she started analyzing his comment, or worse, looking for a different response.

It was tempting to grab hold of her and not let her leave. Tim fought with himself, with what he knew about her and what he hoped for their future.

Patience had to be his catchword, no matter how much it sucked right now.

But even if he was being patient, he was going to play all the cards he could. He couldn't bully Erin into their future, and didn't want to. But he sure as hell could seduce her into it.

He got rid of the condom, chuckling over Erin's discovery

of it. Then he pulled on his robe and slipped out to the living room.

She was tugging her shirt over her head, her pants already on.

"Remind me to pick you for the speed-dressing competition," Tim teased.

Erin paused, a wry smile breaking free as she straightened. And slowed down. "Yeah. I know."

Tim crossed the room to her side, smoothing her shirt over her hips, touching her softly, but intimately. She wanted to escape, so he'd let her. But she wasn't leaving without enough reminders to make her thoughts turn toward him, toward *them*, again and again. "No agenda. You set the pace."

She laughed and tugged on his belt loops. "You just fucked me with your pants on. I was naked, and you were still partly dressed even after I told you to strip. I think me setting the pace is already an illusion."

"Forgive me for wanting to repeat a pleasant memory." Tim curled his hands around her torso and settled her against him, legs spread wide so she was cradled tight to his entire length.

"A good memory?" She looked thoughtful, then shook her head slowly once. Paused. "Oh."

Tim rubbed his cheek against hers. "The first time we made love—I didn't get my clothes off that time, either."

Erin nodded, her eyes darkening as she remembered. "And I was completely naked . . . I seem to be naked most of the times we've fooled around."

"You do naked very well."

Then he stopped the conversation before she could twist things, or head down paths he didn't want to discuss yet. Shadowy places in their relationship that they would need to discuss, but not here or now.

Instead, he kissed her. One hand cupping the back of her head, the other resting gently on her hip. Space between them now, only their mouths touching. Tender and passionate, as if he were giving her a piece of his soul to care for until the next time they'd be together.

The idea wasn't that far off reality.

She matched his intensity, accepting his gentleness. When he pulled away after the final caress of their lips, her eyes were filled with stars.

He walked her to the door. Slipped on his shoes while she got her boots on. Held her hand in the elevator when she snuck her fingers into his.

Walked her to the front doors, and he was already tired of that, but it was right. She wasn't ready for more yet. Maybe neither was he.

But soon.

CHAPTER 10

_{........................}

January

Five A.M. looked rotten no matter which side of the clock you came at it from. Tim rolled from his bed and shuffled his clothes on, the emergency call-out having shattered yet another incredible dream.

He was more pissed off about *that* than the fact it was five in the bloody morning.

One solid month he'd worked with Lifeline now. He'd trained with the team and worked with them, relaxed and played. The job was going great, and he was far more invested in the lot of the team than he'd actually expected.

Erin?

Was driving him absolutely batshit crazy.

They fooled around at least a couple times a week. He'd been doing everything he could to give her space. To allow time for her to figure out that what they had right now, while hot and satisfying on one level, wasn't the end goal.

One moment he would consider ceasing being patient. Just make his demands, and let her discover for herself what he already knew. Then the years they'd been apart would register, and his lingering uncertainty about why she'd left in such a panic would return, and he'd be tossed right back to square one.

Following her agenda, which was unforgettable red-hot sex. Like he should complain.

But . . .

He shook off his frustration and concentrated on the job waiting for him. Early morning or not, a call-out in January was probably going to involve freezing his ass off at some point in the next couple of hours.

Tim pulled into the parking lot at HQ surprised to see that the chopper wasn't being prepped. Instead, a small plane waited on the airstrip.

Something different. Something big was going down.

Marcus met the team in the prep room. "Coastal call-out. There's a tourist excursion gone down in the Pacific Rim Mountains, and the weather is making it impossible to approach the crash site. We'll use the plane to get you out there, then as soon as there's a break in the weather you'll move in. Erin, you'll have a bird waiting at the base out of Comox. Pack ropes and climbing gear, and extra winter equipment in case."

"Coastal should mean less snow, right?" Devon asked as he grabbed bags off the shelves and unzipped them in prep for loading.

"Probably," Marcus slipped back to the radio station. "But you'll cross over glacier territory, so pack for anything. I'll work on getting more details."

The flurry of motion around them moved in waves. Gear being loaded, clothing shoved into packs. Tim pulled aside his prepacked case of supplies from the medical stash, double-checking he had extra of everything. He took the bag along with one from the gear lined up by the hangar door and carried it to the transport.

Erin was already on the plane, chatting with the pilot.

She waved briefly, then ignored him. He did the same until the entire team was settled in the transport seats. The engine revved higher as they buckled in.

Dawn hadn't gotten farther than backlighting the eastern mountains before they were off. Mount Rundle grew smaller as the pilot raced the plane forward into darkness and away from the rising sun, following the TransCanada highway through the Rocky Mountains toward the coast.

A soft touch on his arm pulled him from staring out the window.

Once she'd gotten his attention, Erin leaned back in her seat, her voice over the speakers to his ears. "I need to sleep for a while. Wake me when Marcus has more information."

Tim nodded. Erin turned off her headset and closed her eyes, her breathing slowing as she settled farther into the seat. He snuck her fingers into his, then looked out the window to avoid meeting the gaze of anyone on the team.

He wasn't going to let them stop him from doing this much at least. She was going to know that he was there for her.

Only by the time the headphones rumbled, the noise pulled him from the light slumber he'd fallen into as well. It took a moment to become alert, especially as Erin lifted her head from his shoulder. Her warmth had blanketed him during the time they'd rested. The lingering heat was nice, and made him want to keep her close at all times.

Only now they needed to concentrate.

Anders waved from across the seating area. "Time to wake up, everyone. We've got fifteen more minutes to the airport. Erin, they have a chopper warming up for you. You can finish getting her ready while we transfer supplies."

"This is the one that I used last summer?"

"Yes. Fueled, cleared, and ready to roll."

She gave him a thumbs-up.

"What's Marcus got for us?" Tripp asked.

"They've spotted the crash site, but it's taking a long time to get the local SAR into position going overland. Winds were too high earlier to access the range, and while the conditions have improved a little, they're worried about exposure if the rescue is put off much longer."

"Tricky flying situation?" Erin grinned harder when Anders responded in the affirmative. "Lovely."

Alisha joined them over the microphone system. "Your idea of a good time needs work, my friend."

"Right," Erin drawled. "As if you're not itching to be tossed from the transport hold into a spinning descent at the end of a rope. You're as much a freak as I am."

The women grinned at each other before focusing back on Anders.

Tim took mental notes as they planned their next steps. The plane set down and taxied rapidly toward where the helicopter waited.

Confidence. Camaraderie. Even, yes, a sense of excitement at the rush of the unknown. Tim had always enjoyed his job, and taking chances, but something was different now.

It wasn't him going it alone this time. It was there in the team, and Tim was growing to crave the sensation of being a part of the whole. Wanted to be in a position to gain the admiration of them all.

That in itself was strange. He wasn't usually the one to go looking for pats on the back.

The first part of the approach was straightforward as far as she was concerned. Once they had crossed the Strait of Georgia and started down Bute Inlet, the sharp edges of glacial-topped peaks faced them like a row of massive sentinels, guarding the wilderness interior. Dark green pines broke to dusted white on the front row, the warmer air off the ocean keeping the snow from settling over the entire face. But beyond that, as elevations soared, winter held the landscape in a tight-fisted clutch, beautiful and deadly.

Flying into them was like facing an ancient power—one to be respected and feared at the same time. Friend or foe? From the safety of her chopper, she was a more powerful supplicant than the people they were headed to rescue, yet it could all turn on a breath.

While Alisha and the others strapped themselves into harnesses, Erin brought the chopper closer to the mountain face. Below them the torn carcass of the missing plane desecrated two sections of the steep, rocky crags, the transport torn in two uneven pieces. Broken debris scattered between the main sections clung precariously to the precipice. One person waved, arms moving rapidly as they stood over the still form of another.

Erin eyed the rescue location where she'd have to hover. Of course, they were right at the narrowest section, with two long valleys leading off in different directions. The ultimate worst situation in terms of crosswinds and back eddies off the steep ridges.

It was one of those situations she both loved and hated. The challenge of keeping the chopper in the right spot, of guiding the massive machine over the varying terrain and dealing with shifting wind patterns was something Erin never got enough of.

The fact that they were there because people were suffering wasn't as thrilling. She was glad her skills helped save lives, but the reality of why the team was needed was horrid.

On the more intimate side of the equation, knowing there was someone at the end of the winch line whom she cared about changed the situation all over again. It lent an extra edge of fear and adrenaline that made it more exciting in some twisted way.

Erin listened carefully as Anders called out instructions, guiding Alisha down. The instrument panel gave feedback as well, but Erin's attention remained on her forward focal

point. Nothing to distract her. Nothing but the rescue and
the victims below her who were waiting to be brought to
safety and taken for needed medical attention.

Which reminded her that Tim was there as well, and for
one second the whole idea of sleeping with a team member
became a terrible, horrible idea.

She had grown used to being responsible for Alisha's life.
For the lives of Devon and the rest of the team—used to,
yet not complacent. The sense of awe in the trust they
showed never left her. It might make no sense, but with Tim,
it was different. There was a sense of something—*other*—
lingering every time they worked together.

If something happened to Tim, she wasn't sure what she
would do. How she would respond.

Then there was no time to worry because Alisha was
on the ground, and Erin had to make rapid adjustments to
keep them level. Pressing forward with the controls, listening
to the response of the chopper with not only her ears, but
her body.

"Tim, drop second," Alisha ordered as she hurried
through triage. "Then Devon can bring a stretcher. We have
at least one who will need a ride."

"On my way," Tim responded.

He'd barely cleared the doors when it happened. A hard
gust of wind hit from the north. The change in air pressure
shuddered across the chopper, and they dropped a few feet.
Erin fought to level them, countering the strong crosswind.

A muffled masculine curse carried over the line.

"Tim, you okay?" Anders demanded.

The pause before Tim answered was painful to wait
through. "Fine. Lower me."

Erin clenched her teeth and focused straight ahead. Eyed
the rocky walls ahead of her as they narrowed. Adjusted an
inch at a time toward the north wall to bring Tim closer to
where Alisha waited to guide him to safety.

The chopper danced with her. The subtle changes in

altitude registered not only on the gauges, but under Erin's hands. A rhythm developed as she finessed the massive machine past the narrow rock walls. Easing back, sliding forward. Watching for danger signs and following the steady stream of verbal direction Anders breathed at her as Tim approached the ground.

"I got him," Alisha shouted. "Clear."

Erin let out the breath she hadn't realized she'd been holding.

"Take us up for a moment, Erin," Anders ordered. "I'll get Devon in position."

The short time of respite was long enough to let her pounding heart settle a little. Then she had to do it all over as Devon was lowered, the spinal board with him. Once again there was that sense of anticipation mixed with dread. Erin had to acknowledge what she'd always known yet had become so much more apparent this time around.

What they did mattered, but what they did was dangerous, and there was no way around that fact. It was their life on the line as well. That her job put her in charge over them was unlike anything she'd experienced elsewhere.

She watched the team hustle below her and soaked in the wonder and the thread of satisfaction that rose at the thought. She was powerful. In control. A lifesaver, and in charge of her own destiny.

That wasn't going to change.

Tim caught Alisha's wrist and allowed her to drag him to a safe perch on the rock wall. His hips and thighs hurt like a bugger where his harness had jerked around him—no amount of padding could cushion that kind of blow completely—but he was already on to the next thing.

Alisha snapped out a rapid report. "Peter is the ambulatory victim. He stabilized his friend, but Tony needs your attention stat. I'll help Devon, then climb up to find the pilot. Devon and Tripp can load these two for liftout."

"Stay safe," Tim acknowledged as he detached his cable harness from the winch. He left Alisha and hurried up the mountain to where the first two victims were located, climbing over the jagged terrain with his medic kit in hand. Temperatures had to be hovering around freezing, with the wind slamming the cold against him like icy daggers.

The sound of the chopper echoed off the nearby peaks as Erin moved into position, and this time Devon was lowered. Then Tim turned away from the others to focus on his patient.

Pain skittered across the victim's face as Tim checked his limbs. Possible broken femur, severe lacerations to his right thigh.

"I had pressure on it to stop the bleeding," offered Peter, the one who'd been waving earlier. Tim eyed him quickly, but other than dirt and scratches he seemed in okay shape. It was his friend in trouble.

"You did great. I'll just wrap him up a little extra for the trip out," Tim assured him, working rapidly. He looked into Tony's eyes. "Stay nice and still, and we'll get you out of here in no time."

"What about the others?" Peter asked. "I couldn't leave Tony, but I haven't seen any sign of the rest of the passengers. When the bouncing stopped, we were the only ones on this section of the mountain."

Others? "How many were with you?"

Peter looked confused. "The plane was full. Another half dozen? Maybe a couple more?"

Fuck. Tim engaged his radio. "Anders, Alisha. We've got trouble. There were more passengers on board than the three on the manifest."

"Great. Hang tight. I'll contact the airfield to see if they can dig up more info."

"Anders and I are heading to the upper site," Alisha announced. "Join us when you can."

Overhead the steady sound of the rotors echoed off the walls to produce a syncopated rhythm. Devon joined him, and for a couple minutes they were occupied loading the injured man onto the stretcher.

The man on the carry board had gone silent once the painkillers kicked in. Tim completed putting down a dressing while Devon tightened security straps.

Anders lowered the connecting cable and the stretcher rose skyward.

"I'm heading after the others." Tim pointed uphill. "Alisha's setting fixed ropes."

Devon gave him a thumbs-up, then returned to completing his task.

Tim hurried over the uneven rock toward the back of the half-moon-shaped amphitheater. He paused, examining the area closer now that there were bodies to put the view into perspective.

Above them, Alisha and Tripp were closing in on the nose of the aircraft. The bright red section was wedged into a section of rock, the broken body in twisted shreds as if some giant dragon had used its claws on a new toy. Below him were the tail and part of the body. Cabin walls and padded seats lay in mangled bits, destroyed by their tumble down the ragged mountain face.

There wasn't enough rummage to make a plane. Not if he put all the pieces together in a morbid balsam wood model construction.

He moved to the north, gaze darting over the scene. Looking for the missing clue. A narrow, dark line drew him away from following the team, headed instead farther to the side. He cautiously approached the fissure and peered over it. The rough scree rock had been recently disturbed, a darker trail visible that led down to one side and out of view.

Signs screamed loud and clear that something had slid that direction.

Tim eyed the incline warily. "Erin, take a swing higher and come at this wall from the other side. I have a suspicion someone went down a side route, and I'm hoping it ends somewhere in the open. Look for wreckage, red paint."

The chopper lifted before he'd even finished speaking.

"You find something?" Devon asked.

"We have missing people, and missing plane. It's got to have slid off in a different direction."

"Tim, we're at the cockpit. Pilot is dead." Alisha's somber announcement made them all pause.

"Damn."

"No other passengers in this vicinity. Tripp and I are coming back down."

Devon had joined Tim, and he spoke off radio. "Wait for Alisha and Tripp to return."

Tim nodded. "Let's see what Erin finds. No use crawling into dark places without a reason."

A solid hand clasped his shoulder in agreement as they turned to wait while Alisha and Tripp made the descent and rejoined them on relatively stable ground.

"Getting off this piece of rock is going to be a pain in the ass," Devon muttered, pulling his coat closer around his face.

Tim eyed the cliffs. "We could hang glide."

A burst of laughter escaped his partner. "We can go off Mount Rundle in the spring. Other than that, I'm not into free fall."

"So BASE jumping is out? Damn, you're a lousy date."

Devon winked in response. Normal, everyday chatter between the moments of dealing with life and death—it was what they used to combat the stress. Tim glanced up as the chopper volume increased.

Anders came online. "Oh joy, oh bliss, what we've got

is a sightseeing tour. Pilot registered two for the flight, but had room for more. So either he was pocketing the extra fares, or he booked them on for some special low rate fare as a favour."

"Some favour," Tim muttered, looking around the crash site.

"There's no crash evidence on the far side, Tim."

Erin's smooth tones stroked him, a subtle brush against nerve endings that were set on high when it came to anything about her. Even in the middle of the tense situation he was always aware of her, and not only because the sound of the chopper followed them everywhere.

"They have to be somewhere," Alisha complained.

"Unfortunately, I think I know where." Tim gestured to the ravine.

A whirl of activity followed as ropes and anchors were set, and Alisha made the first descent over the edge.

Devon waited impatiently, Tim holding his safety rope. "Tell us what's happening, Alisha," Devon ordered.

"Come on down. You're not going to believe this. It's like the entire belly of the plane surfed down here and—oh *shit*. Devon, haul ass, I need you. Set lines and descend. All hands."

The radio cut out and if they'd moved quickly before, they were now in high gear, blurs of motion.

"I'll belay you, Devon. Fast trip, call out when you need to slow down," Tim offered.

Alisha was talking steadily again, information regarding the other passengers coming in over the radio as Tripp locked down ropes and tossed lines. Tim focused on the weight in his hands as Devon vanished out of sight below him, the rope skipping out at what would be an alarming rate for most people.

All he got from Devon was a calm, "Ready to slow. Slow down and stop in three, two, one . . ."

Tim braced himself and gripped the rope tighter to bring his teammate to a standstill.

"Nicely done. I'm down. Tie off and descend."

Tim was in midair, dropping toward the others, before he got to see what had caught their attention. The crazed dragon that he'd imagined had clawed apart the plane had taken the middle section and spit it out here. The nearly perfect oval had slid, or rolled, but had jammed to a stop half on a rock lip, half off.

The reason for Alisha's call for speed was clear. There were moving shapes in the wreckage, but the entire mass was close to tipping the final distance. There would be no way anyone would survive that kind of a fall to the watery rocks below.

Alisha had already reached the edge of the plane. "Everyone stay put. We're going to place some anchors, and then we can get you out.

A mass of raised voices greeted her announcement, but she swore, raising her hands in a full stop position. "Guys, anyone speak Japanese?"

"Shit, really?" Devon was up against the rocks, slamming climbers' cams into the cracks as rapidly as his fingers would move. "Head count. We need them out of there."

He gestured at the two passengers who had crawled from their seats earlier and sat huddled together to the side of the wreckage, attempting sign language to make them stay put.

"I see seven, and five are still in the cabin." Alisha dug in the gear bag and began looping chest harnesses to her body ropes. "Do you have a good anchor for me yet, Devon? I'm going in."

"The plane's not secure," Devon shouted.

"She's the lightest," Tripp cut in, not a slap down at Devon, but a reminder of the goal. "Alisha, single rope on each, but we're not going to take anyone out until you've got them chained together. I don't want to tip the balance more than adding your weight."

Tim caught Devon's eye. Confidence was there, but fear as well, as Devon had to watch his fiancée move into terrifying danger. He caught the rope Devon tossed him and waited for the moment he could guide it carefully to Alisha.

She moved with a steady grace, even half buried under her equipment. A hushed silence fell over the area. Excited voices stilled as the plane rocked, a horrifying metallic moan rising from where the metal rubbed the granite mountainside.

One person. The next. Alisha used a strange sort of hands-on comforting and gentle manipulation, but she was getting ropes around each passenger. After she'd done the first, chatter sprang up again as the passengers realized what she was doing. They worked eagerly to help her, arms rising slowly, fingers wrapping around ropes.

The plane settled a foot, and the low murmuring turned to screams. Tim bolted forward as well, unable to stop the knee-jerk reaction.

"It's okay. It's okay. Just stop moving." For a tiny thing, Alisha could sure shout when she had to.

Tripp passed Tim a rope end. "Tie on. I want you ready to move if needed." He spoke softly enough not to be overheard.

There wasn't enough oxygen in the air. Not until Alisha turned from securing the final person and gave the signal.

"I'm going forward," Tim announced. "I can help get them out of the wreckage."

Tripp nodded, then belayed him down the edge. Tim took the time to set his own anchor in the rocks at his feet. A short rope, just enough room on it to manoeuvre.

A dangerous version of a child's playground game began. Standing on the teeter-totter, attempting to balance it, but with the additional stress of working with shifting weights, Alisha directed the passenger farthest from safety to move toward Tim.

Everyone's eyes were wide as he shuffled slowly toward a safer perch. As the first civilian passed him, Tim looped an additional carabiner around the harness Alisha had fastened, and Tripp took control, lifting the man rapidly to a secure ledge. Rinse, repeat. None of them had time for a break, one muscle-aching moment following another.

On the opposite side from where they were removing passengers, Devon held Alisha's rope ready. She turned to the final tourist, and their luck vanished. The plane began a slow, grinding tilt that was too determined to end in anything but a complete disconnect from its perch. Chunks of rock supporting the plane broke away with horrifyingly loud cracks that echoed off the wall behind them.

Tim regrasped the cable he had waiting and made a decision. He snapped the carabiner into his palm, kicked his anchor rope free, and gave Tripp as much heads-up as he could.

"Free fall," he shouted.

Tim jumped, aiming for the open space in front of the two bodies left in the plane. A loud shout rang in his ears as Tripp responded, almost too quickly. Tim slammed the carabiner through the chest loop around the last passenger, then twisted and held on tight to Alisha. She grabbed him with one arm and caught her rope with the other, and the mountainside gave way, taking the empty remains of the plane with it.

Tripp pulled the final passenger over the cliff lip. Alisha and Tim ended suspended in midair, Devon securing them in place. Their ropes slowly twisted together.

A deafening roar rose from the base of the mountain as the plane settled into its final resting place.

CHAPTER 11

'''''''''''''''''''''''''''''''''''''

Tim eased back awkwardly in the plastic seat and let weariness take hold. It was no use pretending he wasn't beat.

After his little leap of faith it had taken an hour to get his and Alisha's feet on solid ground, plus get the entire group of passengers onboard the chopper. Erin pulled off another flying miracle and kept the chopper level in nearly impossible conditions, reducing the panic in the group as they were winched onto the chopper.

They'd shifted the rescued into a medical transport, passing over responsibility at that point, done a quick debrief with the local SAR team, and then Tim had offered to stay behind until Erin completed her paperwork. The rest of the team were shuttled to a nearby hotel for a chance to recover.

That was what seemed like hours ago, and he'd been floating between sleep and consciousness the entire time since. But he wasn't leaving Erin, no matter how much he longed to crash for a few hours.

Soft, warm fingers stroked his arm, and he opened his eyes to discover Erin hovering over him.

"Hey, you."

Tim didn't fight the yawn that welled up as he pulled himself alert. "Hey yourself. You done all your postflight checks?"

"Uh-huh. Plus, I've got amazing news—I get to fly her to Calgary when we leave. They need her out there, and since we're available, we get the gig."

He smiled at her enthusiasm. "That is awesome. Congrats."

She laughed. "You're still half asleep. Come on, we're good to go."

Dragging his carcass out of the seat made him groan lightly as his tight and bruised muscles protested. Erin wrapped an arm around him, and they headed toward the exit.

"The rest of the team settled for the night?" Erin asked.

"They're already at the hotel. And Devon got his wish. Marcus announced we've got a three-day leave."

Erin paused, adjusting her small personal backpack to hang over her shoulder. "Seriously?"

Tim nodded. He tugged her to the side, pulling her strong body against his. "I want to take you somewhere special for the time we've got. Somewhere a little fancier than the local Holiday Inn. You okay with that?"

"Right now I need food." She covered a yawn. "And then anywhere with a shower and a bed is fancy enough for me."

"But you'll go with me?"

"I don't need to hang out with the team all the time," Erin said. "But don't expect me to make any decisions right now. My brain is mush."

Tim tucked her hand in his and led her to a waiting taxi. "No other decisions needed. I'll take care of you."

His aches and pains faded rapidly as she settled beside him in the cab, leaning into him and sighing. He pulled out a phone and connected with Devon.

His teammate picked up on the first ring. "Yo, Tim!"

"You're disgustingly chipper. You already eaten, or do you and Alisha want to join us for refueling?"

"Chipper is because I've had a shower, and we're just headed down to the restaurant. Want us to order for you?"

Shower—*bullshit*. Tim would bet anything Devon had not only showered but bent Alisha over, or had her up against the wall. Only soul-satisfying sex put that tone in a man's voice. "Cover the table with appetizers, and we'll see about the rest when we arrive."

"Deal. Hey . . . while it's on my mind. Going out on a limb here, and I don't expect an answer this minute, but I know Erin's a frequent visitor at The Wild. You ask her to put in a good word, and get Alisha and me an invite to the rooms upstairs sometime?"

Seriously? "Why, Devon, isn't that a little outside your usual tastes?"

A deep chuckle sounded. "Assumptions can come back to bite you, Tim. Maybe Alisha and I get a kick out of keeping it fresh."

And a visit to a sex club was on his mind? Yeah, the man had definitely had sex and now he was gloating. Tim tucked away the phone and pondered how every day brought new and interesting things to light.

Erin nestled in again. "Late lunch with the team?" she asked.

"Just Alisha and Devon. Thought it would be nice to relax with them for a bit." Tim didn't add that his original intention had been to make sure Erin got used to being accepted as a part of a couple. Devon and Alisha worked with the team, but there was an unmistakable connection between them. Something he desperately wanted for himself and Erin again.

A partnership on the field and in the bedroom—strong enough that everyone would know they were together. The details of how they were together and what they were doing in private weren't for others to know, but it was the complete deal Tim was still focused on.

The restaurant was surprisingly busy, delicious smells rushing from the kitchen to assault them as they walked in the door. Devon's call rose over the sounds of happy tourists, and Erin tugged Tim toward the corner booth where Alisha and Devon sat.

The huge platter of nachos waiting in the center of the table pulled a groan from him. "Oh, hell yes."

Erin had a scoop of guacamole on a chip before her ass even hit the cushioned bench. "I dreamed about this the entire flight from Banff."

"We've got enough appetizers coming we don't need anything else," Alisha warned. She held out a plate. "Jalapeño poppers ordered just for you as well. Except Devon's gone through four already."

"It was cold out there. I needed something to warm me up," Devon protested with a smile.

Other than putting in drink orders when the waitress came by, there was little but the sounds of happy crunching for the next fifteen or so minutes.

Devon leaned back, nestled up tight against Alisha as he let out a long, hard sigh. "God, I didn't know I was that famished."

"Granola bars and power gels get the calories in, but they don't count as food." Alisha held up a forkful of salad. "Here—you need something green to go with that carnivore's feast you just inhaled."

Devon rolled his eyes at Tim, then good-naturedly turned to his fiancée. "Rabbit food. Fine."

Alisha might have been the one holding the fork, but Devon was obviously doing something other than it appeared as he accepted the mouthful of food.

Tim watched closely, trying to figure out why Alisha's cheeks had bloomed so brightly. Their body language, the way Devon leaned toward her—everything screamed that they were not only a couple, but a pair who couldn't keep their hands off each other.

It wasn't until Alisha shuddered slightly, though, that Tim discovered the reason for her flushed face. He smiled, hiding the expression behind his glass. Devon's hand was below the tabletop, and Tim would bet long odds he knew what was going on out of sight.

Devon's little question from earlier made more sense now. Tim turned to Erin. "Great job out there today."

"You, too, except for the momentary shot of stupid."

Devon joined in the conversation, no indication that he was doing anything sexual to Alisha while they spoke. "I thought it was no more than what was needed. A touch stupid, but there's nothing wrong with that—"

"Sometimes stupid is what gets the job done," Tim agreed. "Exactly. You can't always wait for the most comfortable situation. Wait for the right place and time—hell, occasionally it's that edge of danger that makes some experiences work better than if you called it safe."

Devon grinned, catching the dual meaning in Tim's words. "That extra edge? I hear some people get off on it."

Alisha sucked in a tiny gasp of air, reaching for her water glass with unsteady fingers. Whatever Devon was doing, she was enjoying it immensely. Or at least enough that she didn't feel safe to join in the conversation.

Erin bumped his shoulder, whispering in his ear. "Did I just miss some guy-talk lingo?"

Tim glanced at Devon. The other man raised a brow but didn't answer. Instead, he picked up a spring roll from the table and offered it to Alisha, feeding it to her as he spoke softly.

All the while continuing to torment her and make her squirm.

Well, hell. Tim had enjoyed Devon's company before, but this was a whole new side that he was seeing. Perhaps they had more in common than Tim originally suspected. It was something he'd have to explore more in the future.

Right now?

Now that there was food in their stomachs it was time for him and Erin to head toward the next thing, and there was no reason not to begin immediately.

He snuck his hand up Erin's back, caressing the strong muscles of her shoulders, stroking the gentle curve with his thumb. He leaned in close so he could speak quietly.

"Your friend is really enjoying her supper today," he whispered.

Erin snorted. "Why are we whispering about Alisha and appetizers? Is this some dark secret because of the deep-frying?"

"Try deep penetration," Tim teased. "Notice where we are? Tucked up safe in this corner? Devon's got his fingers all over Alisha right now, and I bet you she's biting her tongue to stop from moaning."

Erin stiffened slowly as he spoke, instantly glancing away from the other couple. "They're fooling around right here?" she demanded, still keeping her voice low enough not to be overheard.

"That's what I think." Tim squeezed her neck again, dragging his nails lightly over her skin. "You know this. You know people get off on all kinds of edgy play. Voyeurs, exhibitionists. It's a part of what makes people happy. If this is one of their kinks, good for them."

"But it's Alisha and Devon," Erin protested.

"And you've spent how many hours with them over the years?"

"Enough, but I didn't know—I mean, I don't *want* to know what turns them on."

"You trust them with your life; they trust you with theirs. You've played together as well as worked—enjoyed a good meal. A good movie. Sexual pleasure is simply one more thing we appreciate as humans. Knowing what they like doesn't mean you're jumping in and getting hands-on, either."

He ignored her and faced the table. If Devon and Alisha were playing right out in the open like this, he was going to take advantage of the situation. Plus, there was something deliciously sensual in helping them take it one step further.

He caught Alisha's gaze, making sure he was wearing a completely nonjudgmental expression, but he also didn't let her look away. "Alisha. When you drop on the cable, especially in high winds, I've noticed you don't seem to spin as much as I do. Got any secrets to share?"

Alisha swallowed hard but wiggled herself a bit more upright. Devon's soft smile showed his approval and delight as he also met Tim's gaze and waited for Alisha's answer.

"It might have something . . . to do with our weight ratio. I don't present as big of a target since my—" She sucked for air, her lashes fluttering. Only a second later she pulled herself together, voice shaky as she continued. ". . . My mass is smaller than yours. Try flipping between staying compact, and using a ballet dancer's snap to focus your . . . torso on one point. That slows . . . *oh, god* . . . the rotation."

She pressed both hands to the table and her eyes went unfocused for a second, lips slightly open as she silently exhaled. Devon was fully engrossed in her now, his mouth close to her ear as she got caught in the maelstrom of what Tim judged to be a very nice orgasm.

At his side Erin squirmed, a good indicator of just how much this was affecting her.

Erin wasn't a wiggler.

"You'll have to work through that with me in the gym sometime." Tim raised his glass to Devon. "Demonstrations are the best way to learn."

"Fun as well," Devon agreed. He raised his hand to his mouth and deliberately licked the wet fingers clean, all the while staring at Alisha.

"Holy shit," Erin breathed, leaning against Tim. "This is all wrong, but I'm so turned on right now."

Hallelujah. "Nothing wrong, love. Our friends have healthy sex drives. They know what they like, and they're good having some fun. Sounds like pretty much the perfect situation."

"It feels . . ." She shook her head. "Not here."

He squeezed her leg, leaving his hand on her thigh. "We'll talk about it in a bit, then."

She nodded.

Tim wanted to jump up on the table and cheer. Instead he focused on the rest of the time together with Devon and Alisha, making sure it was ordinary and everyday as possible. Just friendly team members, taking a break. Enjoying the start of a couple days off.

But when they got out of here? He was picking up the conversation and running with it. And he was sending a bottle of really good whiskey to Devon the first chance he got.

Tim followed her into the back of the taxi. He didn't crowd her, yet his presence wrapped around her so hard she broke into an instant sweat. His scent, his nearness.

Just *him*.

Erin was a mess of emotion, all tangled up with urgent sexual desires that needed to be dealt with right now. Only she wasn't sure exactly what she wanted to do with herself.

Watching Devon and Alisha fool around shouldn't have driven her so crazy. Or maybe that wasn't the truth—Devon was a good-looking guy, Alisha good-looking as well, and seeing them together was far better than your typical pornstar mash-up. But seeing them getting turned on had been far more exciting than she'd expected.

For one second she'd wanted to slip over to the opposite side of the table and join in. Add her touch to the hand stroking Alisha—and girls weren't the normal go-to for Erin's turn-ons, but they'd been so into what they were doing. So intent on finding pleasure that the situation had just screamed for Erin to be a part of it.

She'd been so wrapped up in her pondering that she missed what Tim said to the driver.

"We're not staying at the hotel with them?"

Tim shook his head. "You agreed I could take you somewhere else. Three days of R and R on my dime. If you'll allow me." He lifted her hand and kissed the back of her knuckles.

Erin could no sooner stop the shiver that rocked her than stop the blood from rushing to her erogenous zones. "You did catch the part where I said I needed a shower and some sleep?"

"And food. Don't worry. I'll make sure we cover all the bases."

The heat wasn't just there inside her. Tim's gaze drifted over her face, more than a touch of anticipation clearly there for her to witness. "You're acting twelve. You'll be making comments about hitting a home run next."

"Anything to score with you." He winked at her groan. "Don't worry, I intend sex to be involved, but I'm exhausted as well. I'll be a perfect gentleman until we've both recovered."

Erin ignored the fact that the driver could hear them. After Alisha and Devon's little scene in the restaurant, being overheard talking about sex wasn't nearly as risqué. "The idea of you being a gentleman makes me laugh."

"Gentleman pirate?"

She chuckled softly. "That I could see. You scoundrel."

He leaned her head against his chest and cradled her close. "At your service. It's what scoundrels do best."

She thought she'd fall asleep, what with the winding roads and the long day of travel and work. Instead she found herself awake but relaxed, the steady beat of his heart under her ear. The rhythmic touch of his fingers as he stroked her braid. Fingertips light on the strands as it hung down over her shoulder.

Outside the grey sky filled with clouds, harsh against the deep green of the evergreens on the mountainsides. They were out off the highway and headed into the higher ground of the island. "So not into Victoria City?"

"What's that?"

Erin rested a palm on his chest and held on lightly. "I thought you'd take me into the big city. Find us a fancy hotel so you could impress me."

"Too easy. And too much like being back living in a tourist town. Banff is great, but I want some time away from the constant influx of strangers, even if we're a couple of them."

Good point. "Rustic cabin in the woods?"

"Just about." Tim pointed ahead of them.

Erin leaned forward to follow the line. "Holy shit, Tim. Rustic doesn't mean castle-sized."

"I do everything bigger." Tim laughed when Erin's hand curled into a fist, and she playfully tapped him on the chest. "I can't help it. I've been gifted in so many ways."

"Gift of oversized ego, that's for sure." Erin stared out at the rapidly approaching estate and wondered why she wasn't screaming harder about being kidnapped. "Tell me what is this mansion we're headed to. Because that doesn't look like a hotel."

"It's a private residence. Someone I know who has a few places, and offered for me to stay anytime I wanted."

Oh, right. She gave him a look. "You just happen to know someone who just happens to have a place on Vancouver Island that is like a million-dollar setting, and without even calling, we're going to be welcome for a few days?"

"Multibillion-dollar."

She snorted. "You are so going to have to tell me what you've been up to over the past years."

"Making friends." He shrugged. "There's a lot of money in and around the oil industry. In this case, though, knowing how to save a man when he was having a heart attack during a visit to the platform got me the connection."

"Oh, that makes sense." Erin relaxed a little. "He got sick while doing a tour of the station, and now he's eternally grateful to you?"

"Something like that. Add in the fact I'm a charming fellow, and I get invited to a lot of parties."

"I bet you do." Erin eased back. "Fine. I'll trust you."

Utter silence followed the statement, and panic threatened to rise in Erin.

Trust. She pretty much had always trusted him. Except when her actions had led to his one shitty retaliation. For the rest, when things had gone sideways, it had been far more about her fears than him doing anything wrong.

Far more about losing control and losing herself.

The car pulled up to the front of the long drive, stopping under the protective roof of a massive overhang. A few lights were on in the house, and a well-dressed young man came forward to open her door and offer her a hand.

Erin waited silently, a little uncomfortable until Tim joined her.

"Is Matthew home?" Tim pulled Erin to his side, soothing her fears with his confident approach.

"Unfortunately, you've missed him. He'll be home tomorrow."

Tim held out his hand. "Timothy Dextor and Erin Tate. Matthew said for me to drop in. We'll be staying for three nights."

The man shook hands. "I'm Jason Lord. Let me help you with your bags, and I'll show you to the sunroom. You can relax while I see about getting your suite prepared."

"I'll deal with the taxi." Tim gestured for Erin to go ahead. "I'll be with you in a minute."

Jason extended his arm, and Erin wrapped her fingers

around the cool black suit with hesitation. "There's not a problem with us stopping in unannounced?"

"Mr. Haven enjoys the spontaneity of new guests," Jason assured her. "I'm sure he'll be delighted."

Then Erin got lost in the three-storey ceiling and massive roman columns arranged in a circle around the grand foyer. "Holy shit," she whispered. "We're not in Kansas anymore."

Gold. Textiles. Dazzling colours and comfortable leather. It was like watching *Homes Beautiful*, international version, only instead of being on the TV it was right freaking there in front of her.

She was a little shell-shocked by the time Tim joined her in the sunroom. An unpretentious name for a room the size of her main floor that was filled with greenery and exotic blooms.

"You comfortable?" Tim grabbed a bottle off the side counter and poured sparkling liquid into two fluted glasses waiting there.

Erin's jaw snapped up as she fought to find words. "What the hell is going on, Tim?"

He shrugged. "I told you, Matthew and I go back a ways. He's got money, and I like spending it for him. We get along fine."

"So Jason isn't off summoning the police right now?"

Tim shook his head and handed her a glass, the stem cool against her fingers. "Of course not. I'm sure he left the room and immediately phoned Matt to make sure we were on the up-and-up, but seriously. Think about it, Erin. Would anyone really show up out of the blue and announce they were staying for three days if they hadn't been invited?" He raised a brow. "Right? I mean, that would take more chutzpa than even I've got."

"True." Erin accepted the glass and sniffed cautiously. "Only you have to admit this is far outside my usual lifestyle."

"I don't live this way on a daily basis, either. Makes it

more enjoyable when I do." Tim raised his glass to her in salute. "To three days of luxury and relaxing."

Their glasses touched, and a crystal click echoed off the walls. Erin could no longer hold back her grin. "To three days of decadence."

The flash of desire in his eyes promised that their time would be enjoyable for many reasons.

Heat trickled up her spine as Tim strolled through the room, but she answered his casual comments with matching nonchalance.

For the past month he'd done everything he'd said he would. He'd let her be in charge, hadn't pushed for more in the bedroom than what a typical vanilla couple would enjoy. And he was talented enough that she'd had fun. But—

The look of ecstasy on Alisha's face only a few hours earlier had changed things. Rocked the world that Erin had been fighting to maintain—a world where she didn't step outside the very clear boundaries she'd set.

Yet the longing to accept more from Tim was real. While that scared the hell out of her, Erin tucked up her fears and let the other side of her desires escape.

Maybe it was wrong, but for this short while, in a new and somewhat unreal setting, maybe the rules she'd been following so closely for so long could be slightly bent. Maybe, as with Alisha and Devon, there was a place for her to simply take what it was that gave her the most pleasure.

Now she had to work up the courage to let Tim know the rules were temporarily changing.

CHAPTER 12

,,,,,,,,,,,,,,,,,,,,,,,,,,,,,,,,,,,,

Jason led them up a staircase that could have fit in any royal manor, the wood surfaces polished to a sparkling shine. All the while the man at Erin's side distracted her more than the opulence glittering around them.

He waited for her to enter the room first before accepting a key from their guide. Tim closed and locked the door silently behind them.

If she'd thought Tim's condo was over the top, this remote palace was another step up the incredible scale. Only the carpets and leather couches and gilded-framed mirrors didn't have a chance when she was fixated on something far better. Tim stood at her side, his fingers playing softly with hers as they stopped in the center of the living room.

"Our backpacks look very out of place," she noted, retreating to the floor-to-ceiling windows.

"Backpacks don't care." He grinned. "Come on. You said shower and sleep, so let's get ourselves a little of that. Jason informed me he'll send up breakfast, and Matt should be back sometime well before noon."

"Lovely." Erin twisted her fingers together before deliberately jerking them apart. Bullshit if she would turn into some wilting flower just because she was about to ask for . . .

God, am I really going to ask for . . . ?

Tim tilted his head. "What's wrong?"

"Nothing."

He caught her hands in his, calm and reassurance in his presence. "Trust me. Matthew is a great guy, and we're not going to be kicked to the curb in the middle of the night. Or staked in our beds, or anything weird."

Erin took a deep breath. "I trust you."

She stepped away slowly, his gaze still pinned to her as she separated their fingers. Then she lifted her hands and undid her top button. Pulled the fabric free from her pants.

"Erin?" The word was a smooth, low rumble that teased her senses and heightened her anticipation. His smile kicked up a notch, the concern fading away.

Her heart didn't seem to be beating properly, and the air in the room seemed very thin.

"I trust you," she repeated, shedding the fabric and letting it fall to the floor. The button on her waistband was undone, the zipper lowered slowly. Tim didn't move until she'd eased the material over her hips. Then he held out a hand and supported her as she stepped away from the pile of clothing left behind.

Naked but for her bra, panties, and socks.

All the stress of the moment vanished as she looked down at the specifics of what she wore, laughter escaping in a somewhat hysterical burst. It was the *least likely to be considered sexy* outfit she'd ever seen. A serviceable bra, plain undies, and a pair of the thickest socks she owned that she'd dragged on this morning before first light. "I picked the best day to decide to do this."

Tim held her fingers in his and refused to let her go. Instead he moved closer and lifted her chin. His blue eyes danced as he examined her. "And what exactly are you doing?"

Her pulse skipped. "Trusting you."

His volume dropped even further. A sheer whisper that scratched along her nerve endings and made them tingle. "Not enough. Erin, why are you stripping down like this? Did you want to make love?"

The bastard was going to make her say it. After all the time they'd spent together during the past month, she should have expected he wouldn't simply take over at the first gesture on her part.

Her breasts rose and fell rapidly with each shaky breath, yet his gaze never fell below her chin as he observed carefully.

Waited for her to respond.

Erin closed her eyes to shut out all distractions. "I want you to take control. I don't want to be in charge of what we do, and I trust you to make these days special."

A soft stroke slid over her cheek and chin, then his lips brushed hers. "Open your eyes, kitten."

She obeyed, lifting her lids to discover him only inches away as he gazed lovingly at her.

He stroked her cheek again. "I agree to one day. We take one day, and then we see where we're at. What do you think?"

The offer surprised her. "You don't want . . . ?"

Tim paused. "I want the best for you, Erin. I don't want you to feel pressured or upset if you change your mind. So let's take twenty-four hours and see how we feel. We're adults, we can talk things through. Make right decisions at the right time."

Unexpected as his suggestion was, something inside her lightened. A fear lifted as if attached to helium balloons, floating off her. "I agree."

He curled his hand around the back of her neck, his strong thumb stroking the sensitive place where her pulse once again pounded out a rapid rhythm. "Safe word the same as always?"

She nodded.

"Say it."

Sympathy twisted her smile. "I was trying to save you a cringe."

Tim eased in and kissed her, his laughter brushing her skin as softly as the contact between their lips. "I'll survive. Say it."

"Spider."

His involuntary shudder wasn't funny, but it was. Erin cupped his face in her hands and kissed him tenderly.

His hands circled her waist, palms warm on her bare skin as he separated them a few inches. "At least you know I'll never say it unless we're in dire straits."

He looked her over for the longest time as her anticipation rose. When he finally moved, it was to slide a strong hand down the back of her leg until he knelt at her feet.

Blue eyes trapped her, his smile growing by the minute. "Thank you for trusting me, kitten. Now lift your foot."

Erin rested her hand on his shoulder for balance as Tim carefully removed her woolen socks. "You're serious?" she teased. "Only a Newfie would have a woman at his command and go for her socks."

"Living in Newfoundland does not make a soul a Newfie." Tim stroked her calf as he settled her foot carefully on his thigh. "Besides, 'tis not the Newfie in me, but the Irish. I'm after your dainty dancing feet."

Erin moaned as he dug his thumbs into her tired arches. "You can have them. I'll dance prettily for you if you promise to rub me right."

He surprised her, standing and scooping her up. "Rubbing you right is definitely on the agenda."

Erin caught hold around Tim's neck, snatching glimpses of the rooms they passed en route to wherever he was carrying her. "Not to be changing the topic, but Mr. Matt the billionaire? What does he do exactly? And how big is this set of rooms they put us in, because this is crazy. I'm going to get lost finding the bathroom in the dark."

"Matt owns a refinery or two. And you won't get lost." Tim swung her to the floor and held her until she found her balance. "I'll show you the way."

Another gorgeous room to admire, only Tim gave her no time. Instead he had her stripped naked and under a cascade of warm water before she could utter a single word about overdone but fantastic bathing areas.

She lifted her hands to remove the elastics from her hair, waiting for Tim to join her.

Only as she combed her fingers through her braids to loosen them, Tim didn't strip down any further. Instead he stood and watched her, his gaze easing over her like a hungry cougar eyeing his dinner.

"You having a shower?" she asked. "There's definitely room for two in here."

Waiting for him to make the first move was going to drive her crazy.

The temptation was to jump in right away. To follow her into the shower and use his hands and mouth and cock to work her into a state of utter exhaustion. Sated and fucked to oblivion. But as much as his body screamed for him to follow through on his carnal impulses, that wouldn't highlight the truth he desperately needed her to realize.

She might have given him control, but she was ready to wrest it back at a moment's notice. He knew it, and that was the battle to be won.

Twenty-four hours to prove that here, in the bedroom, she wanted him. More than wanted—she *needed* him to call the shots. It wasn't nearly long enough to put everything in motion so all the dominoes fell the right way.

But he'd do his damnedest.

"I'll shower later." Tim leaned his hips against the thick

granite counter and got comfy. "Right now, I'm enjoying the show."

Water cascaded down her torso and made her skin glisten. The smooth curves of her breasts, the scooped indent of her waist. She teased her hands up her body to briefly cup her breasts before stepping back and lifting her face to the spray.

Tim admired her muscular body, calves and thigh muscles flexing briefly as she shifted position. Strong biceps, firm shoulders. All of her strength contrasted beautifully with her softer womanly curves. Dark nipples pulling to peaks in spite of the heated water washing her clean.

She knew he was watching.

Erin twisted her back to him, lathering shampoo into her hair. Sections draped over her shoulders, and he itched with the desire to grab hold. To tangle the long strands around his fingers as he made fists and held her in position. The long line of her back arching toward him as he pumped into her.

Soon.

The scent of coconut drifted out, and he laughed. "You're already good enough to eat. You don't need to add to temptation."

"It was that or tea tree oil," Erin commented as she faced him again. "I'd prefer to smell like an exotic drink."

"Summertime. The scent of a hot day, lying in the sun with nothing to do but listen to the ocean and let the sun bake your senses."

"Oh, poetic." She crossed her arms, framing her breasts perfectly. "I'm clean. You want the shower, or what?"

Tim didn't answer. Just stepped barefoot into the enclosure with her and ignored her gasp of surprise. Everything he wore was instantly soaked as he crowded her against the tiled sidewall, fully clothed to her naked skin.

She tilted her head and met his kiss full on. Accepted his hungry assault as he took possession of her mouth. He kept his hands pressed hard to the wall on either side of her head to stop from clenching her. To resist the urge to shove her to her knees and drive his cock into her mouth.

The feral animal inside him wanted to seize and control. The man took what she would give, and waited.

He pressed harder, his body alone pinning her in place. Kissing continued. Passionate bites and licks as he moved to torment the tender section under her ear. All the while he refused to allow her to retreat.

Erin moaned, a gasp of longing and anticipation. She'd caught his shirt and held on tight, her strong fingers squeezed into fists. She couldn't move him, and he wasn't about to leave, but she held on just the same, struggling to make the connection between them more intimate. She wiggled, but her hips only shifted minutely from side to side.

Tim slowed his kisses and dragged in a breath of air. "You want more?"

"Yes," she hissed, desperately attempting to make him do something.

He was on to her game. "You want to come?"

"You decide. Bastard."

Tim laughed. "But you seemed determined to get something here. Shall I take what I want? Or give in, and let you have your way again?"

A string of curses scorched his ears before she paused and let out a long, slow breath.

Then relaxed.

All the tension she'd been fighting him with washed away, as if flowing out of her limbs and down the drain. Her tight-fisted grip on his shirt loosened, and she rested her head on the tiles, eyes seeking his.

He nodded slowly.

Tim ran his hand down her side. He caressed her hip, then caught her under her knee and lifted the leg upward. "Wrap it around me," he ordered.

Her body was open to him, and as he leaned back slightly, there was enough room to sneak his fingers between them.

Just far enough to separate the folds of her sex and tease with a fingertip as he kissed her. This time the hunger between them was different. He took control, and she accepted what he gave her. Savoured it. Eased her neck back so he could dance attention on the sensitive curves, lave his tongue in tiny circles as he headed toward her ear.

All the time he kept his fingers moving. Increasing pressure on her clit, firm thrusts of his fingers into her wet core.

She shivered as he sucked on her earlobe. "God, I'm getting goose bumps in the shower."

"You need this," Tim breathed softly. "Letting go makes every part of you more sensitive. When I stroke your skin"— he brought his left hand down her collarbone, over her nipple, until he caught hold of her hip—"you don't just feel it where we connect. The sensation dances all over, like an electric pulse. A net of intense pleasure. When I touch your clit, you know I can make you come. But every part of you wants my touch. All of you craves my attention."

"Yes," she whispered. This time the word meant so much more. There was no command in it, just sheer desperate desire.

Tim adjusted them slightly so the water fell over her, keeping her warm as liquid splashed freely over her breasts, the fine spray like a thousand tiny fingers caressing her skin.

Erin's head fell back and her eyelids slowly lowered, her lips shaking lightly as they settled into an open pout.

He rested his palm on the upper curve of her ass to brace her. Fingers spread wide, maximum contact between him and her bare skin. With his other hand he continued to play, teasing between her folds, pressing his fingers deep. Curling his fingertips inside her until a long, low purring rumble escaped her.

Her body tightened around him, waves rocking her torso. Tim watched, fascinated, as her orgasm unfurled. Slowly, intense. Her pulse pounded in the hollow at the base of her neck even as she gasped out small, panting breaths.

Astonishing to witness. Addictive as well.

When she stopped shaking, he kissed her one more time. "That was beautiful. Thank you for sharing with me."

Her smile twisted upward. "Anytime."

Tim made sure she was stable against the wall, then took a pace backward and the next step forward. "Undress me."

Erin didn't hesitate. She reached for his shirt and tugged it free from his waistband. Her hands skimmed up his abdomen, nails teasing as she reached around him to finish the job in the back. Then she caught the bottom edge and lifted it upward as far as she could before he had to take over, dropping the sodden mass in the far corner of the shower enclosure.

"Do you mind if I explore while I work?" Erin asked.

"Be my guest." Tim waited to see what she would try. Was this already an attempt to regain control on her part?

But she merely pressed gentle kisses to his chest. Examined the slight scars marring his body from years of rescues and active adventures, and left each one after giving it loving attention.

She went to her knees before him, water streaming over her shoulders. Tim looked down at her and fought to keep from shouting his delight.

Erin stroked the outline of his cock where it bulged the material. "Have I mentioned how much I like that we don't have to use condoms anymore?"

"That's my line," Tim teased.

The snap of his pants gave way, then the zipper. His cock pressed urgently against the front of his briefs. The next few minutes were a combination of sensual torment and laughter as the wet material clung to him, and Erin had to work hard to strip away his pants. Her muscles flexed smoothly as she leaned lower, tugging each pant leg free one at a time from his feet.

Her hair lay in ribbons over her back, the long black strands showing more of a curl as the moisture wicked into them. The long line of her spine curled gently, glistening and smooth.

Then she turned and faced him, eager hands rising to grasp the edge of his briefs, lifting away the fabric to release his cock. Gently brushing her fingers over his length to free him so she could again remove his final clothing.

His cock stood upright, and he longed for another touch of her fingers. What he got was even better as she knelt upright, her task complete. Her gaze stopped at his hips as if fascinated with what she discovered there.

"Taste me," Tim commanded. "I want to feel your lips around me, and nothing else."

She'd already been reaching for his length, but at his words she changed tack, resting her hands on his hips instead, firm fingers wrapping around to press into the muscles of his ass. Erin took a deep breath and extended her tongue, making contact with the base of his cock. She licked upward, the slick heat of her mouth so different from the water cascading around them.

More intimate. More intense. More *everything.*

The height difference between them wouldn't allow her to capture him easily without the use of her hands, but Tim waited to see what she would do. How she would follow his directions without breaking free.

She didn't try to surround him. Not at first. Just worked his length with her tongue. Captured his balls and sucked lightly until the tingling at the base of his spine warned he'd better make a decision or it would be torn from him. The sight of her there at his feet—it wasn't that she was powerless, not when she had the ability to make him lose control so readily.

Tim caressed her cheek softly with one hand, and with the other he angled his cock toward her mouth. She opened eagerly, stopping short of engulfing him. Instead she twirled her tongue around the head, playing along the sensitive edge of the crown. Only when he was a second away from driving forward did she seem to sense his need.

Erin glanced up. Their eyes connected. That was when she leaned forward and took his cock as deep as possible.

Tim shuddered at the intense sensation. At the hard suction she used on the slow retreat. Every nerve in his body seemed connected to his cock at that moment, and Erin was the one holding him enthralled.

He tightened his fingers and tilted her head slightly. Pulled her forward just a touch more on the next plunge. Her nostrils flared as the tip of his crown briefly hit the back of her throat. Tim retreated, but did it again, pushing a little farther, his limbs going weak from the exquisite pleasure she was giving him.

Erin relaxed again, her throat loosening as she let him support her. He slowed, long full strokes again and again as he allowed his full length to stretch her lips. Feeding every inch of his shaft into her so deep that her nose touched his groin on each motion.

His hands on her head controlled her.

"Fucking you is always incredible, but this?" Tim groaned, letting her hear the primal creature she reduced him to. "You should see what I see. Strength and beauty. Giving, and being taken. I like fucking your mouth, love. You make my brain go numb, and I want to drive into you until my seed fills your mouth. See you swallow around me, fighting to keep every bit. Will you do that?"

He pressed her head higher and she stared at him, eyes glazed with passion as she'd relaxed into the act.

Once more he pressed deep, and with them completely connected, he paused. Just for a second, but long enough she had to hold her breath. There was no way for her to take in air. Her only two choices were to fight for freedom or trust him.

A second only, but if she didn't believe in him it would seem an eternity.

Staring into her eyes he saw nothing that worried him. Nothing but trust, and he pulled back until his cock head rested on her glistening lips. Erin breathed around him, her heated gasps rushing over the wet length and tormenting him that he still hadn't found release.

"Suck," he commanded.

Instantly she closed her lips, cheeks hollowing in response.

The sensation dragged a raw curse from him, urgency rising. He pulsed his hips forward in short, ragged stabs that, combined with what she was doing, guaranteed an explosive end all too soon.

"Maybe instead, I'll mark you. Paint your pretty face and body. See my seed glistening on your skin."

She swayed slightly, nostrils flaring.

Oh, yeah. "You like that idea, don't you."

Her response was to suck harder, fingernails edging into his flesh.

He moved quicker, only seconds remaining. "Like pearls against your dark skin, love. Lift your head."

Tim pulled his cock from her lips as the first blast escaped him, a line of seed coating her tongue, her open lips. The second sprayed down her cheek and throat, and he wrapped his fingers tight and jerked every last drop free until her skin glistened with trails of semen over the moisture from the shower.

He put the wet head of his still-hard cock to her mouth. "Open."

Her lips separated only slightly, rubbing his length as he filled her once more. She swirled her tongue over the sensitive head, sucking him clean. Pulling pleasure from him until he was barely able to stand.

He leaned down and brought her to her feet, draping her against his body. They stood there as he smoothed his fingers over her, washing her with his seed. Marking her even as he cleaned her.

Soft and sated. At peace.

A long contented sigh escaped her, and she relaxed against him even more.

"I liked that," Erin whispered. "Way too much."

"Oh, love. Stop judging and enjoy. You liked it, I loved it—there's nothing more to think about. Not now." He stroked the hair away from her face, and kissed her tenderly. "Come, it's time for bed."

CHAPTER 13

The door opened and Tim sauntered in, his bright smile lighting the room as much as the sun. He had a food cart in front of him and a bag over one shoulder. "Hey, lazy bones. Haul ass."

Erin grabbed the comforter and pulled it to her chin, ignoring the scent of coffee that had followed him into the room. "I'm on holidays," she complained. "Go away."

"Ha." He tossed the bag to the floor, then took a flying leap and landed on the bed beside her. The mattress bounced her upward, and before she could react, he had her trapped.

She stared up as he hovered over her, his hands closing around her wrists. He pinned them on either side of her head, and with that one motion he turned her inside out. She couldn't move, couldn't escape—

Didn't want to, either.

"I missed your usual enthusiastic wake-up call." No matter how firmly she attempted to say the words, they came out breathless and lust-filled.

He leaned in and kissed her. So soft and gentle it was hard to remember that he held her restrained. The contrast between her power and his made her insides turn to jelly.

Tim sat back and pulled her upright. "All sex and no play makes for a holiday you can't brag about to your friends. Matt had a brilliant idea."

"He's home?"

"He is. He's suggested loaning us some winter gear—if you'd like to go skiing?"

"Serious?"

"Hell, yeah. He's got some nice hills right in the area, and a snowcat to take us up. Jason will drive."

"Sounds great, if Matt's got the equipment to handle all of us."

Tim raised a brow. "You making a dirty reference to Matt's equipment? I like how your brain works."

"Jeez. That was a perfectly ordinary comment."

He waggled his brows and pulled a laugh from her. Then he proved he was practically perfect by pouring her a coffee.

Moments later they sat in the overstuffed chairs in front of the window, staring over the wintery Hallmark-worthy scene as they consumed fresh-baked muffins and delicate slices of fruit served in crystal goblets.

Erin wasn't sure if she'd really woken up. "Remind me to be nicer to the people we rescue from now on. Tim, this is not the real world."

"It is for some people, obviously." He added another scoop of whipped cream to his fruit, his grin widening. "And there's nothing wrong with us stepping into their reality for a short while."

"No, I guess not."

The muffin was still hot enough to melt the butter, little pools of decadence forming in the second before she put her teeth to it.

"Oh. My. God."

Tim leaned forward, his gaze intent on her instead of out the window. "Damn, you keep making those kind of noises, and we'll be late for skiing."

Erin drew out another long moan, deliberately licking her fingers one by one.

His gaze was hot enough to burn. "Stop now, or face the consequences."

She mock-pouted. "But I want to go skiing."

His laughter eased over her as he put another muffin on her plate. "Eat. Make sex noises. I'm enjoying this very much."

They exchanged smiles, then Erin sighed, deep relaxation sinking in.

"I needed this. Hey, anything I need to know about our host?" Erin asked.

"Matt?" Tim considered for a moment. "He's probably younger than you're expecting. The heart attack I mentioned was caused by a preexisting defect he didn't know about, not age or abuse. Old money. The rest of his family still lives in Alberta. I've gone backpacking with him as well as gambling."

"Nice. So he's not just all this." Erin gestured to the formal decor festooning the walls.

The place was a touch on the gaudy side for Tim's tastes. "I have a feeling someone else decorated this, not Matt. But we can ask him later. He's a straight shooter. As impressive as the house and the location are, you don't have to mind your manners around him. He's just a guy."

"A guy with money."

Tim grinned. "Lots of money."

They eventually made their way to the walk-out basement, Jason guiding them into the room before abandoning them. "Matt will be here in a moment."

Tim opened a set of storage doors and whistled. "Hot damn, he's got snowboards as well."

A new voice broke in. "Of course. Knew you'd be joining me someday."

Erin faced the entrance and was surprised all over again. The man who walked through the door was not only a lot younger than she'd have expected if not for Tim's earlier warning, Matt was drop-dead gorgeous. If Tim had the scruffy, dark scoundrel looks she loved, Matt was an angel with dirty eyes. Blond hair long enough it stood upright as if he'd been dragging his hands through it, silvery grey eyes that took in the room quickly. He was in his late thirties, or early forties at the latest, his well-cut ski clothing covering a trim body.

This holiday got better and better all the time. Erin had no objections to having lovely eye candy to enjoy.

Tim stopped his exploration of the room and strode toward his friend. "If you didn't hide in the bush, you'd get more visitors."

"This way only the good ones stop by," Matt offered. He thumped Tim on the shoulder. Then he pulled back and examined Erin with a growing smile. "And now the good gets even better. Tim, why did you let me waste time talking to you when there's a goddess in my house?"

Tim slipped his arm around Erin's waist. "Erin, this is my good friend Matt. Matt, meet Erin Tate. She's the chopper pilot for the SAR team I'm with."

Matt's brows rose as he took her hand in his, the heat of his fingers rolling up her arm in an alarming manner. "Pilot. Well, now. Beautiful *and* talented. Welcome, Erin. I hope you enjoy your stay."

"You've been very generous letting us drop in out of the blue. Thank you."

He tossed his hands in the air. "Not like I don't have the room to put you up, right?"

She smiled. "It is rather spacious."

His eyes sparkled briefly before he turned toward the storage cupboards. "Let's get our gear and hit the slopes.

We've got perfect conditions, and I don't want to waste a moment."

A fountain of snow flew skyward before slowly settling to the ground, not nearly disguising the deep hole Tim had made when he fell.

Matt's laughter rang out, bouncing back from the hillside to dance around them. Erin grinned as well once Tim's sheepish smile appeared over the edge.

He pulled himself to vertical. "Laugh it up. You now have the marker to beat for the best fall of the day."

"We don't try to one-up disasters," Erin mocked.

"Sure we do," Matt interrupted. "During drinks, after the skiing is over."

Erin waited for Tim to extract himself, taking the time to look over the terrain with a rising sense of satisfaction and wonder. Tall trees displayed snow-capped limbs against the pale-blue sky. Around them endless powder lay undisturbed except for the traces of trails to the north where they'd done a run earlier. Not a single soul but for the three of them, with Jason waiting at the bottom to run them up the mountain again when they were done. "You've got a piece of heaven here, Matt. Absolutely amazing."

"I figured it was worth the cost." Matt leaned on his ski poles as Tim joined them, doing the weird hop-hop motion his snowboard forced upon him. "After Tim here saved my life, it didn't seem right to spend the rest of it in an office fighting tooth and nail just to make more money."

Tim connected his free foot, then brushed the snow from his sleeves. "I was in the right place at the right time, that's all. And you're still making plenty of money."

"True. But I'm spending it on things that make me happy now rather than worrying about increasing my net value and rising in the ranks of the Fortune Five Hundred."

"Good for you." Erin took a deep breath and enjoyed the icy bite in her lungs. "You're in good health now, it seems."

"Better than before. Surgery to fix the problem, and then I got in shape." Matt casually adjusted his stance. "Better shape than you two—race you to the bottom."

He was gone, a war cry echoing into the air, his skis aimed straight down the hill.

Tim caught her arm before she could take up the challenge, dragging her against him for a heated kiss. Their helmets knocked briefly before they lined up properly, but by that time she was laughing too hard to kiss him without her amusement getting in the way.

He smiled against her lips. "You having fun?"

"Uh-huh." She slipped one arm free, planting it carefully on his chest. "You?"

"Absolutely." Tim eased back slightly. "So, what do you think?"

She pushed as hard as she could, and he went sprawling for a second time. His expression was wide with shock as she quickly stepped out of reach and poled down the hill. "I think I'll meet you at the bottom," she shouted.

He was already rising to his feet, so she focused on the hill before her. Matt's tracks wove through the trees in as close to a straight line as possible, and she followed them, turning aside to enter a gully that opened into clear territory.

Matt was visible ahead of her, leaving wide, controlled tracks. He was obviously not racing now so much as having a good time, and Erin joined in, turning in opposition to his marks. The snow rose around her boots, leaving a perfect record of her passage, and together their trails formed one perfect figure eight after another.

It was exhilarating to be in the mountains under her own power. So often she brought the team into remote places and stayed with the chopper, which was her role. But it was good to be on foot this time. Far into nature, and right smack-dab in the action. She needed to do this more often.

Her cheeks were slightly numb from the icy air rushing past by the time she approached where Matt had pulled to the side, waiting for them to regroup before reentering the trees. His contented expression had to match her own.

"Nice. I like the artistic touch on the hillside." He pointed at the tracks they'd laid.

"Now we need to see what Tim does," Erin warned. "I can see the showoff driving a straight line through the middle."

"You could be right," Matt admitted.

She soaked in the scenery, admiring the low foothills rolling off into the distance, clouds covering their feet where they met the coastline. Behind her and Matt, the mountainside was one massive bump completely filling sky and horizon.

"Or"—Matt grabbed her arm and pointed above them—"he could be taking the elevator down."

Far above to the right was the near-level surface that she would have skied if not for selecting the gully. There she'd had a slope gradually descending her to the level where they now stood.

Tim had missed the turn. Deliberately or not, she wasn't sure, but he was in the clearing on the very edge of the precipice, headed for the cliff.

"Is he serious?" Her heart gave one giant pound, then seemed to freeze in her throat as Tim made a couple of casual turns but didn't change paths.

"Landing could be interesting."

She jerked her eyes off Tim for one second to gape at Matt. "*Interesting?* That's a . . . what? Sixty-foot drop?"

"Tim can do it. He's got a fantastic line to follow, and enough of a run out. If he lands it."

The absolute calm Matt projected helped, but didn't erase her fears. She snapped her gaze back up to Tim with dread weighing her down. "Thank you for that, Mr. Warren Miller."

It wasn't her imagination. Tim was going off the edge.

He had built up a lot of speed before he left the mountain ledge, body in a controlled position. Then instead of falling as she'd expected, the asshole added to her heart attack.

His snowboard spun skyward, his body straightening until his head was down, feet up. The rotation continued slowly, seeming to pause when he was belly down and rapidly descending toward the earth.

She would have sworn, but all available air was stuck in her chest behind a closed throat. He tucked in his knees and finished the rotation, the smooth surface of his snowboard making contact with the snow. He coasted. Arms stretched wide, snow flying everywhere as he moved rapidly forward until the deep powder pulled him to a stop a short distance below them.

A long loud shout of delight broke free as Tim threw his fists in the air and shook them in triumph before spinning toward them, his sheer enthusiasm visible even at this distance.

"You still planning on killing him?" Matt asked.

"Making him hurt, oh hell yeah. Death, I'll give him a reprieve—looks like he's cheated it twice today."

They grinned at each other, then added their cheers as they headed to Tim's side to finish their trip down the mountain.

One thing was for certain. Tim had a far broader definition of what constituted a good time than she did.

CHAPTER 14

''''''''''''''''''''''''''''''''''

A screaming hot shower and a short nap followed their full day of marking up the powder. Rested and damn near starving, they were definitely ready for dinner.

Both of them eyed their clothing bags with a bit of disgust.

Erin held her cleanest T-shirt gingerly between two fingers. "I think I'll be dining in the room so I can wear a towel. As much fun as this impromptu holiday is, I didn't pack much more than a change of undies. I'm not wearing any of my stinky stuff down to a formal dinner with Matt."

"First, stop with the *formal* and *Matt* thing, but I agree about the clothes. He said we're free to check the closet and use whatever we want."

She tugged open the door to the walk-in closet and flicked on the light. "Sweet Jesus, is Matt a cross-dresser, or does he often have women show up he needs to dress?" Erin whirled to face him. "These aren't his ex-wife's clothes or something, are they?"

Tim tugged forward a sleeve to show a price tag was still attached. "I'll ask him, but I get the feeling this is like the decor. Someone bought the lot because closets are supposed to hold clothes. I wouldn't worry about it. They're here, let's find something that fits."

She ran a hand along the garments as she paced forward, the fabric swaying as she released it. "Matt's world is a whole different place than the one I live in," she repeated.

He kissed the back of her neck, then pulled a blouse forward. "Get dressed. I like that colour."

"You should try this on." She tugged a hanger to one side and raised a brow.

Tim grinned. "A kilt?"

Erin patted his ass as she grabbed a couple of hangers and headed into their room. "I wouldn't complain."

By the time Tim escorted her down the stairs to the main dining room, there was a spot inside him that could only be called contentment.

Erin leaned against him easily, all the fight and bluster that usually hovered around her faded to a low level. It wasn't as if she were weaker, but the bristly side she tended to display in public was muted.

Tim wondered if she even realized how often she tended to put on a tough façade. He hoped for the next couple of days she'd continue to allow herself to relax, not only in private behind the doors of their suite, but out in the real world.

As real as mansions in the high alpine were, ones with suited servants and a professional chef.

Jason strolled into the room only a moment after they'd arrived. His dark eyes flashed as he smiled at them. "Good to see you looking more rested. If you're ready, I'll have dinner brought in. Matt's been delayed by a phone call—he suggested you start without him."

"We can wait," Erin offered.

"No need, although he did mention he hopes to join you

by dessert." Jason tilted his head politely, then left the room, vanishing like a shadow.

Erin picked up a full water glass from the elegantly set table and raised it toward him. "To rest and relaxation."

Tim joined her in the toast. "Two more days of luxury," he agreed. He examined the room, a happy sigh escaping as he spotted his target. "I hope you don't plan on sticking with water the entire time."

She made a face. "Tim, I'm already wearing clothes out of Matt's guest closet. I don't feel comfortable drinking his liquor as well as crashing at his place, not unless I'm contributing to the cost."

"Good point, but I doubt he'll take cash in payment. I'll ask, though, if it would make you more comfortable." As Erin settled into a chair, Tim walked to the side table where a selection of wine and alcohol covered the surface. "Matt and I have the kind of relationship where he calls me up on Tuesday to announce he'd like to go parachuting the next day. I set it up, and that's it until the next time we get together."

Erin laughed, the bright tones dancing through the room. "Great, two daredevils. No wonder you get along so well."

Tim had just grabbed a bottle of whiskey and turned toward her to answer.

She'd leaned back in her seat, the thick braid she'd woven her hair into leaving her face shining and bright. No adornment, no makeup. Both the borrowed blouse and skirt he'd convinced her to pull on were far more puritanical than the naked he'd prefer to see her in, but in spite of all that, Tim stopped cold and stared.

She frowned. "What?"

"So damn beautiful."

Her pleasure at the compliment was clear as she fidgeted slightly. A smile lingered on her lips as she gestured to the bottle in his hand. "What are you going to ply me with?"

"Grey Goose. Or if you'd prefer, I'll open a bottle of red wine."

"Hmm." Erin templed her fingers together as she leaned her elbows on the table. "Decisions, decisions. Maybe I should have a taste of each."

She jerked back, teasing expression vanishing as Jason reappeared, a trolley of food before him. "May I suggest the Merlot? The chef is grilling steaks for your main course."

"Of course he is."

Erin choked down a laugh at Tim's comment.

Jason had no qualms about sharing his amusement. His deep rumble of laughter rolled over them as he uncovered plates and placed them on the table. "We've made an assortment of things for you to try, since we had no idea of your preferences."

Amazing smells rose from the platters. "It looks delicious," Tim commented. "Open a bottle of the Merlot, and I'd like my steak medium rare."

"The same for me." Erin scooped up a shrimp with her fingers, dipping it in the rich sauce before pausing. "Jason—I don't know how this works. Would you like to eat with us?"

He lowered his chin briefly. "Thank you for the invitation, but I ate earlier with the rest of the staff."

Jason moved smoothly to the sideboard to open the wine, and Tim took advantage of the distraction to ease a couple more tidbits onto Erin's plate.

Five minutes later they were alone, music playing in the background, candles lighting the length of the table.

Tim raised his glass.

"Another toast?" Erin asked.

He shook his head. "Taste."

He held it to her lips, tilting the glass slowly as the dark liquid moved toward her mouth. Her gaze fixed on his eyes as she parted her lips slightly, a small sip of liquid all he allowed before stopping the flow.

She licked her lips, her tongue darting out to gather the lingering drops. "Lovely."

Hmm. Her voice had gone sultry and low, a tantalizing brush more potent than the wine. "Here. Try a pastry."

He chose one of the tiny tarts from her plate and lifted it as well, waiting until she leaned forward and took a bite, her teeth nipping through the flaky crust. Small crumbs scattered and he brushed them from her carefully, letting his touch linger on the curve of her breast under the silky blouse.

"Tim," she whispered.

He popped a stuffed mushroom cap into his mouth and enjoyed the burst of flavors for a moment before lifting the glass for her again. "We're alone. And I want to take care of you."

He watched her consider his words as she took another sip. She hesitated, then relaxed. She snuck one hand over and rested it on his thigh as she leaned her head on his shoulder.

Cheering wasn't appropriate, but reassuring was. He pressed his free hand over her fingers and squeezed encouragingly. "Thank you for your trust, kitten. I promise to help you enjoy yourself."

"Just don't go—" She pulled herself to a full stop, dark eyes glittering as she jerked upright so she could stare at him. She shook her head. "No, I won't do that. I won't make rules to try to influence what we're doing."

She said it plainly but in a hushed tone, as if she didn't want her confession to intrude into the world they had stepped into.

"You're braver than I am," Tim admitted. "I like influencing what's about to happen."

A spark of mischief danced in. "Then we're both in a good place, aren't we?"

"Exactly." Tim leaned back in his chair, looking her over carefully. The food was going to get cold if they didn't enjoy it soon, but there was one more thing . . . "Since we've established I'm in charge, and that I'm planning lovely things for your pleasure, then you'll have no problem handing me your panties."

CHAPTER 15
''''''''''''''''''''''''''''''''

Of all the sexual games she'd been expecting, Tim had surprised her yet again.

He waited, hand held out, palm up.

She opened her mouth to protest, then covered the move by reaching for her own glass of wine and taking a deep sip. It wasn't that bad a request, and somehow the thought made her achy.

"I suggest you do it now, or Jason will be back with our steaks before you've finished straightening things."

Erin pushed back her chair. The borrowed blouse and skirt were slightly large, but she still needed to wiggle hard to get hold of her underwear to pull it free. She passed over the warm bundle of fabric, then turned her attention to the table, ignoring the heat flushing her cheeks.

Tim slipped her panties into his pocket, the material creating a bulge.

Or maybe the extra fabric he was storing wasn't the cause. She caught his eye and teased. "You should have worn the kilt."

"My cock would have appreciated the extra room right now," he confessed easily.

"Jeez, Tim." She glanced over her shoulder, but the door to the kitchen remained closed.

"I'm pretty sure Jason has heard the word *cock* before, love. I'm also pretty sure he's got one. Might even use it upon occasion."

Erin ignored her burning ears and sampled the food. Tim laughed as he joined her, chatting easily about a madcap adventure he and Matt had taken part in up in Labrador once.

He was refilling her glass as Jason walked in with their main courses, perfectly done steaks with king crab legs arranged on top.

It was all Erin could do to not stare at Jason to see if anything had changed. His expression, his body language.

Did he know? And why could she not stop thinking about cocks and other dirty words? It was as if Tim had hypnotized her, and having been triggered by the smutty side, her brain had trampled off for a nice little exotic holiday.

She jerked upright at a touch to her hand.

Tim leaned toward her. "Jason asked if you needed anything else."

A simple head shake seemed like a hell of a lot more work than it should have been. "Thank you, no."

"Mr. Haven will be done in about ten minutes. He'll join you for dessert, if that's all right."

Tim nodded, and Jason left as Erin attempted to stop squirming in place.

The heat between her legs was unreasonable. Made no sense. All that was different between now and a million other dinners she'd enjoyed was that she was sitting bare-ass naked under a long skirt. No one could tell—

And she was still going up in flames.

She managed to cut a few pieces of steak and get them down, each bite savoury and delicious. But her appetite wasn't there.

"You've grown very quiet." Tim caressed a finger up the back of her arm. "Is the food not what you'd hoped for?"

"I think I'm intoxicated," Erin confessed. "There's no other explanation."

"You're not drunk," Tim assured her. "But you are ready for more. Open your legs."

Shit. She gripped the edge of the table and slowly obeyed, the soft sweep of fabric falling against her thighs. "You're not going to do anything now, are you? Jason said Matt could be here at any time."

"So?"

A sweep of light-headedness rolled over her. Her breathing picked up, but it wasn't panic. Nothing that would make her call him out and call it off.

"You're a bastard," she noted as plainly as she could.

"You've told me so before, and yet here we are." Tim leaned over and tugged her chair to face him slightly. "You like your men with a little bastard in their blood. Admit it."

Her breathing picked up a notch. "I like you."

He smiled in approval, then rocked her control even further. "Pull up your skirt so I can see your pussy. Now."

Her fingers were moving before her brain fully registered the words. She rolled the fabric upward and cooler air from the room brushed her, and she sighed.

Tim pulled something from his pocket. "Damn. So fucking gorgeous."

When he dropped to his knees and pulled her hips forward, she bit her lip to keep from shouting. His tongue stroked between her folds, wet heat circling her clit. The scruff on his chin rubbed her inner thigh, his upper lip a tempting abrasion that made everything more sensitive. She caught hold of the chair arms and dug in her fingers to stop from fisting his hair. She wasn't sure if she wanted to keep him there or tear him away. The door could open any second and Matt could walk in—

She was seconds away from having an orgasm at the thought, and the realization rocked her hard.

Only Tim pulled back far too soon, a final lap over the sensitive tip of her clit making her legs shake. He stared approvingly.

"One more thing," he added.

The mysterious item he'd brought from his pocket. It was U-shaped, and he licked one side, that talented tongue wasted on an inanimate object.

Then he pressed it into her body, slipping the moistened end between her folds so it rested inside her sex, and the other half nestled against her clit.

"You'll enjoy this," Tim promised. "It's not so big as to hinder you from moving, but you'll be aware of it all the time. Especially when I do this."

He sat back in his chair and pulled out a small remote control. She didn't see him do anything, but suddenly the item between her legs vibrated.

Soft, low pulses, inside and out. "Sweet mercy, Tim. What the hell?"

"You like it?" He pulled her skirt back into place and gently levered her knees together. The motion only increased the pressure, and she gasped. "Nice. That's what I thought."

Oh *God*. "You're not going to—"

Again she caught herself. Of course he was going to play with the damn controls while his friend was in the room. That was the point.

She deliberately reached for her wineglass and tipped it back, finishing the final couple of swallows as she fought to keep the toy from destroying her mind in under two minutes.

Tim clicked something else and the speed of the pulse reduced to a pace that allowed her to breathe again. He placed the control on the tabletop beside his plate.

"What? No timeline or demands that I don't have an orgasm until after coffee is served?" Erin eyed the sideboard with the liquor and considered whether a couple of shots of tequila, straight up, would take the edge off the impending earthquake.

He stared into his glass, swirling the final inch of wine remaining. "Where's the fun in denying you orgasms? That's not your thrill, Erin."

"And you know what is?" She wiggled slightly, causing the angle of the damn vibrator to adjust enough so she could talk without her voice shaking.

"Some of them." He looked her straight in the eye, mesmerizing and captivating. "I won't push too hard, too soon, but consider this. Matt is a good friend I trust, but he's not someone you ever need to see again."

A myriad of possibilities raced through her mind. "What exactly are you proposing?"

"Right now? Nothing. But keep an open mind."

"Which is no answer." Erin held her breath as Tim reached for the control and palmed it.

He raised a brow. "Have you had enough to eat?"

"I have. Thank you."

There was no use in insulting him, not when she had given him control. Only the edge of fear had returned. One step beyond what she thought she wanted was one step further than she would ever accept going. The line in the sand frightened her.

How close to the edge could Tim take her without pushing her over?

He stood and held out a hand. She rose to her feet, adjusting to balance the strange sensation of the vibrator.

Tim's smile softened as he waited for her to stop wiggling. "Does it feel strange?"

"Edgy. Different." Erin glared at him. "If it falls out while your friend is in the room, I'm warning you now you're the one who has to explain."

"It won't fall out," Tim soothed her, walking her slowly

toward the living space with the massive leather couches. "It's made so you can wear it while we have sex."

Oh.

He grinned. "And if it did fall out? Matt already knows what it is—I found it in our room. Brand-new out of the box. There was a nice assortment of toys to choose from."

Choice swear words flooded her brain. "Maybe it was his personal shopper at work again stocking the shelves, did you think of that? Or do you *know* he's a sex toy connoisseur, and if you do know that for sure, that's pretty damn kinky."

"Why?" Tim asked. "Are you going to wonder if he knows that you're excited? Will he look at you and imagine seeing you panting with excitement, trembling on the edge of orgasm?"

He clicked the on button as he spoke, and the lightest of caresses resumed. Even on low, Erin had to deliberately relax to complete the journey to the couch without stumbling.

Adding the sensation of the vibrator to Tim's words lit her brain and body on fire. "And does Matt like to watch?" she murmured, twining her fingers in his.

Tim seated her, then joined her on the buttery-soft leather. "Matt is a voyeur, yes. That's one of the things he enjoys very much."

The thrill of excitement rushing her had to be tempered with reality. "No cameras in our suite, are there?"

Tim shook his head. "He's not rude, Erin."

The door opened before she could respond, and a hearty hello rang out as Matt joined them.

No longer covered by layers of winter clothing, Matt was even more impressive. Erin instinctively glanced between the two men, contrasting the easy power they displayed. Tim wore his confidence like a well-aged leather coat, and she could imagine him at ease with brass knuckles and a knife visible at his hip. Another quick peek let her admire the five o'clock shadow he hadn't bothered to shave. The strong

hands he used to dole out caresses with the same competence with which he handled a scalpel or a rope. Dangerous
from the first glance—dangerous and delicious.

On the other side of the equation, Matt was a boardroom
knight. Pristine except for his hair, which was a shambles
again. White button-down shirt, dress pants. Clean-shaven
and clear eyes as he glanced around the room, then focused
directly on them. The kind of decision maker who would
make million-dollar choices without breaking a sweat. The
kind corporations wanted on their side, not bidding against
them.

The lone downfall to the rest of his cool, debonair
appearance—Matt had rolled up his sleeves. Just like that,
Erin got entangled in staring at his forearms and hands—
and wasn't that just wrong, to be turned on by the sight of
strong forearms with their dusting of hair?

Matt strode across the room, unaware she was sexually
objectifying his arms.

"Did you have enough to eat?" he asked, coming to a
stop by her feet.

She pulled on her best manners, hoping that her strange,
instant attraction to the man hadn't made her drool. It had
to be the vibrator turning everything around her into one
giant aphrodisiac. "Dinner was incredible. Thank you for
your hospitality."

Their host dragged a hand through his hair, and Erin
smiled. She'd guessed that part right—the gesture was obviously a habit with him, and totally explained the ends standing every which way as he twisted to the sideboard. "And
that's enough politeness for one night. Relax, make yourself
comfortable. What are you having in your coffee, or with
your coffee? I saw Jason in the hall and he's bringing in
some ghastly sweet thing made of chocolate and whipped
cream in a minute."

Erin opened her mouth to answer.

Tim adjusted the speed on the vibrator and instead of air

going out she gasped, fingers tightening on his. She coughed lightly to cover her tracks, then tore her gaze off Tim's grinning face to look into Matt's questioning expression.

"Pour us all brandies," Tim suggested, his tone just shy of an order.

Matt hesitated. He glanced between Erin and Tim, and his smile widened.

Whatever secret codes the guys had going, Erin hadn't missed the crystal-clear message—Matt wasn't the least surprised by Tim taking charge in his home, and more than that, Matt didn't seem to mind one bit.

There was no mistaking the increased heat in his tone as he moved to comply. "Stay where you are. I'll bring them to you."

"Erin will help." Tim urged her forward, his hand resting intimately on her lower back. He leaned in to whisper in her ear. "I'm glad you like Matt. He seems to like you as well. Perhaps we need to explore this a little. Yes?"

He pushed her toward the sideboard.

Sweet mercy, she was going to die. Erin worked on her breathing as Tim reclined on the couch and proceeded to torment her with the damn remote control.

What did he mean, *explore*?

He didn't give her time to adjust. Matt asked some innocent question, and Tim flipped the vibrator to an uneven pulse. She answered, unable to keep her words from trembling.

Matt held out a goblet filled with gold liquid, wrapping her fingers around the glass. "Let your body heat warm the brandy. That's the best way."

His strong hands lingered on hers as he waited for her to take hold. Erin checked over her shoulder, but Tim was still smiling as he observed. Matt held out a second glass and Erin reached for it.

The pulse between her legs bounded to high as Tim changed vibrator speeds again, and a moan ripped free from her lips, a quiver rocking her. The brandy shook, sloshing over the edge onto her and Matt's fingers. Cool liquid over heated flesh.

"Now you've got the brandy at true body temperature," Tim teased. Then his words turned husky, much lower than usual. "Matt, don't let it go to waste."

Erin froze, then let the wildfire racing over her burn. Tim was in charge, and while this wasn't what she would have picked—hell, *yeah*.

Matt lifted her hand and while they both still held the glass, he slowly licked the brandy clean. Silvery grey eyes stared into hers as his tongue stroked the sensitive area between her fingers.

Decadence. Animal attraction. She wasn't sure if she was turned on because Tim had started her motor ages ago, or if the lure of the supposedly forbidden was going to destroy her right where she stood.

Matt hummed happily as he sucked her fingers clean one at a time. Heat rolled from his body, his broad shoulders shifting slightly as he turned her toward Tim.

"Don't forget you have a glass in the other hand as well," Matt warned. "Or perhaps, do forget. If you spill more, I'm willing to help clean up. Any time. Anywhere."

Tim sprawled on the couch, the heavy bulge at his groin far too obvious as Erin found her footing and stumbled across the short distance between them. Any sense of knowing what was going on had vanished completely, and she waited, nearly breathless, to find out what would happen next.

Every step forward they took just encouraged him to go faster. Tim had planned to keep things slow to avoid going into overload, but Erin had not only taken his simple commands in stride, she was blossoming.

With Matt a willing participant, the possibilities for the next two days were endless.

But first, Tim would stick to his original plans for the evening.

Erin passed him his drink and settled gingerly beside him. He'd turned the vibrator down again, but not off, and as her ass met the couch she made another one of those noises that melted his spine.

"Feel free to put your feet on the couch. We don't stand on ceremony around here." Matt proved his point by sitting opposite them, kicking off his shoes before stretching his long limbs over the leather surface. "Tim, you said you and Erin work together. I guess this means you're not available to go scuba diving with me in a month?"

"Probably not." Tim eased Erin against his chest and stroked her hair softly. "I'll need a little more warning for tropical getaways, but I have found a great place for a future whitewater trip if you're game."

"Awesome." Matt sipped his brandy, then turned his gaze on Erin. "Your boyfriend is the source of endless hours of entertainment."

Her low chuckle carried one-hundred-percent Erin attitude. "So I'm learning."

That remark earned her a click on the remote control. He turned the vibrator to medium, a steady pulse that should have made her clit ache. He lifted her chin with a finger and kissed her, ignoring Matt, ignoring everything but her soft lips. She sighed as his tongue slipped into her mouth, and he tasted the sweet brandy she'd sipped only a moment earlier.

He caught her lower lip in his teeth briefly before easing back, staring into her eyes. "Entertainment. Pleasure. There's so much to experience."

She watched him carefully, as if eager to see what he would ask of her next. He stroked her cheek. "Soon," he whispered.

"You're killing me. I need . . . more." She spoke softly as well, but when they turned back to the center of the room,

Matt's eyes were lust-filled and his gaze roamed freely over Erin.

Admiring. Wanting.

Tim deliberately took the conversation to general topics for a while. Dessert and coffee arrived as they discussed what there was to do in the area. How Matt had been keeping himself busy. All the while Erin tried to appear interested, but the constant squirming was a giveaway her mind wasn't on the conversation.

Matt had just finished a story when Tim chose to move. "Would you excuse us? Erin hasn't seen the view from the observation deck yet."

"Take your time. The light switches for the gardens are on the south wall." Matt swirled his brandy. "I'll just top this up."

Erin held Tim's fingers tight enough to make them go numb as he led her around the corner and onto the deck he'd discovered earlier while she'd showered.

"Observation deck in the dead of winter?" Erin asked. "It's going to be cold," she warned.

"Not this one." Tim closed the door behind them and flipped on all the feature lights, showcasing an enormous landscaped path system below the house. He left on only one of the dim overhead lights in their area, moving her to the side so they stood half in the shadows, but still visible.

If someone knew where to look.

"Ahh, a closed-in sunroom. Very pretty. It's . . . *oh.*" Erin clutched the window frame. "That damn vibrator. I hope you're having fun."

"Not as much fun as I will be in a moment." Tim stepped behind her and fisted the fabric of her skirt, shoving it over her hips as he pushed between her shoulders and positioned her to his liking. "Keep your hands on the sill."

Erin glanced back, her gaze darting down to his hands as he tore open his fly and pulled his cock free. "Seriously?"

"Very." Tim slipped his fingers along her sex. "Jeez,

you're wet. Now I don't know if I want to fuck you or lick you clean."

Erin squeezed her lips together as if not wanting to influence his decision, but with her bare ass presented to him, there really was no better choice. He lined up his cock and thrust.

She cried out, but pressed back to meet him as he withdrew and thrust again. "Oh my *God*, do you feel that?" she asked.

He'd turned the vibrator to high and while it added some sensation for him, it was obviously much more for her. "Hitting your G-spot, is it? I just feel your tight, wet cunt squeezing me." He reached one arm around her waist and the other under her thigh, and pulled her upright, fucking into her body with short, hard strokes. Erin reached up and hooked an arm around his neck, her breath escaping in passionate moans and little pants.

It wasn't just the vibrator that had gotten her so wet, and Tim knew it. "Did you like it when Matt licked your fingers? So dirty, right out there in front of me. Another man touching you—that get you hot?"

"Yes." Erin confessed. She protested as he slowed his strokes, switching to long, full plunges as deep as he could go. "But only because you were there," she added.

Her honesty floored him, and cheered him on. "You get off on being touched when I can see. Trying to drive me mad, kitten?"

"You enjoyed it, too," she whispered. "You like seeing me turned on, no matter who gets me going."

"Guilty. It's pleasure, and I want it for you." Tim twisted them slightly, pausing with his cock just clinging to her passage. "Desire comes in all sorts of packages. Who are we to say what is right and what is wrong? Would you deny yourself pleasure because someone else says it's not proper?"

"My life. My body," Erin stated clearly, and Tim wanted to roar in approval.

Instead he twisted her face toward him until he could take her lips with a hot and heavy kiss. Possessive, and being possessed all at one time. He shoved a hand under her top and ripped up her bra so he could grasp one firm breast. She squirmed, fighting to get his cock deeper inside.

When they broke apart for much-needed air, Tim smiled and spoke softly. "When I bend you over again, look at the windows on the right. You can see our reflection. Watch me fucking you, loving everything about you."

Erin's pupils grew wider. "Windows?"

"Yes." He flipped her back into position and leaned her over, pulling back on her hair slightly to make sure she was looking in the right direction. "The windows of the living area where we were sitting a few minutes ago."

He powered into her body, her passage tighter than ever as she noticed what he'd seen the entire time. Their reflection was there, that was true, but if you looked *through* the window you could clearly see into the room. A dim light in the distance revealed Matt, legs stretched out on the couch as he sipped his refilled brandy. His gaze fixed on their location on the equally dimly lit deck.

"Oh, fuck. That's Matt. He's . . ." Erin shuddered, then rocked her hips back, driving Tim's cock deeper.

"Yes, he's watching"—Tim thrust again—"wishing this were his cock"—another thrust—"feeling your passion"—another—"fucking you hard."

Erin moaned, her knuckles gone white on the ledge she clung to. *"Yes."*

"But you're mine," Tim warned. "Even if others watch. Even if they touch, it's because they're a part of me. Because I give you to them for that time only. But you're *mine*, not theirs."

She was shaking now, the vibrator pulsing against her clit. Tim clutched her hips and fucked her relentlessly, deep and hard until she screamed, her body jerking so violently he nearly slipped out.

He instantly turned off the control, slamming in for the final few strokes it took to trigger his release after holding back for so long. He fucked her through her orgasm, through his, prolonging the waves of pleasure rippling through her. Dragging more from himself than he'd thought possible.

Sheer decadent pleasure driving them both beyond the limits.

Good thing his tastes ran to being watched as well, and Matt certainly had never complained before.

Erin moaned as he pulled her upright, his cock slipping free. Moisture met his groin as he held her to him, his semen and her wetness escaping to trickle down her legs. Still he supported her until their breathing calmed.

He turned her to face him, examining her carefully for any sign their little romp had been more than she wanted. All he saw was happy, sated contentment.

Then she cupped her hands around his face and kissed him. A full-on, breathtaking, soul-shattering kiss that left him reeling as hard as his entire climax moments earlier.

CHAPTER 16

''''''''''''''''''''''''''''''''''''

The second full morning of their time off began with the sun streaming over the bed, the curtains at the window wide open. Erin rolled over to discover she was alone.

A quick examination of the room didn't turn up any signs of Tim, so she crashed back into the pillows and wallowed in the unfamiliar luxury of sleeping in.

Last night had been one of the best sleeps she'd ever had.

After their explosive adventure in the sunroom, she'd expected to have to face Matt, but the living room had been empty when they returned, and Tim had whooshed her back to their rooms and basically put her to bed.

She'd been fine with it. Fine with *all* of it. Talking through the adventure right away would have ruined the intoxicating buzz rushing through her veins. Settling into Tim's arms for the night had been the perfect end to the most unusual day. And the unusual would continue today.

He'd asked for one day, but there was nothing to change her mind about wanting him to keep going. Not really. Last night had been so far up the scale of what turned her on that another pulse of desire struck just thinking about it.

Okay—maybe there was one thing to discuss. In all their playing years ago, the one thing that they'd never done was include anyone else in the picture.

Matt changed things.

If she was going to be honest with herself, the idea of fooling around with Tim *and* Matt did crazy things to her brain. Sex was pleasurable, but she could only imagine what it would be like to have two men focused entirely on making her feel good. Remembering the hot slick of Matt's tongue over her fingers made her shiver and think *good* was far too insignificant a word.

Tim appeared out of the bathroom, strolling slowly toward her with nothing but a towel wrapped low around his hips, and she wasn't thinking anything anymore but *damn*.

He paused in the middle of rubbing his hair dry. "You hungry?"

She licked her lips, deliberately looking him over.

A short burst of laughter escaped. "Insatiable."

"You know it." She hesitated for a moment. "So, about last night."

Tim raised a brow. "I say insatiable, and it reminds you of last night. I like the way those topics connect in your brain."

She took a mock swing at him, and they ended up back on the bed, play wrestling for control. Erin played dirty, and Tim must have let her win, because she ended up on top of him in the reverse position from where they'd been earlier.

Somehow the towel had been lost in their struggles. *Strange.*

Erin rested her hands on his abdomen and enjoyed playing lightly with the treasure trail under her fingers. "All kidding aside, I'll tell you straight out. Nothing about last night upset me. It was hotter than hell, and I'm game for the rest of the trip to be on your call."

His eyes flashed as he ran his hands from her hips to her waist. "Thank you for sharing that. I promise whatever we do will be with your pleasure in mind."

She nodded. "I trust you."

Quiet descended on them, the only sound their soft breathing. Erin's mind raced as she tried to imagine everything Tim would lead them into.

A gentle brush over her cheek brought her back from her mental ramblings. Tim had curled himself up and was staring intently into her face. "You're so far away. Stop thinking so hard about it all. It's not that difficult, kitten. Just enjoy yourself."

She nodded. Took a deep breath, then let it out slowly. "You're right."

"Of course I am.'

A laugh escaped and she wrapped her arms around his neck and kissed him fiercely.

Tim gave her nose a tweak. "Come on. Breakfast awaits."

Matt waved hello as they entered the room, but other than gesturing to the table he didn't say a word, his attention pinned to the computer tablet sitting beside his plate.

Guilt hit Erin briefly. "I should check my e-mail."

Tim made a rude noise.

She snorted. "*You* should check your e-mail as well. Bastard."

He held a hand up by his ear. "What's that? You're mumbling. I think you said something about bastards, though—that sounded familiar."

"What if you're the missing heir to the throne of some tiny nation you've never heard of, and they're desperately trying to track you down to crown you?"

"More likely find a bunch of Viagra offers, which I don't need."

He leered at her, and Erin laughed.

Jason stepped into the room, coffeepot in hand. "If there's anything you need from the kitchen, let me know. The chef is making a cold lunch, and he's taking requests for dinner as well."

"God, I like how rich people live." Tim held out a chair for Erin. "I like how I live when I'm with them."

"Tim," Erin scolded.

"What? Matt knows he's loaded. It's not really a secret." Tim pulled his cup forward for Jason. "And I have no requests—let the chef do his magic and surprise me."

Jason paused after filling Erin's cup and leaned in to speak softly. "Tim's right. Matt knows he's loaded, and I like how I live when I work for him. It's all good."

Erin laughed as Jason pulled back to his formal distance. "I like you."

He tipped his head and retreated from the room with a smile.

Tim took his time prepping his coffee, watching Erin out of the corner of his eye. She sipped her juice, then pulled her phone from her pocket, glancing at Tim as if daring him to say something. He just smiled and grabbed a couple of pastries from the table, before eyeing the covered plates resting in front of Matt.

She'd said she was fine with last night. Given him the go-ahead to keep things rolling, which was incredible. But part of accepting responsibility for their bedroom games meant being in tune with what she wasn't saying. The subtle or not-so-subtle hints that she was giving off.

If her words said she was okay but her body screamed for them to stop, he'd call off his plans in an instant. Nothing was worth hurting her, and the last thing he wanted was a repeat of years earlier when she'd taken off without explaining the true reasons why.

Matt closed his computer and put it aside, turning with a satisfied sigh to the table. "And that's done for the day. No more work to deal with for a week."

A muttered curse escaped Erin. She glanced up, frustration in her eyes.

Shit. That didn't look good. "Trouble?"

"You were right." She slouched back in her chair. "I shouldn't have checked my e-mail."

"Something wrong?" Matt asked.

Erin made a face. "Not wrong, but our holiday time here is cut short. They need the chopper in Calgary by tonight. We have to leave."

"Seriously?"

She nodded.

It was Matt's turn to make a rude noise. "Can I admit I'm disappointed? I was looking forward to your company for a few more days." He cleared his throat and damn near flushed. "And I mean that without any ulterior motives."

"Of course not," Tim reassured him. "You've been a great host and . . ." It was a wild idea, but why not? "Why don't you come with us?"

Matt and Erin both straightened.

"If we're just making a delivery, why not?" he reasoned. "We still don't have to report for work for a couple of days. And there's more than enough room for Matt to join us even with the rest of the team."

"No team," Erin added, eyes on her phone. "It looks like it's just you and me."

"That's crazy." Didn't anyone know how to relax anymore? "Did everyone else sprout wings and fly home without us?"

His sarcasm pulled a reluctant laugh from her. "Check your e-mail. There have been a whole slew of updates from everyone since we left them at the airport. Tripp and Anders actually went home yesterday morning to spend their time off in Banff."

"That makes sense." Tim spoke down the table toward Matt, who had rested his elbows on the table and was listening intently. "Tripp's boyfriend isn't out here. He'd want to be with him," he explained.

Matt nodded.

Erin was still scrolling through e-mails. "Get this, though. Devon found out there's a training session being offered by the coast guard next week, and somehow convinced Marcus it was vital for him and Alisha to stay and take part."

Amusement hit instantly. "Poor Alisha. Does this mean she has to use a scuba suit in the Pacific at this time of year?"

"Probably. Devon I expect that kind of insanity from, but Alisha is into tropical temperatures." Erin shuddered. "She's going to freeze."

"They're in love—that's more than enough to keep her warm."

Their gazes met, and for a second hope stirred in the dark, beautiful depths before Erin jerked herself away, as if hiding from him.

Some things they weren't ready to even think about—he got that, but her quick denial seemed harsh.

He focused back on their current dilemma. "Then that makes it even easier to fit Matt in."

Erin glanced at his friend. "Would you be interested in flying with us? Like Tim said, there's no reason you couldn't come along. It's about a four-hour trip, and I can guarantee some great views. You'd have to find a way home, though."

Matt waved a hand. "If you're headed to Calgary, I can take advantage of the opportunity and book meetings for next week. I would love a semiprivate tour of the glaciers."

"Then we're settled," Tim said. "Erin, you want to set up a liftoff time with the authorities?"

She nodded, far more relaxed than a moment ago. "Two hours from now? Three?"

"Three. No need to rush out of here, and the trip is short enough we'll still be flying in the light even if we leave later."

Tim gestured toward the hot plates in front of Matt. "You planning on sharing any of that?"

Their host smiled happily and held out his hand. "Let me load your plate for you."

"One second." Erin typed quickly, then smiled as she put the phone down on the table. "Done. I've requested a leisurely departure time just after lunch. I'll check back after breakfast to confirm we're a go."

They played pass the plate, Erin handing off to Matt then returning it on the way back.

Matt held her plate for an extra moment. "Sausage? Bacon? Your choice."

"Anything is fine," Erin answered.

"You didn't ask my preferences," Tim pointed out, waving a sausage-loaded fork in the air.

Matt snorted. "Your plate is full. That's what you'd ask for. I know you too well, my friend. Only Erin is a new guest, and she needs to ask for what pleases her most."

He turned his attention on her, no trace of teasing as he waited.

Erin eyed the food. "Extra bacon, please."

"Ahh, an excellent choice." Matt loaded her plate with bacon and scrambled eggs. "And after we eat, I'll make arrangements for Jason to drive us to the airfield."

"Sounds great."

"Tim, you need to do anything to prep for leaving?"

"Nothing more than stick my dirty clothes back in my bag."

Matt turned to face them both, his expression gone serious. "And finally, I figure I should ask. Is there an elephant in the room who's also going along for the ride?"

Tim appreciated his friend all the more in that moment for bringing up a potential issue before it became a real issue. He knew from past adventures with Matt that a bit of voyeurism wasn't a problem for him. Erin had given him the same assurance this morning.

Matt and Erin hadn't yet spoken about what happened last night, though.

A burst of laughter escaped Erin as she glanced at Tim. "Well now, that's one way of asking."

The small edge of concern that had still hovered was wiped clear by her obvious amusement. If she was teasing about being watched during sex, things really were fine. "We should tell him it's a pet. And it's about this high"—Tim held out a hand at shoulder height—"and bright purple."

"With polka dots," Erin added.

Matt dug into his breakfast. "If it can pack light, I've got a carry-on for it. Otherwise, it has to stay home without us."

Erin eyed Tim, then rose to her feet, crossing the short distance to Matt's side.

He stood as well, wiping his mouth on a napkin. "Yes?"

She shrugged. "Just wanted to say an official good morning."

Erin wrapped her arms around his neck and hugged him tight. Matt's brows shot skyward, but he returned her embrace, looking over her shoulder to Tim for a sign that what was going on was kosher by him. Tim nodded at his friend, allowing his approval to show in his expression and voice.

"There's your answer," Tim assured him. "No pachyderms traveling with us today."

Matt guided Erin back to her seat before resuming his own. "That's good because there really isn't room in the limo for more than four people anyway."

CHAPTER 17

Jason drove them to the airport, pulling to a stop outside the transport building. He smiled sincerely as he passed them their bags. "Come for a longer visit next time."

"We'll take you up on that," Erin promised, not at all certain how or when, but sincere in the hope she'd get to return.

The whirl of prep for flight began. Tim let her take care of the technical details while he guided Matt to the chopper. He showed his friend around, how to use the headsets and harnesses, went over emergency procedures.

Once Matt was comfortably settled, Tim returned to see if she needed anything.

Erin motioned to the hangar. "There are a couple of boxes in the office that we're transporting. You can grab them and lash them down in storage. Other than that, I'm nearly ready."

He nodded, then paused at her side, kneeling to kiss her.

Hard. One hand thrust into the hair at the back of her head, fingers tightening. He tugged her lips higher so he could reach her better, and a rush of sexual endorphins floated through her bloodstream.

There was a marked contrast between the intense concentration she'd been using to prep for flight and the total lack of brain cells she was currently engaging. Intense and exciting in two completely different ways.

He backed off and left her gasping for air. "Dammit, you make my head spin," she complained.

"I'm still on holidays," he joked before heading off to load the supplies she'd mentioned.

The chopper rose smoothly under her control, the incredible break in the weather continuing as she took them in a direct line off Vancouver Island, headed for the shortest route home.

The terrain changed moment by moment, the icy waters of the Pacific under them dotted with numerous islands, everything from places large enough for a single-family dwelling to those with tiny communities, their only access off and on by boat.

A buzz broke in over her headset. "You need me to do anything?" Tim asked.

"Not right now."

"Good. Then Matt and I will play tourist. I haven't seen the view this clear in years." Tim adjusted his angle to join Matt in staring out the window, forehead resting against the glass as he gazed downward.

Matt clicked on the line. "It is a great view. You know how seldom I get to see clear skies on the coast?"

"Best part of living in Banff," Erin teased. "No coastal weather. I don't miss the grey skies all winter long."

"The never-ending winter winds that sweep the east coast drive me insane," Tim confessed. "Erin, you know this—if it's not tied down or fastened to the Rock, there'd be nothing left in Newfoundland after a long hard winter with the winds licking over the Wreckhouse flats."

She shuddered involuntarily, remembering all too clearly

even after her years away. "God, it chills to the bone, doesn't it?"

They all fell silent for a short while, admiring the sunshine glinting off the wave-painted surface of the water. From this height each indentation appeared to be lit from within, turning the entire ocean into a sparkling, multifaceted diamond. It was glorious, and mesmerizing, and she nearly hated to exchange the water for the shoreline, rising over the trees and heading through the passes that provided the straightest route while avoiding the major cities.

A world of shimmering silver was exchanged for the purest white of upper-range snow. Here among the peaks there was no one to disturb the virgin white. Rare even was the thin line of an animal track marring the endless fields of snow as they headed higher and broke through the teeth of the Selkirk Range.

"Amazing." Tim reached over and clicked her radio to a different line, not the one they'd been talking on with Matt. "It's a piece of heaven, love, and I'm so grateful for the chance to see it with you."

With one sentence he melted her. She took a deep breath and refocused on the instrument panel to stop from blurting out anything that was too soon to be saying.

But she was thinking it. Hard. It would be too easy to completely fall in love with her scoundrel if he kept on being so damn fascinating.

Too much baggage was involved to be thinking that seriously. So much they still needed to discuss.

They topped the next ridge, entering a sea of mountaintops, and Erin gloated in the glory that was her job. "So beautiful."

Black snow-free peaks jutted skyward, breaking the pristine landscape with sharp slashes of dark against the light. Erin adjusted altitude to follow the level of the glacier field below them, the earth racing past in a rush of wild magnificence.

"Makes me want to leap out and make some tracks," Tim shared. "Leave behind a sign that we've been here."

Matt shook his head. "It would only last for a few hours. The wind would have the slopes buffed and polished before you even reached the bottom."

"*I'd* know I'd been there."

Tim twisted to catch her attention, brilliant blue eyes as beautiful and compelling as the scenery below them.

She smiled back. "You do leave an impact wherever you go."

She'd planned a flight path that took them north of Whistler, heading in a near-straight line toward home. Tim fell silent, and she just enjoyed being with him. At one point he leaned in the opposite direction so he could lay a hand on her thigh, his gaze still fixed out the window in fascination.

They'd been in the air more than two hours, the huge chopper easily eating up the distance. Another hour and a bit and they'd be landing. Drop off the chopper, find a rental car, then they could discuss the next thing.

Their holiday break was needed in more ways than one. For the first time in a long while, Erin could honestly say she was on her way to being truly relaxed.

They closed in on the secondary pass, a narrow passage between the towering cliffs. Erin increased their altitude slightly so as not to get caught by an updraft off the opposite side of the mountain. The shadow of the chopper followed them on the snow below, a dark silhouette growing larger and smaller as the terrain changed.

They broke over the ridge, and the world changed.

"Holy shit, what's that?" Tim pointed to the south.

"Tracks. What makes tracks that big?" Matt asked.

The ground was exposed in a near-straight line running northwest to southeast, the snow shoved aside like an enormous shovel had been dragged over the surface.

Tim stabbed a finger at the window. "There. Broken landing gear?"

Erin headed for the cliff Tim indicated, the situation far too similar to recent memory. "Damn, looks like a plane crash. Think it went over the edge?"

"Possibly. I'll get our gear ready." He unbuckled and headed into the back.

"Hey, slow up, buddy. We have some decisions to make first."

Tim stopped dead in his tracks, reversing direction and planting his butt in his chair. "You're right. Sorry for jumping the gun. Matt—you okay with us stopping?"

"Of course. My God, there are people down there. I'll stay out of your way, or help if you tell me what to do."

"Good man," Tim said. He turned to Erin. "Anything on the radio?"

"I'm not picking up anything."

She manoeuvred them toward the thick line marring the pristine snow. Tim leaned against the glass, a set of binoculars in his hand as he scoured the ground.

Erin double-checked instruments and made a few notes in the log. "I've got our location. We spot anything, and I'll call it in."

"Still want to go down and— There, over to the right more."

It wasn't a cliff crash, but it wasn't good. Whoever had been piloting the plane had managed to land it before the entire level of the glacier surface dropped a good twenty feet, leaving the plane at an impossible angle, not just for takeoff. Most of the body was still intact, and as they buzzed, a flash of bright orange appeared in the doorway.

"We've got survivors," Tim announced.

Erin checked the site. "Not a lot of room to land, and there's no way in hell I'm letting you go down a line without a winch man."

"Land on the upper slope and we climb down?" Tim was itching to get moving, she could tell.

"If we have snowshoes. Otherwise at this elevation you try a step forward, and you could be up to your neck."

Tim was already headed to the back. "I'm sure we have a bag of them in the gear section. We brought all that stuff when we came out, remember?"

Erin hovered, wanting to turn them toward the landing spot. "Give Matt your binocs. I need the numbers off her to call them in."

Tim did as she'd asked, then moved out of sight behind Matt, equipment being shifted.

"What do you need?" Matt asked.

She explained, then waited as he called out the plane's identifiers, jotting the information down before prepping for the next step. "I'll have us down in a minute. Once we're on the ground, Tim's in charge. I haven't run a rescue for years."

"Matt will be staying at the chopper," Tim announced.

"No problem."

Matt's quick agreement was the only acceptable response, but Erin couldn't help but worry.

This was no longer a relaxing sightseeing trip. Things had gone real bad, real fast, and she only hoped they got better just as quickly.

Tim threw gear bags into rows based on what he thought might be needed. He pulled out spare gloves and a thick coat for Matt and Erin as well as himself. In the background, Erin was on the radio, giving information to the authorities in the hopes they could identify the downed plane.

This was something totally new they were headed into, not only because Matt was along and Erin rarely went on the ground portion of a rescue. Those issues were bad enough, but the sheer isolation added a ton of risk as well. Any mistakes were amplified tenfold simply because they were so far away from additional backup.

The sooner he knew what they were dealing with, the better.

The chopper settled, the heavy noise beating in his ears

at the same pace as his heart. The rotors slowed, and Erin scrambled out of her seat, hurrying to pull her hair back and lock it out of the way under a warm hat.

He held out a helmet, and she rolled her eyes, pulling it to her and exchanging it quickly. The volume outside decreased until she could speak without using the chopper radio system. "I forgot about the helmets. Thanks."

"Here's your remote radio. Matt, I don't know if the range will be good enough that you can hear us, but listen in best you can. Don't talk unless we specifically ask you a question."

"Got it." Matt was tucked to one side, pulling on the extra gear he'd been handed and trying to stay out of the way.

"Channel three for everything, backup on channel four. If I need to talk to you in private, or there's an emergency, flip to two lower than what we're on."

Her eyes snapped up to meet his. "You expecting problems?"

"Always. But I love it when I'm surprised and there are none."

Erin cracked a smile. "Did I mention it's been a few years since I was actively on the ground during a rescue?"

Tim zipped up his coat, then pulled on an oversized harness. "Like falling off a cliff—you'll remember soon enough. I'll deal with the medical, you make decisions regarding getting them home safe."

"Which bag is for me to carry?"

Tim pointed, and Erin hoisted it. "No problem."

He helped her into a harness and checked straps as he explained how they'd use the chopper as a secure wall to run their ropes down. "That way we don't have to worry about setting anchors in the snow or ice."

Erin settled her pack into place. "The chopper's not going anywhere."

Tim turned to Matt. "You hear that? The chopper's not going anywhere, so don't take off for Hawaii and leave us here or something."

Matt nodded. "Deal. Stay safe, you guys."

Tim shot him a thumbs-up before looking Erin straight in the eye, his hands tight on the front of her harness. "You good?"

She nodded. "You?"

"Nauseated, and butterflies the size of hummingbirds are fighting in my belly. About like normal."

She laughed. "Good luck, and be careful, okay?"

He kissed her quickly before stepping back. "Ditto."

Ice-cold air rushed in when he opened the door, and he and Erin both cringed a little, but the rush of anticipation couldn't be denied.

"Oh, hey," he tossed at Matt. "Once we leave, close this door and then you make sure you keep moving. Best way to burn off the calories we're going to consume for dinner."

"Go. I'll be fine," Matt insisted.

It changed the situation enormously, having a passenger on board without more of the team around, but they'd just have to deal with it. Matt was being as cooperative as possible, and they really had no choice.

There were a whole lot of unanswered questions, though, that he'd better find out answers for, and fast.

Tim hooked a pulley system over the side struts, attaching one on either side of the door. Ropes were added before he tied Erin in, and then himself.

Final step? Snowshoes. Less fun than skis or snowboards, far more efficient for their needs right now.

Was it only the day before they'd been out playing on the slopes with Matt? Tim shook his head at the unreal sensation.

"Go first, I want to watch your self-belay," Tim ordered.

Erin nodded, caught hold, then stepped back off the chopper deck. It was only a few feet to the ground, but she did everything right.

"That wasn't so bad." Erin lifted a thumbs-up at him.

Tim joined her on the ground, testing his balance and

the snowpack. "Looks like we've got a nice firm base for walking on. Keep your rope taut, though," he warned.

Erin's voice over the radio was firm and confident. "You want me to drop over the cliff first?"

"Nope. I want you on the edge, watching me. If I tell you to bug out, you go. Head back to the chopper and get it ready to leave."

She glared at him but didn't argue, which was good. If he found out the plane was about to explode, he wasn't letting her anywhere near it. If he found any manner of things gone wrong, he'd be ordering her to get her ass out of there as fast as possible.

They waddled their way to the edge, following the hard-packed trail the plane had carved into the frozen surface. Tim stopped them a few feet back to make sure they weren't walking over a cornice, one of the dangerous snow ridges produced by high winds, but the plane had done a good job of removing everything at the edge down to bare rock.

"There's someone," Erin pointed.

"Two someones. We've got room for how many?"

"Twelve if they need room to spread out, sixteen if it's a short flight, but that size of plane shouldn't have had more than six on her."

He nodded. "I'm going down."

It was only a twenty-foot drop, not long enough to get any kind of adrenaline flowing, but he already had plenty of that, stepping into the unknown.

The drop was long enough to look over his shoulder at the couple of men approaching his landing spot. Thick winter coats, snowshoes—they weren't unprepared for the conditions.

He landed on the lower level, detached his rope, and locked the lines in place to use on the upward journey.

"Hello."

Tim turned and lifted a hand in response to the shout.

"I'm Tim—paramedic with Lifeline Search and Rescue. You need some help?"

The men exchanged glances. "Search and rescue? Damn, you got here fast."

"You just went down?"

"Two hours ago—we think our pilot had a heart attack. We've done what we could, but he's passed out inside the plane."

Shit. "Okay, let me take a look at him. Anyone else hurt?"

"No. Can you take us out of here?"

"How many are there of you?" Tim asked, stomping forward to examine the plane. "And how is the engine? Any leaks or other dangers to worry about?"

"Except for she's not sitting on a runway, and we have no one to fly her, I think the plane is fine. There are four of us."

Erin's radio crackled in his ear. "Tim? Can I come down yet?"

He responded softly. "One more minute to clear."

"Roger."

Tim stomped up to the plane, eyeing the men who had moved to stand on either side of him. "I didn't catch your names."

"John and Ken." The shorter of the two gestured. "I'm Ken."

"I want to check you guys out as well," Tim commented, "but first, show me where your pilot is."

He ditched his snowshoes outside the door, then willing hands pulled him onboard as another face was added to the mix. This guy was a lot bigger than the other two, and Tim made sure to put on his least scary expression. "Paramedic. Where's the pilot?"

The man pointed, and Tim hauled his way down the narrow path to where they had the man supported in a nearly reclined chair. He went to work, but first he called Erin.

"Leave your supplies at the chopper and exchange them for a stretcher. Shove it over the cliff, then come on down.

We've got three able-bodied and one not so good. Their pilot."

"Got it," Erin responded immediately. "Time for me to check the radio for a response from emergency?"

"Matt? Has the radio up there made any noise?"

A short pause—Matt was probably trying to remember how to use his radio. "Oh, no. Nothing but you guys."

"There's your answer, Erin. The authorities know where we're at, that's all we need right now."

Tim worked steadily, but one fear had faded after he'd entered the plane. The distinct lack of boxes and bags meant at least they hadn't stumbled upon a group of smugglers. Because getting mixed up in a drug transport situation couldn't end well.

"I need some information," he called. "Any ID on the pilot? Age, anything else you can tell me? Was he complaining about anything before the crash?"

"Nothing unusual. Said he wasn't feeling well, and the next thing we knew we were way lower than we should be and headed for the ground." John slipped into the chair next to him. "Just a pilot we hired out of Anchorage. We're headed for a private home outside Seattle."

"Grab me his ID from up front," Tim ordered.

John hesitated. "I don't know where it would be."

"Root around. See what you can find. Trust me, he's not going to be upset with you—I'd like to know if he's got medication somewhere."

"Don't you usually have a much bigger team to go out on a search and rescue?" Ken asked. "Just one guy, flying all alone?"

Tim paused with his fingers on the victim's pulse, not liking how low the count was. "You caught me coming back from a holiday. I can't imagine how long it would have taken a team to respond to your SOS—you're in a hell of a spot here."

"There's another person coming down the hillside," the unnamed third man announced.

"Another part of your team?" Ken snapped. Either he

was beginning to freak out now that rescue was happening—some people did that—or Tim had made a horrid mistake.

"That's our chopper pilot. There's one more waiting on the chopper—a good friend of ours. Don't worry, though, we've got plenty of room. Ken, go grab the stretcher from her, and you—what's your name?"

"Red."

Guy was shaved totally bald. He had either a sense of humour or delusions of grandeur. "Red, stuff the most important things you guys need into a couple of bags—no more—and we'll get you on the chopper and headed home ASAP. John, I need you to help me get the pilot ready for transport."

Three people headed in three directions. Tim glanced out the window at Erin, who was at the bottom of the slope, securing her ropes together as he'd done. Once this was all over, he owed her a huge dinner and a massage and hell, another damn getaway, just the two of them.

The pilot wasn't responding, his skin gone ashy white. Tim didn't like the looks of it at all. Still, he did what he could.

He clicked on his radio. "Erin, I don't know if Ken reached you yet. If he did, give him the stretcher, then turn around and get the ropes ready for a stretcher lift."

There was no response.

"Erin?"

He shot to his feet and looked out the window, but there was no sign of her.

Hell.

A body blocked his path as he headed for the door. "Move. I need to check on my partner," he snapped.

Red stepped aside just far enough to reveal that Ken now stood beside Erin at the back of the plane, one hand clutching her arm, the other holding a gun to her head.

CHAPTER 18

||||||||||||||||||||||||||||||

Had she really thought spending more time in the middle of the action was something she wanted? She cursed the gods who obviously had a sense of humour about such things.

Fucked up, stupid, scary world. She'd never had a gun pulled on her before. She didn't like it one bit.

At the opposite end of the small plane, Tim lifted his hands carefully in the air. "Don't hurt her," Tim ordered. "She's your only ticket out of here."

"Agreed. I thought you were the pilot, but since you're not . . ." Ken tossed her radio headset to the ground, then nodded toward the front of the plane. "John, take care of him."

Erin drew in a quick gasp as John pulled out a gun and casually pointed it at Tim.

"Oh my God, *no*. Don't, or I won't fly you anywhere." Erin struggled to get free. "I mean it, hurt him and I'll damn well leave you to freeze."

"Gutsy." Ken jerked her again like he had when he'd come up to her and surprised her, snapping off her headset before she could get out a call for help to Tim. "Fine. Don't shoot Tim. But we need to get out of here before anyone else shows up. Get rid of the baggage, John."

John tilted the gun slightly lower, adjusting the angle before he pulled the trigger. The body resting in the chair beside Tim jerked, and Erin screamed involuntarily, her hands flying up to cover her face.

Tim shouted as well, reaching down to cover the blood welling up. "Dammit, that wasn't—"

He slammed his mouth shut and pulled his hands back as John once again turned the deadly barrel toward him. "Keep your mouth shut, and we'll let you live. Since she's so keen on it."

"Red, get our things. Tim, Erin. Lead the way. And you know better than to do anything stupid." Ken stepped aside, allowing Erin access to the exit.

She glanced across the distance separating her and Tim and wondered how their world had turned so rapidly from the twenty-four hours before. Her gaze drifted to the body at his side, the signs of death growing as the man no longer stirred, and something went numb inside her.

Whatever she and Tim had stumbled onto, these men were willing to kill to avoid getting caught. Being kidnapped was a far better option at this point.

"We'll go along peacefully," Tim promised. "There's no need to hurt anyone else. Let me see the pilot again—"

John pushed him toward the door. "He's deadweight. Move now, or you'll join him."

Tim turned reluctantly, a sound of pain escaping him. But he hurried down to her and ushered her out the door. "Nothing fancy—no attempts at being a hero," he cautioned as they hooked on their snowshoes.

"You, too." She snuck in a quick squeeze to his arm, glancing over her shoulder as the other men crawled out of the plane, following after them too close for even quiet conversation. She had to risk one word, though. "Matt?"

"Working on it."

The three men didn't have much with them. Not other than their obvious desire to not be near the plane when any authorities arrived. Erin plotted ways to get a message out, but the entire time they traveled to the chopper she had one or another of the guys at her side.

She was worried sick their crash victims were going to shoot either Tim or Matt, and there seemed to be nothing she could do. Tim seemed to have gotten in some muttered conversation time with his friend, but the crisis situation only increased by the minute.

It took puzzle-solving skill to get all five of them up the short distance to the same level as the chopper, none of them wanting to be the last, not wanting Tim and Erin left alone without someone at their side to ensure good behavior.

"I need to get the chopper warmed up," she warned. "I can't hop in and turn it on like a car."

"You'll wait until I'm there to watch you," Ken warned. "You'll have time once we've got your friends in position."

That didn't sound good at all. Erin met Tim's eyes again, and the bastard actually winked, probably attempting to give her what assurance he could.

Only there were no guarantees he could make right now. There was only dealing with one moment to the next. Belaying up the hill, crossing the distance to the chopper, and stripping off unneeded gear.

Tim stopped before opening the door. "In case you were thinking of shooting our friend, don't. He told me to mention he's worth a mint. You can easily make some money if you treat him well."

"Thanks for the information." Ken laughed. "Good friends like you are hard to find. Now tell him to sit down and hold his hands in the air where we can see them."

"Matt?" Tim spoke into the headset. "Company coming aboard. Sit down and don't try anything. Hold your hands up, and trust me."

Ken ripped the headset from Tim and dropped it into the snow. "You won't be needing that anymore."

The door opened slowly, and Erin held her breath, bracing herself for the report of a gun. Fearful of it coming, afraid there was no way to avoid it.

Instead she watched as Red climbed aboard and closed in on Matt.

Tim's friend was obediently seated, hands toward the ceiling. His eyes were wide with fear, but he said nothing as his hands were shoved to his sides and Red pulled a roll of duct tape from his pocket.

A hard shove hit between her shoulder blades. "Get this chopper moving," Ken ordered.

She crawled in and hurried toward the front, only to be jerked to a stop, Ken pulling her nearly off her feet.

"Your friends don't have to stay in good condition," he warned. "If you try anything, and I mean anything I think looks wrong, they're going to get hurt. Don't call anyone, don't answer anything—"

His message was clear. "I got it. Do you know anything about flying, though? I have to do lot of things that might look suspicious, but they're—"

"Explain, or don't do them." Ken motioned her forward. "Get going."

She was in her seat, glancing back to make sure they were doing as they'd promised and keeping the guys safe. "Lock everything down," she called, snapping to a halt as Ken raised a hand above her.

"Don't talk to them. Tell me what needs to be done, and I'll decide if I pass it on."

"It's just normal takeoff procedure," she explained. "Tying things down, making sure they're secure so if we hit turbulence there's nothing flying around inside the cockpit with us."

"Get this thing going." Ken twisted to the back. "John, watch Tim—tell him to do the normal things to get ready to fly."

There was always a buzz of excitement that accompanied the slow speeding of the props. Now for the first time there was also dread. As she went through start-up, Erin's fears grew. She couldn't see a way out of this without someone getting hurt, and if she was the one who made a wrong decision that led to Tim or Matt being injured or killed, she didn't know how she'd survive.

It was one time she really didn't want to be in control.

The one time she had absolutely no choice.

She glanced into the back. Tim must have finished putting things in place. John had taken a second roll of duct tape and was lashing Tim to another chair as far from Matt as possible. With their wrists pinned to the chairs, there wasn't much that either of them could do to deal with the three men moving freely around the cabin. Erin struggled for the next idea.

"Ken, I need to put on my headset. I need to listen to my instrument panel . . . some of the signals I use to fly are auditory. And I need to know where you want to go, so I can calculate if I have enough fuel."

He pulled out a paper. "That's what we gave the other pilot. It's a private airstrip, so you don't need to contact anyone to land. And no, you can't wear your headset."

Dammit. Options were fading fast. The rotors were at nearly full speed now, and the volume loud enough to deafen everyone. She checked the coordinates she'd been given and punched the data into her navigator. Then she ignored the fact that she had three unwanted guests and took off without any further warning.

If they got bumped around, so be it.

And then the damn gun came back to mind, and she stifled her instinct to send them into a wild tailspin. She might be okay with the resulting loss of balance, and Tim would be okay, especially since he was locked down. Matt would probably get sick, but that would be fine if it meant they were safe.

But that gun changed things. She headed south, leaving behind the remains of the plane and a man who was dead or dying. Their proven willingness to use violence was far too strong an incentive to follow her captors' orders.

Tim had given up trying to guess what came next. Locked in position, he could do nothing but hope his next breath wasn't his last. As far as he could tell from his position in the center of the hold, Erin did nothing but take them in a straight line to the private field.

There'd been a second when he wondered if she was going to try something, but a glance over her shoulder had her stopping as soon as she spotted the gun John held pointed in his direction.

He wasn't even sure what he would tell her to try.

The glimpses he had out the window showed they were passing out of the Rockies and into the lowlands, closing in on the U.S.-Canada border, the thin thread of a river widening into a long stretch of lake that Erin followed for a good fifteen minutes.

Sure enough, the no-touching zone appeared ahead, the swatch of trees cut in a nearly straight line the entire length of the forty-ninth parallel. They were almost out of Canada. There were no major roads visible. No communities.

Little chance they would be spotted and reported to curious border authorities.

Ten minutes past the border, a small clearing in the trees appeared. They were high in the mountains again, this time the less rugged and more rounded Columbia ranges that were common along the BC-Washington or Idaho line. Erin let them down, the pressure and noise in her ears dying away, but a low ringing remaining.

Erin was escorted to the door, where she jerked off Ken's grasp on her. "I'm not going anywhere without the guys."

"They're coming with us. Insurance for your continued good behavior."

"You have no reason to hurt any of us—" Erin started.

"Shut up. We'll put you somewhere safe."

The duct tape was cut away, freeing Tim's wrists from the chair. Before he could even think about making a move, a new set was applied, locking his hands in front of him and leaving him a lot more helpless than he wished. On the opposite side of the plane he caught glimpses of Matt being given the same treatment.

Then Matt disappeared, led away by Red. John held Tim in place at the side of the field as Erin worked alone to refuel. "It would go faster if I helped her," he offered.

The man at his side shook his head, crossing his arms as he looked around the ranch area. "No rush. We're not leaving anytime soon."

And then he closed his mouth and didn't say anything else.

Frustration, fear—Tim had it all. They'd killed a man already. What reason could they have for keeping any of them alive once they were no longer useful? Matt's insistence at being offered up as a hostage had been a necessary evil, but even that didn't provide insurance for either Erin or himself.

Red emerged from the cabin where he'd disappeared, wood smoke curling from the chimney. He was alone, and Tim's stomach flipped with worry.

"Where's Matt?"

"He's safe. If he is who he says he is, we'll treat him well."

It was the longest time before Ken escorted Erin across the field. An icy chill was settling into Tim's limbs from the lack of movement and the tight tape around his wrists.

Erin met his eyes. "You okay?"

"Yeah."

Ken pushed Erin toward the small metal shed beside the cabin. "In you go."

"Tim—"

"Is going with you."

The short glimpse of light while the door was open showed that there was nothing much in the place but a couple of barrels. Tim shuffled forward awkwardly, uncertainty rising again, but the fact that they were together was good.

Good yet still terrifying. Matt wasn't with them, and they only had the word of killers that his friend would stay safe.

If he could have turned back the clock and never offered the suggestion of the getaway, he would in a second.

The door closing them into the small shed didn't help.

After the past hours of high-volume noise, his ears rang with imagined sound. Still, both he and Erin stood silently for a moment, straining to hear footsteps moving away. Listening for some sign they were really alone.

The cabin door slammed—which was no assurance, but was probably the best they could expect. Tim turned toward where Erin stood, thin lines of daylight sneaking in through cracks near the ceiling.

"Oh, God." Erin shook violently, then reached for him. "Let me take the tape off you."

"There's a pocketknife inside my coat. Right inside breast pocket."

Her eyes grew wide. "Seriously?"

"They weren't concerned about frisking me, just in getting here."

She bit the tip of her glove and pulled it off, unzipping his coat and slipping her hand inside to find the blade. "I'm sorry. I couldn't think of anything to do that wasn't going to put you guys in danger."

"There was nothing you could do. We need to get out of here, though, because once we're not needed . . ."

He didn't want to bring back images of the pilot. Deadweight, Ken had said.

At what point did he and Erin become deadweight?

"You did good," he assured her. "And they had you refuel the chopper—so maybe they still need you to fly them somewhere."

Erin lowered her voice. "I was considering a spinout. I thought about stalling. I thought about taking us straight to a manned airport—and I didn't do any of them because I was afraid—"

"For good reason." He pulled the last of the tape from his wrists and wrapped his arms around her, hugging her tight. "Oh God, Erin, I did the same mental wrangling, and there was no solution. If you'd done any of those things we might all be dead right now."

Erin slipped her hands up to his chest and pushed him back slightly. "Do up your coat. How are your hands? It's cold, and if we're going to have a chance to get away, we need to be as warm as possible before we go out there again."

Both of them were deliberately ignoring the impossibility of getting Matt out from right under the kidnappers' noses.

"Look around in here, see if there's anything that can help us." Tim tucked things back into place, slipping his knife into his main right pocket.

She had her coat open and was placing the strips of duct tape she'd cut off him onto her clothes. "Just in case we need them later," she explained. "And I know it's no use right here, but there's a gun in the chopper."

Well, now. "You knew about that, did you?"

Erin closed her jacket while she answered. "Of course I knew. Marcus and I had a bit of a fight over it initially, but in the end he agreed it was a good idea."

For the first time in a while Tim actually felt like smiling. "I wasn't talking about you having a gun. I was talking about the one I have hidden in my medical supplies."

"You're shitting me."

"Nope."

She snuck under his arm briefly, putting their heads close together. "I knew I liked you. You're devious."

"So are you. We fit well together."

Their smiles faded, though, as the reality of their situation grew clearer again. "Look around, right?" she asked.

There wasn't much there. A couple of smaller old barrels. A bunch of rags. Tim tried the door, but for a run-down old shed, the thing barely budged, even when he slammed his shoulder into it. There was nothing that could get them out. "Great. Well, we can burn the place down around our heads if we want to."

"Let's save that one for tomorrow," Erin suggested.

He tipped the empty canisters over and created a seat of a kind. The rags became a layer of cushioning that he sat on, then he tapped his lap. "Come, conserve body heat."

She slipped in next to him and curled up tight. They tucked their hands between their bodies and tilted their heads down, a small bundle of humanity keeping as much of their body heat in as possible.

"So. Any plans?" she asked.

"They need you to fly them somewhere else. That's the only reason I can think of for the refueling." Tim made sure they were speaking softly enough to not be overheard even if someone stood right outside the shed. "Sounds as if they're treating Matt a little better—looking for the extra cash."

"I hope he's okay." There was real fear in her voice.

"I hope so, too, but he's a smart guy, and he does have the money if it comes to that. But mostly we're trying to buy time for someone to help us."

"Which is not going to happen very quickly, Tim." She sighed. "I never got out a distress call—I was too scared to try anything. That means the chopper not showing up is our only warning to anyone. Which means no one will even be out looking until tomorrow."

"Which is why I think your idea of the nearest airport is a good one. Doesn't matter if Matt and I are lashed to chairs. Go in low, out of air traffic range but high enough to get on radar. You set down on the edge of a runway, and our kidnappers will have nowhere to go but through the security that will show up."

"There's a ton wrong with that, though. Even with security blocking them, they could hole up in the chopper. They could shoot you. They could shoot Matt. What the hell are they running from, anyway?"

"I thought smugglers first, but they said they were out of Anchorage and headed to Seattle. There were no drugs on the plane, and they barely took anything with them when we left."

"Bullshit on them being out of Anchorage." Erin's breath brushed his neck, a steamy stroke that warmed him deeply. "The pilot had to have registered the flight, but there was no way they would have been passing over the mountain they were when they went down. Anchorage to Seattle is an all-coastal route, and we were inland far too much, even changing direction to head toward the new coordinates once they were in the air."

"Interesting." Tim pulled his arms free to rub her back slowly. "Possible starting points?"

"Major airports? Offhand, only Whitehorse comes to mind. Yellowknife, maybe—the route would make sense if the pilot was trying to avoid cutting over any main air traffic routes, staying off the radar. Private airstrips could be anything between those two points." Erin sighed. "I wonder if he had the heart attack because of being hijacked."

He soothed her the best he could. "Don't. We can't change it, and we're not going to focus on that now. Now we're all about getting out of here in one piece."

"Okay. Landing at a major airport—safer for civilians than a shopping mall or main highway."

"They can't take off and hide as easily, either," Tim pointed out. "But if a highway is all you get, take it."

"They can still shoot you. I don't think they have much respect for life at this point."

He agreed, but that wasn't what she needed to hear. He lifted her chin and looked into her eyes. "I wish this hadn't happened. I wish to God we were back home and safe. But we will get through this. We'll keep our eyes and ears open, and the next chance we get, we're going to do what we can to get out of here."

She slipped her hand from her glove and cupped his face, her palm warm against his cheek. "We'll do what we can."

CHAPTER 19

''''''''''''''''''''''''''''''''''

Erin fell into an uneasy doze, relaxation coming in spite of her fears. There was nothing to do in the small space, no room to move around, and the tight position she and Tim ended up in grew warm enough that she'd closed her eyes and actually slept. The darkness around them felt like a tangible thing, dimming sounds, blurring her mind. No matter how hard she looked she couldn't see anything, and the sensation of total blindness was strange.

"Erin. Someone is coming." Tim pushed her upright gently. "There's been not a lot of noise for about an hour, but I just heard something from toward the cabin. Sounded like a bit of a scuffle."

She slipped to her feet and helped him up, the two of them wiggling slightly, moving their feet in an attempt to get the blood flowing again. "How late is it?"

"About ten. Be ready."

Her ears ached from listening. Was that a footstep? The wind? All the clues seemed muffled.

"You awake?" A deep voice, not Ken.

"We are. What do you want, Red?" Tim asked.

No sound for a moment. "We need to get out of here. If I let you free, will you drop me off somewhere safe? I have a gun, and I will use it if I have to, but—"

"Where are your friends?" Tim snapped. "Why should we trust you?"

"They're in the cabin. I tied them up with that duct tape we used on you. I'm opening the door, and I have the gun. We need to move now, though."

"He's telling the truth." Matt's voice.

Shit. "Matt? You okay?"

"Yes, so hurry up."

Erin raised her voice. "Let us out."

The door swung open a bare inch. Tim pushed it open all the way, revealing the big man with, as promised, a gun pointed at them. Matt stood a little ways away, his hands still taped in front of him, but a grin on his face shining in the faint line.

They were still in deep shit, but the sight of Tim's friend eased a small spot of panic. "Good to see you, Matt."

Red shook the gun. "Talk later, we have to leave."

"Point that thing some other direction," Erin snapped. "I'm sick of people sticking guns in my face when they want my help."

Tim cleared his throat, but she was too pissed to care.

Red motioned with his head to the chopper. "I tied them up, but if they get free, we're in trouble. The chopper is ready to go, right?"

They were headed toward the chopper, her feet stinging as blood rushed back into them. "It'll take me five minutes to get off the ground. Where do you want to go?"

"Edge of the nearest small town is good. Just give me a way to get away from them, and I promise not to hurt any of you."

They were running now, racing for freedom. Erin pulled herself in and started the routine to get the bird off the ground.

Matt was right behind her. "Anything I need to do?" he asked.

"Belt yourself in, put on a headset so you can hear what's going on. Then shut up."

He took the closest seat to hers and followed orders. She was too busy to regret snapping at him.

Behind her, Tim moved a little slower, talking to their supposed rescuer, who still held the gun trained on his back. "You're going to be in trouble with your partners for letting us go."

"They weren't my partners. I was hired, like the pilot. There was no need to kill him," Red said.

"Ahh." Tim paused. "Figured out you were probably next?"

"Yeah. If they killed him, they have no reason to keep me around, either, not once they get where they're going." Red spoke louder as the noise level rose. "Please, don't use the radio. Don't turn me in."

"Right now you're our best friend, Red." Erin pulled a headset from the dash and held it in the air. "I won't call the authorities, but if you put one of these on, it will save all of us our hearing. Tim can show you how it works. Liftoff in two minutes."

Then she concentrated on making the final preparations.

The normal actions of getting the chopper ready soothed her. Calmed the panic flipping through her veins as the reality of what could have happened flicked like trailer shots through her brain.

The unexpected freedom was nearly giddy-making.

Bullshit on not calling in details, although she'd wait until they were actually off the ground. On this one she agreed with Red—the farther they were from the men with the happy trigger fingers, the better.

The radio flicked in her headset, Tim's voice coming in. "Push this button to talk. Channel three, okay?"

"Got it." Red spoke softly. "Hurry."

Tim settled into the second seat, pulling the seat harness across his chest and slipping on the headset. "Nearly ready."

Light flashed briefly from the left, and Erin swore. "What's that?"

"Company. Take off now, Erin," Tim shouted. "Shit. Shit, *shit*."

She pulled them skyward, rotating the chopper as she lifted, attempting to get out of range as quickly as possible.

Curses rang from beside her. "They're shooting at us. Leave, now."

Erin throttled forward, sensing the bullet's contact with the chopper body more than hearing it. The faint light pouring from the cabin door showed two bodies standing in the beam, hands raised, as she headed over the treetops and away from their captors.

She took a deep breath, then eyed the control panel. "Nothing major showing up as hit so far."

"How long to somewhere to put Red down?" Tim asked. "It's an emergency."

Those were the prearranged code words Tim had established before they'd started the rescue—Erin already knew what he had in mind. "Let me check the map." She clicked channels to number one to speak privately to Tim. "Really put him down?"

Tim answered immediately. "Yes."

Dammit. She hadn't expected that response, but she switched back to the open channel immediately before their passenger knew she'd been gone. "Outside a town, right, Red?"

"Anywhere I can get a ride."

"They'll be after you," Tim warned. "We'll tell the police where Ken and John are, and hopefully they're caught, but if they get away, will those two know how to track you down?"

"They don't know much about me. I was hired to transport a bag to them. Then they asked if I wanted to do one more job. I was supposed to be a bodyguard. They didn't say anything about shooting anyone."

"Where did you fly out of?" Tim asked. "Will they be able to track you by going back there?"

No answer.

"Hey, you don't have to tell me. Was just curious, but don't worry about it." Tim turned and faced forward as Erin mentally suggested he shut up and leave this one alone. "What's the nearest point you can do a touchdown, Erin?"

She was having a harder time than usual keeping things in a straightforward direction. "There's a town about fifteen minutes for us, hours by road for Ken and John in case they had a vehicle up at the cabin. Hang on, though, I'm having issues here."

Tim sat upright. "What kind of issues?"

"They shot something, Tim. I'm not sure what, but I'm losing control of my tail rotor in spurts."

"That's not good?" Red asked.

"Not good at all," Erin confirmed. "I can land, but it might get bumpy before then. Strap yourselves in, guys, I'll see what I can do."

Tim glanced at their passenger. "You know what to do?"

The man was scrambling with the chest harness, twisting it the opposite direction to what needed to happen. "No."

"Do you want some help?" Tim offered.

Red glanced up, and now instead of just seeing the massive size of the man, Tim spotted how young he was. "Yes."

Tim was out of his seat when they lost altitude. Just a bump, but enough to drag a shout from all three of them; him, Matt, and Red.

"Sorry, guys. Between whatever the shot busted up out there and the changing temperatures, I don't know how steady this flight is going to be," Erin warned.

"You want to take us down the soonest possible?" Tim suggested as he made his way back to Red, clutching seatbacks and tie-downs as he moved in case there was another unexpected jolt.

"I want us down near civilization," Erin muttered. "I've had enough of backcountry landing strips for one day, thanks."

"Don't be too picky," Matt ventured.

Tim pushed Red back into his seat so he could straighten the harness webbing. "I agree with Matt. What if you lose pieces of the chopper altogether?"

"Then we'll land sooner than anyone expects," Erin taunted. "Stop fussing, old man, I know how to fly her, even if she's having a bad day."

Tim found a thread of amusement in the middle of his stress. He clicked the final straps together on their passenger, glancing up at Red's face. "Notice she's talking to the plane like it's alive? See what I have to deal with all the time?"

The man didn't smile, but he didn't frown, either.

Tim gestured to the gun in Red's hands. "Why don't you put that away? If the trip does get rough, the last thing any of us needs are holes in vital places. Those kind of concerns make it tough to concentrate."

Then he stepped away, slipping into one of the side seats and buckling himself in.

The fact that his medical backpack rested in the seat to his left was a big part of his choice of seating.

He strapped himself down. "Erin, did you put out a call yet?"

"No. I was waiting until we drop off Red."

Shit. He glanced over at the young man. The gun was thankfully no longer out in plain sight. "Your call here, Red. The sooner Erin gets a location to the authorities, the sooner the guys might get caught."

"But . . ." He frowned. "Yeah, I see that. Can you not tell them about me?"

"No problem," Erin cut in. "I'm not going to do a ton of talking, only give them the coordinates of the cabin. The police will want to talk to us after we land, but you can be gone by then."

Nice. Tim nodded reassuringly along with Erin's words.

Red paused, then gave his approval. "Do it."

"Thanks, Red. I have to change to a different channel, but we should be down in a few minutes."

Tim had his backpack turned toward him, the thin hidden zipper along the bottom edge opening easily and allowing him to slip his hand in and make sure what he needed was ready. "Good job, Red. When we touch down, you head wherever you want, and we won't even watch you go. We'll take off and hit the closest airfield for the rest. Got it?"

"Yeah."

"And just a suggestion?" Tim made a face. "Check out your prospective customers a little more carefully."

Red's answer was lost in the sudden change of volume outside the chopper, and a huge drop in altitude.

Tim instinctively clutched his chest harness. "Erin?"

"Working . . ." Her words died off into an unintelligible mixture of grunts and vicious complaints.

"That sounds more like swearing to me," he responded. "Tell me what's happening."

"Nothing good."

Then she ignored him, the chopper bouncing hard from side to side.

"Hold on tight, Red. This could get bumpy." Tim followed his own advice, making sure he had his pack strapped in as well. He didn't need a heavy weight slamming into him unannounced at any time.

Under them lights were appearing more frequently. "We're into busier airspace, Erin," he warned.

"Really. I wondered what all those shiny things were. Now shut up, and let me do my job."

He glanced over his shoulder at Red. "She loves me, really she does."

"Oh *shit*, hold on."

Even her warning wasn't enough. It was like being back on a cheesy ride at the fair. The ones that spin in a circle, throwing you to the outside of the seat with a sudden jerk before crushing the inside person into the poor sod on the outside edge. Tim was pushed back in his seat, only the left side of his harness webbing preventing him from being shoved any farther. A rapid rotation followed—eerie and hard to handle in the daylight when there were visual cues to help pull his equilibrium back to normal. Now in the mostly dark, it was a Disney ride gone evil. No idea when it would end, or how it would end, or at least that had to be what Red was thinking.

"Make it stop now," the man begged.

"My *God*." The words shook free from Matt, taut and fear-filled. "Erin?"

"Lost the tail rotor," Erin snapped. "Trying . . . I think . . . Just wait."

She swore again before cutting off the radio, leaving him, Matt, and Red alone on the line.

"She's good," Tim reassured the others, even as he clutched his thighs and concentrated on breathing through the rising nausea that was inevitable with the spin. He'd told Marcus long ago he had a cast-iron stomach, but he still had to work to keep in control.

Also, Erin was brilliant.

The overhead noise cut to a whistle, and the pitch of the chopper changed. Instead of spinning violently, they were moving forward and down, rushing rapidly into the darkness.

Tim's head was still spinning. Matt was groaning. Red . . .

Their kidnapper was throwing up.

The sounds of his misery faded as Tim clicked to line one. "Erin, we landing soon?"

"Sooner than you'd like. Which tends to happen when you have to turn off your main rotor. We're on autorotation."

Shit. "This wasn't some great ploy of yours?"

"Negative. We have no more tail rotor, and I'm aimed at

what I think is a grocery store parking lot. Hope there's no twenty-four-hour Laundromat or something in the area."

Tim leaned forward so he could see out the front, but from his angle it was nothing but levers and knobs, and a small windshield that was full of pitch black.

Out the side window the only clue of their forward speed was the flickering lights rushing past, the small balls of light growing larger at an alarming rate. The rush of dizziness had completely left him, a new flood of adrenaline washing through his system and preparing him for anything.

Which hopefully didn't mean too hard a landing.

He snugged his straps as tight as they would go, then waited, trusting the woman behind the controls to get them through this.

Trust. There it was again, and in this situation there was no one that he'd want to deal with this more than Erin. Once they were out of this hole he'd be happy to spend all the time it took to convince her of that fact.

The lights grew larger still.

Erin came back on the radio. "Brace yourselves, guys. Changing angle in three, two, one . . ."

The aircraft tilted. After moving forward at a nose-down position for however long she'd had them in autorotation—free-fall using the rotors like a parachute, their nose tipped up, slowing their descent and bringing the skids into landing position.

They were in the middle of a parking lot, the tall lights at the corners of the lot creating a fantastic runway as the skids touched down and they basically landed like an aircraft, rolling forward briefly over the snow-slicked concrete. Erin brought them along so smoothly Tim wasted no time. He unsnapped his harness and grabbed his gun, out of his seat the moment the chopper tugged to a stop.

He turned on Red and got the gun into position. "Don't move."

The man's expression of misery barely changed. "What the hell?"

Outside, flashing red-and-blue lights were converging on the chopper. Erin came back online. "Police are here. Sorry, Red, but there are some promises that aren't meant to be kept. Anything that starts with a gun involved would be one of them. But we'll tell the authorities exactly how much you helped us, and what we know you did and didn't do. The rest is up to you, and how much information you have to give them."

"Shit."

Erin had shut down everything and stood in the cockpit, a gun in her own hand. "Tim, go talk to the police. Matt and I'll keep an eye on Red here until they can take him away."

There was the usual scramble of dealing with the police made much easier because their kidnapper-turned-rescuer wasn't interested in struggling as he got put into the back of a squad car.

Tim was ready to burst from pride. They still had a ton of details to deal with, but for now? They were back in civilization and they were alive. There was no way this could be considered anything but a win, and Erin had been a major part of it.

Matt leaned on the car hood beside him. "I had no idea glacier tours were so . . . invigorating."

Tim laughed. "Yeah. Erin knows how to show a guy a good time, doesn't she?"

Erin slipped into his arms and squeezed him tight. "Maybe we can avoid the being-kidnapped part next time." She held out a hand to Matt, and he leaned in and caught it. "I'm glad we made it out of that in one piece."

"With my money still intact," Matt added with a laugh.

"Hey, you notice your money got you a spot in the cabin instead of the shed. See how handy that was?" Tim teased. Erin leaned harder against him, and he cherished her warmth. The affirmation that she was alive.

That they were all alive.

"No more cabins. No more sheds," Erin stated firmly. "And you two are responsible for finding us a way home from here. I'm done driving for the day."

CHAPTER 20

'''''''''''''''''''''''''''''''''

Marcus peeled open the door a crack, glaring out at the three of them on his doorstep. "You really expect me to let you in after the mess you made of my chopper?"

"Idiot." A towel hit him in the back of the head. "Open the door."

He winked before stepping aside, the door swinging wide.

Becki rushed forward, stooping to pick up her towel and welcome them. "Ignore him and come inside."

She offered a hug to Erin, which, all things considered, Erin gratefully accepted. "Thanks for the lunch invitation."

"Are you kidding? I was ordered to invite you over because everyone wants to hear the entire story." Becki squeezed once more before rotating her on the spot.

The rest of the Lifeline team, minus Alisha and Devon, stood in the living room, a few extra bodies hovering on the edges. Tripp's boyfriend, Jonah, waved from the couch. Anders's best friend shifted positions where he stood beside

Anders. Marcus's brother David was there as well. The owner of the local search-and-rescue training school stepped forward from the kitchen area, lowering a tray of snacks to the table.

"Dammit, I thought you'd all be busy with other things," Tim complained. "There's nothing interesting here. Move along."

"No? I've never been kidnapped in the middle of a rescue. That takes some serious talent." Tripp gestured them forward. "You may as well give us full disclosure all at one time rather than having to repeat it multiple times."

"But Tim was planning on getting a barbecue dinner out of each of you while he shared the story over and over again," Erin drawled. "You've gone and ruined everything."

"Oh shit, *barbecue* . . ." Marcus darted across the room and through the deck doors, throwing open the lid on the massive grill. A cloud of smoke rose upward. He grabbed a set of tongs and poked around for a moment before waving the metal hooks reassuringly at the house. "No problems. All under control."

Becki laughed. "Don't worry, we have extra. But first— you must be Matt."

He accepted her hand, then glanced around the room. "Nice place you've got. Thanks for including me in the invitation."

"Hey, we're an equal opportunity barbecue provider. You get kidnapped, you get the same goodies. Make yourself at home." She picked up a platter from the side counter and held it toward Tim. "Any of you men who want to go do some male bonding, feel free."

Tim had already been inching toward the doors, but he paused, taking the tray from her. "Is it that obvious we're dying to be involved in making charcoal of good food?"

"It's a genetic thing. We get it," Erin said. "Go, have fun making fires."

Suddenly the room was empty of all but Becki and Erin.

"We really need to do something about the lack of female population around here," Becki complained.

"Definitely a good idea, but notice they're the ones standing in the cold while we've got the warm house?"

"Because we plan ahead." Becki held bottles in the air. "Beer, wine? Something harder?"

"Tequila shots at noon. I don't think so."

A lazy shrug lifted Becki's shoulders. "Don't consider it noon, consider it *early in the day during your extended vacation*. Marcus is giving you extra time off, did he tell you that yet?"

"No, but that's great news." Erin pointed at the beer. "One of those would be fine. And extra days off would also be fine."

Becki twisted the top off and handed the bottle over. "You deserve it, and besides, Devon and Alisha aren't back from training until Wednesday. So unless there's a dire emergency that requires your flying abilities, Lifeline remains on break."

Erin curled up in the corner of the couch. "Thank you. I'm pretty sure you had a hand in convincing Marcus that was a good idea."

Becki settled beside her. "Maybe a little. How are you doing?"

"Tired," Erin admitted. "By the time we dealt with the police, and the helicopter, and the media, and transferring all the Lifeline gear, it was past midnight. Tim got us dropped at a hotel for the night. We rented a car and drove home this morning. We stopped at Lifeline to dump gear, hit my place for a minute, then used Tim's apartment to clean up before heading over here."

"A whirlwind. You do need some extra holiday time. Is Matt flying home later today?" Becki asked.

Erin hesitated. The discussion had remained very generic for the entire drive, at least the parts she hadn't slept through. She wasn't sure if it was because Tim didn't want to talk in front of Matt, or the guys didn't want to talk in front of her. Or maybe they were all just overloaded with their own thoughts after the heart-pounding adventure.

For whatever reason the trip had been mostly filled with bad radio reception and conversations about food. "You know, he didn't say yet. There was talk about the meetings he has in Calgary, but I don't think that's until next week."

She briefly went over what had happened, Becki's eyes widening in appreciation at the appropriate moments.

"Damn. You did everything right *and* you were really lucky."

"If Red hadn't decided to help us, I'm not sure what we would have done. It's not something I'd like to experience again anytime soon." Erin shivered briefly.

"Agreed." Becki leaned back on the couch. "Marcus said you've already got the helicopter dealt with."

"Get this. One of the cops had a tow company on speed dial, the kind that deal with big rigs when they get into trouble. They loaded the chopper onto a flatbed, and she was on the road to Calgary before we were on our way to the hotel." Erin laughed. "I bet Marcus told you that the chopper was safe before he told you about us."

"Don't be stupid." Becki slapped her leg lightly. "He was worried. We all were."

"I know, I'm just kidding. It was pretty scary. Scarier than any rescue I've done, and we've had some wild ones."

"Another reason for a bit of a break," Becki said.

"I thought the rule was get right back on the horse?" Erin let her gratitude show. "We'll be fine. And hey, I proved I'm still up on my emergency chopper manoeuvres."

Becki gave her a high five. "You are classy, and talented, and I'm glad you're home safe."

"Me, too."

"Becki, where are the buns?" Marcus shouted from the doorway.

"My favourite ones are in your pants," Becki called back,

rising to her feet and winking at Erin as laughter poured in the door along with the cold air. "One second, I'll get them."

Erin relaxed where she was, sipping her beer while she stared out the window at the guys congregating around the grill.

Extra time off. She wasn't sure what they would do with it.

Her stay with Tim at Matt's had been—she hated to be cheesy and say *magical*, but it certainly hadn't been real life. Maybe that was why she'd been so willing to let Tim take control.

I let him take control because that's what I wanted.

And there it was again. That edge of honesty that cut into her fear. There really was no going back. It wouldn't be fair to either of them. Either she confirmed what she'd said to Tim before about enjoying what he'd arranged, or she needed to call this relationship off and let them both move on.

Only confirming that she wanted more of what they'd shared on the island also meant they had to have a serious discussion, and soon. Their past wasn't going to vanish without a trace, and the longer she held off discussing it, the harder it got.

Tim caught her eye and straightened. All his attention focused tightly on her. Watching, assessing. Like he did during sex. Like he did all the time. The cheeky wink he tossed her did nothing to answer her dilemma, except . . . it was such a purely instinctive Tim move, she had to smile in response.

Maybe that was her answer. Things with Tim would move forward, and they'd see what came next. What came naturally.

And at the end of it all, she hoped she still had herself as well as him.

It was crowded around the grill, but Tim didn't mind. He was in his glory. Erin hadn't been far off in her tease about him getting maximum mileage out of sharing their adventure.

Their time with the group was also a great distraction from having to make the next set of plans. He knew what he wanted, but first he needed confirmation from Erin for the go-ahead.

Getting the catch-up time with the team was important, but he was itching for the next step.

"You had far more luck than you should have," Anders pointed out, a murmur of agreement rippling through the group as Tim, along with Matt's enthusiastic additions, finished their story.

"Luck was a big part of it." Matt pointed in the window. "Luck and that lady. When I heard the propellers stall I thought we were going to plummet straight down and be gone in one huge explosive fireball."

"Erin's the best." Tripp leaned on the wall, one arm around his boyfriend. "Although I can't imagine autorotation becoming a popular method of transportation."

"Better than the spinning thing she had us doing a minute earlier." Matt shuddered. "God, I need another drink just thinking about it."

Tim slapped him on the shoulder. "You did great. Most people react like Red. You only whimpered for your mommy."

"Ass," Matt replied without rancor.

Marcus laughed. "I'm glad everything worked out."

"Not everything." Tim didn't want to dwell on it, but he was still wondering. "I wish I could figure out what those guys were doing in the middle of nowhere. It wasn't drugs, but it was obviously something important enough they felt the need to kill a man and kidnap us to get off the mountain before the authorities arrived—it makes no sense."

"Did the police pick up the guys at the cabin?" Tripp asked.

Tim shook his head. "Got a call this morning from our contact. The police made it to the cabin before morning, but the men were already gone. Must have had a car in one of the outbuildings. Good thing we got Red arrested—it's probably the only thing keeping him safe right now."

Tripp frowned. "You and Erin aren't in any danger, are you?"

"Nah," Tim reassured him. "There's no reason for them to want to see us again. They're probably thankful they don't have to deal with us."

"I don't even want to think what *dealing with us* might have meant," Matt said.

Tim patted him on the back. "We're safe. End of story."

"And it's a good end," Marcus affirmed. "Matt, if you need a hand while you're here, I'm yours. I can drive you to Calgary if that's where you're flying home from."

"I'll let you know if I need anything," Matt promised. "Oh, that reminds me."

He passed something to Marcus.

Marcus then glanced down, confusion drifting across his face. "Your business card. Thanks."

Matt pointed to the corner. "That's my assistant's direct line. Call her, and we'll see what we can set up in terms of a donation or two to the team."

"Hang on." Marcus shook his head. "No, I mean I feel bad enough—"

"I'll warn you now, arguing with Matt about money is a losing cause," Tim cut in. "Just say thank you, and call the man's assistant on Monday."

"And if you don't, I'll call for you." David tipped his head to Matt. "I'll speak for my brother, who's too busy sticking his foot in his mouth. Your offer is not necessary, but donations are very much appreciated. Government funding only goes so far, so thank you."

"Agreed. And since I know personally how important it is to have search and rescue on hand, I'm always on the lookout for places to support." Matt tossed Tim a dirty look. "Someone should have mentioned sooner he was with a new team."

Tim shrugged. "You need mysteries in your life."

"Alisha and Devon are on Skype," Becki interrupted from the doorway. "Tim, come in. They're waiting to talk to you and Erin. The rest of you, everything else is laid out on the counter, if Marcus has finished sacrificing the first burgers."

Marcus grinned sheepishly. "You're never going to let me live down burning those steaks, are you?"

Becki passed Tim a smile on her way to drape her arms around her lover's neck. Marcus slipped his arm around her waist, pulling her close to kiss her passionately in spite of the crowd stepping around them on their way back into the house.

Tim watched for a moment before heading inside, hungry for that kind of relationship. Longing for the connection he saw in the people right around them, and the urgency to get to that stage with Erin grew.

All through the visit with Alisha and Devon, all through the meal, he pondered his dilemma. Wanting to push harder, make the moves.

Maybe it was time to simply take what he and Erin both needed. It had been far too long coming as far as he was concerned.

Their lunch finished, they said good-bye and headed out the door, pausing on the path leading back to Tim's truck.

Matt cleared his throat. "Before it becomes a huge topic of discussion, I'd like to announce my assistant found a great place to rent about an hour from here."

"So you'll be staying in the area for a few days?" Erin asked.

"Yes, but I was thinking . . ." His friend dragged his fingers through his hair, a wry smile sneaking out. "I know this might seem a touch crazy, but the place is big enough for all of us. To make up for having to abandon my place on short notice."

Tim hesitated, listening to what his friend wasn't saying. "You have things to do in Calgary—when?"

"Wednesday."

Which meant he'd be holed up by himself until then. Tim

squeezed Erin's fingers and considered how this changed his plans for their extended holiday. It was the perfect way to kill two birds with one stone.

He turned to Erin, but she was staring at Matt, a frown on her pretty face. "You'll be all alone until Wednesday?"

"Erin. I'm a grown man." Matt shrugged. "I spend a good deal of time by myself."

"Not right now, you don't," Erin flashed back.

Tim's smile only widened as Erin twirled toward him. "Want to keep holidaying with Matt?"

"If it's okay with you?"

"Spend more time with this jerk? You're a glutton, aren't you, kitten?

A subtle smile snuck out. "Only for some things."

Matt's pleasure that his suggestion had been accepted was clear. "I'll get the directions."

Erin held up a hand. "Wait. Before we head off to places unknown, we're swinging by my house so I can grab some clean clothes. I insist."

"No problem." Tim leaned forward and kissed her cheek, unable to stop the teasing whisper. "Although why you think you'll need any clothes is a mystery."

Her eyes widened—her interest and excitement obvious. She swallowed, and her gaze flicked ahead of them where Matt was waiting with the truck door already open.

A rising sense of pleasure and hope mixed together. Whatever the next couple of days would bring, Tim was looking forward to it immensely.

CHAPTER 21

,,,,,,,,,,,,,,,,,,,,,,,,,,,,,,,,,

The house wasn't quite as big as Matt's.

Almost, but not quite.

Having established that fact, Erin wandered into the kitchen with a sense of awe stalking her. "How is it possible to make one phone call and end up with a house like this to rent for a few days?"

Matt shrugged. "Money makes things happen."

Money. *Man* . . . "Matt, it's got a pool. And a workout room."

"And a stocked bar and fridge." Tim closed the fridge, hands full of drinks he lowered to the counter. "And there's a chef coming over later to make dinner." He pointed at Matt. "That one's on me, you hear?"

Matt accepted the bottle from Tim. "Fine. You can pay for supper. I arranged for massages for this afternoon."

Tim laughed. "You didn't."

"Well, I didn't. My assistant did," Matt confessed. "But

we're getting pampered at four thirty. That gives us plenty of time before the feast begins."

Decadence at its finest. Erin eased against Tim's side, trailing her fingers over the counter in amazement. "You two are hired to pick all my vacation spots from here on. Did you see the yard?"

Both the guys smiled approvingly. Tim slid an arm around her and guided her into the open living space under the storey-and-a-half ceiling. "It's not a yard, it's an *outdoor entertainment area backing onto a wilderness reserve.*"

"Oh, excuse me. My mistake." Erin squeezed him tight, then had to haul up a hand to cover her yawn. "Sorry about that."

Tim eyed her. "Last night knocked you for a loop. Come on. We'll explore later. Matt, I'll be back in a bit."

"No hurry, no agenda, or at least not until four thirty." Matt had settled on the couch, playing with a remote control. "I'm very happy right where I am."

His grin grew bigger as the fireplace flickered to a warm glow. Satisfaction in his every move, he put his feet up on the coffee table and dragged a magazine into his lap.

Then Erin couldn't see anything more because Tim had her out of the room and down the hall to the master bedroom Matt had insisted they use.

Tim had her shirt off before she knew what he'd planned, and he was working on her pants. "Take a shower, take a nap. Like Matt said, there's no agenda here other than to relax."

He was right. She had no set ideas for her afternoon, and being stripped down and kissed tenderly was definitely a good idea. He cradled her against him for a moment, and she shivered.

"Cold?" He went to pull back, but she clung tighter to stop him from letting go so soon.

She licked her lips. "I'm naked again, and you're fully

clothed. That does something to me." Her confession came out husky.

"Hmm." He stroked lazily over her back and hips, moving the barest bit against her. The caress kicked the sensations licking up her spine into overdrive. "It does something to me as well," he breathed against her cheek.

Logic wanted her to explain away the extreme relaxation in her limbs. It had been a long day. She'd been up early, and while it was only one thirty in the afternoon, it seemed like a lot later between the transport back to Banff and the time spent at the barbecue with the team.

But honesty made her confess that it wasn't sheer exhaustion leaving her limbs relaxed to the point of being jelly. It was the mellow sensation in her gut.

Her mood had changed. The fear of the kidnapping, the stressful hours that had passed since—all of that faded until there was only the two of them, Tim's strong hands guiding her forward until they stood beside an enormous porcelain tub.

"Shower?"

"I changed my mind. You get to relax, I get to enjoy you."

Erin sank into the oversized soaker tub, her eyelids growing heavier by the minute as Tim turned on the water and proceeded to wash her. His touch was sensual, not sexual, hands stroking slowly, the rougher texture of the washcloth rubbing her skin and leaving a heated pulse everywhere.

Somewhere in the house a faint chorus of music had begun playing. Classical, with powerful upsweeps of strings and bass. She was being seduced to the strains of songs that had been performed before kings and queens.

She felt every inch a pampered royal.

Tim helped her stand, then indulged her by wrapping her in a huge fluffy towel. Her hair was wrapped in a second towel, so she was nestled in warm cotton as he placed her tenderly on the massive king-sized bed and proceeded to pat her dry. The room was cool, but the brush of his hands with the soft cloth made her skin tingle.

He lifted the edge of the comforter and she crawled under it, her naked skin on the sheets the whisper of a caress. One detail made her smile. "Flannel, not silk?"

"It's winter," Tim offered. He stripped down rapidly before joining her. Heat streamed from his body to chase away the slight chill as their bodies warmed the sheets.

He pulled her against him and kissed her temple and adjusted his hold to half drape her over him, settling them in place. "Sleep."

"You told Matt you'd be back shortly."

"Matt will wait. I want to hold you."

"Hmm." Erin teetered on the edge already. "Don't let me sleep away the entire holiday."

He laughed. "No chance of that. I promise I'll wake you when it's time. For now, a couple hours of rest come first."

It felt oddly greedy to allow her eyes to close and sleep to take over, but if this was part of what he wanted—

Give him control. Let him call the shots.

It was difficult to stick to her plan, but while they hadn't officially restarted their adventure, she was sure he'd gotten her message. She'd left behind a few fears in the tub, washed away with his touch.

I want more.

The thought slipped in as she fell asleep.

It seemed only a moment later she was being rolled to her back, hands tugging her under him. "I want you," Tim whispered. "I need to be inside you, now."

Dream or reality? Erin didn't care. She opened her legs and welcomed him as he settled between her thighs. Naked skin brushed, his cock nudged her core. Fingers fumbled for a moment as he guided himself between her folds.

And paused, the head of his cock nestled just inside her sex. She opened her eyes as he pulled her hands over her head, stretching her beneath him. He tugged until she arched, body curving upward.

His fingers curled around her wrists, pinning her in place. With his free hand he caught her hip and lifted. Slowly he joined them. She was wet already, easing his entry as his cock pressed her apart.

He worked in all the way to the root, fully buried. Pleasure rippled over his expression as he pulled back and thrust forward more rapidly the second time.

Erin relished the sensation. The fullness. Knowing that he was enjoying her body even as her own passions rose.

She couldn't move except to lift her legs, and she did that now, wrapping herself around him and gasping as the new position allowed him to press deeper.

Tim smiled. "Keep your hands where they are."

Oh, shit.

But she nodded, linking her fingers together to remind herself not to move. He slipped his hands free of her wrists.

He rose to his knees and caught hold of her hips, changing the angle as he plunged harder into her core. Her heels dug into the muscular cheeks of his ass, but it was the relentless thrusts that threatened her sanity. With most of her weight balanced on her shoulders, Tim drove his cock in again. Hard, his fingers squeezing the delicate skin of her hips and ass tight enough to bruise.

Erin struggled to keep her hands over her head, the temptation to reach down and grasp his shoulders shaking her. The urge to touch him was so strong, the desire to stroke his body. To hang on tight as he possessed her. But he'd ordered her to leave her hands up, and locking them together to do that forced her to take the pleasure he gave without adding to it on her own.

Every time he thrust, his heavy cock stroked her clit, and every time the deliberate rub brought her that much closer to coming. She didn't expect the pleasure. For some reason she hadn't expected him to make sure she came as well. It was just as satisfying to look up and watch him, to see the play of desire dance over his face. He froze, cock filling her completely as his hips jerked and he found release.

He lowered himself slowly, his body blanketing hers, the sheets long abandoned to the floor. She was more than warm enough as he panted softly, his lips finding her neck. His chest rubbed her lightly, the tight curls on his chest abrading her sensitive nipples.

"You are too tempting," he scolded, the words a teasing caress past her ear. "And I'm not nearly done with you."

"Umm, I like that, but don't we have a massage appointment soon?"

"Soon enough." He tugged her hands apart from where she'd been keeping them in place by clutching the mattress cover. Tim kissed her knuckles, then used her hand to brush his cheek.

His five o'clock shadow tickled and tantalized. She loved to feel that rough scratching sensation over her entire body. Have him leave rash lines between her thighs—the possibilities were endless.

Only what he did was rock backward, finding a spot on the side of the mattress. His heated gaze carried over her. Mischief and fire all mixed up into one.

"You didn't come," he noted. "I was too quick."

"It's okay."

He shook his head. "I don't want you having to endure your massage all turned on and unsatisfied."

Erin wiggled up onto her elbows. She lifted her hair and twisted it out of the way, laying it to the side of the pillow, the still damp strands distracting her for a moment.

She waited as Tim stroked her leg from the knee down to her ankle. "Why do I get the feeling you're up to something?" she asked.

Another stroke, this time upward, the drifting touch making goose bumps rise ahead of his fingers. "Just want you to be happy. Do you want to come, Erin?"

"Well, if you insist."

His eyes flashed hotter, but he sat back on the mattress instead of moving closer. "I do. Make yourself come, Erin. I want to watch."

Oh *shit*.

She pulled the pillows under her head and shoulders, propping up at enough of an angle so he wasn't looming over her. Only his expression was intense enough to burn her no matter how equal their body positions.

There was no doubt who was in control at this moment, and it wasn't her.

She fell into his command. Pushed aside everything that said this was too much or stupid, or the wrong kind of thing. He wanted her to come?

Game on.

Starting slowly seemed right, even though she was already turned on enough that a few touches might be all it took to send her over. She trailed her hands over her breasts. Lifting the heavy swells lightly before pausing to circle her thumbs over her sensitive nipples. The tips were already hard, and her light caress made them tingle.

She drifted one hand down her torso, fingers spread wide to allow the heat banked in her body to flare again. The other she kept raised, playing with her breasts as Tim's gaze darted back and forth between the two points.

She was slick with her own moisture and his release, and her fingers skimmed smoothly through her folds. Small circles, longer dips into her core, the entire time increasing pressure on her clit as Tim rose to his feet, his stare intensifying. It wasn't going to take long, not with how close she'd been during their earlier session.

And his eyes. Lord, the way he watched her made everything . . . *more*. More intense. More sensual, until it wasn't her fingers on her clit, teasing and rubbing, it was his—*his* hands pinching her nipples to make them sting for a second before a wicked flush of pleasure washed through her and edged her higher.

When he knelt on the bed at her side and leaned closer to take her lips, nothing mattered except the wave of desire that was ready to break over her. His kiss arched her upward, desperate to keep their mouths in contact. He moved to her neck and sucked, right there under her ear, and it propelled her over. Dizzy delight rushed in, tangling her limbs. Shaking her hard as her body responded to all the tactile pleasures meeting together in one perfect moment. Touch, taste—the sensory overload made her giddy.

She relaxed back on the pillow, gently guided there by his strong hands.

"Whoa." Erin cupped his cheek, enjoying the tease of his whiskers.

Tim stretched out beside her, his hands drifting over her face, her hair. Pulling strands back from her forehead as his gaze danced over her. "Lovely as always."

Some smart-ass remark would be appropriate, but she couldn't find one she liked. The mellow sensation from earlier had enveloped her completely, leaving her only response a smile. "Massages soon?"

Tim nodded. "We have a few more minutes, but we should be getting ready."

Erin stretched, pleasure rippling through her veins. "I need to finish waking up."

"For a massage? Don't bother." He kissed her nose, then rolled away. "Have a quick shower, pull on a robe—that's all you need."

She wasn't sure if his expression was one of satisfaction for what they'd just experienced, or if he was already anticipating the next thing. Either way, she liked what she saw, and this time she was willing to admit it.

Things were about to get real interesting.

CHAPTER 22

Tim paced down the hall to Matt's room. Logistics for the massages plus a few other things were on his mind. If he was going to take full advantage of this holiday, now was the time to set some things in motion.

Matt was the perfect person for what he had in mind, as long as his friend was willing. And chances of him not being willing?

Slim.

He put his knuckles to the door and got an instant response.

"Come in."

Tim eased the door open to discover that Matt had obviously been prepping for his massage as well. Fresh out of the shower, his blond hair was still disarrayed in ragged spikes as he tightened a robe belt around his waist. "What's up?"

"Massages. Are they here yet?"

"No, but I was headed to the living room. I'll let them

in." His eyes darkened. "You want a private room for you and Erin to go at the same time?"

"Couples massage?"

Matt shrugged. "I don't know how much interaction you'll have, but you may as well be in the same place."

"Sounds great to me." Tim walked beside Matt silently for a moment, considering the wisdom of what he was about to do. It really wasn't that tough a decision. "Personal favour to ask. You willing to help give Erin a fantasy or two over the coming days?"

There was no doubt of Matt's response. His eyes lit up, and his body language all but shouted *yes*. "Tell me the lines, and I'll stay behind them."

"The lines are going pretty damn far." Tim examined Matt closely. "I'm trusting you with someone very precious to me. It's taken months for her to step to the point of giving me control."

"You're a lucky man." His friend nodded slowly. "I'll follow your lead."

"Which means you might take the lead at times. Other than that, I don't know what we'll end up doing." Tim waited until Matt had stilled. "You're a good friend, and I trust you. I know Erin well enough I won't let you do anything that takes it further than she's ready for. I won't let you do anything that would hurt her. So if she calls it off, we stop. No matter what point we're at."

"I understand the rules." The touch of excitement in his voice was apparent as they entered the living room. "Is it gauche to say thanks for including me? And I'm serious, I didn't offer the rental in the hopes of something like this happening."

Tim laid a hand on Matt's arm. "I know your offer was made with only our best interests in mind."

Matt nodded. "I'm glad. Your friendship means a lot to me, and I don't want to do anything to get in the way of that."

"This won't. Not if we keep it all about Erin—making what she needs happen."

"Of course."

Erin had gone boneless. Gentle music played in the background while soothing hands worked her over and teased out all the sore places she didn't even know she had.

On the table next to her Tim let out a long, low moan of satisfaction.

His masseur chuckled. "You want me to massage anything else?" Charlie asked.

"Sounds like you're already getting into obscene territory," Monique, the woman doing Erin's massage, teased.

"I'd be moaning, too, if I had the strength." Erin stretched slowly, careful to not shift away from where Monique was using her thumbs and doing repeats down the tired muscles in the back of Erin's thighs. "I'd offer to marry you if it would do me any good."

"Sorry, don't swing that direction. But thanks for the compliment."

Another near obscene noise escaped Tim, and Erin pushed up on her elbows to take a closer look. "What are you doing to him?" she asked Charlie.

"He's pushing his thumbs into my ass cheeks like he's digging for diamonds. I don't know if I should moan or scream."

"Nearly done. You've got a ton of knots back here. I'd suggest whatever you've been doing, take a break from it for a while," Charlie said.

"I'll pass that on to my boss. He'll be thrilled."

Charlie and Monique finished up and left, music still playing in the background.

Erin lay still, utterly content. "I'm never moving again," she sighed happily.

"That will make flying the next rescue difficult," Tim noted.

She pulled to a sitting position, legs dangling from the massage table as Tim rolled to his back.

She stared at him, at all his firm muscles flexing as he moved. His lean torso had a light dusting of hair on his chest, a trail leading down to his semi-erect cock. He reclined like a Greek statue, and she soaked in the sight, enjoying herself immensely.

Tim smiled. "What?"

"I'm taking stock of my blessings. Today has been one incredible thing after another. Not to mention that we recently got out of a scary situation unscathed." She leaned forward, resting her elbows on her knees. "Thank you for taking such good care of me."

"It's been my pleasure." His gaze drifted as the robe she'd marginally draped around her for privacy slipped off one shoulder, revealing her breasts. "Anything for you."

She artfully shrugged so the other side would slide away as well. There was a low level of pleasure riding in her veins. It didn't matter that it had been someone else who'd been touching her; her skin had grown more sensitive from knowing Tim was all but naked, two feet away.

Erin tilted her head. "Did it turn you on to get the massage?"

"Charlie?" Tim considered. "It felt good no matter who was touching me, but the sheer-out pain he caused there at the end—I wasn't kidding when I said it hurt like hell."

She examined him closer because she could. "I'm turned on. I'm a little surprised—I didn't think girls did it for me, but that's twice in the past couple days that the idea of being with a woman hasn't frightened me."

Tim shook his head, pulling his robe back on and sadly covering up her lovely view. "It should never frighten you to find someone attractive. It's not only physical beauty that makes us look twice, either. Sometimes it's an attitude, or a skill set. Both can lead to good old honest lust."

Erin took his hand and let him help her off the bench.

She leaned against him as he guided them back to their rooms. Between the conversation and her utter relaxation, she found it tough to concentrate. She pulled on the simple wraparound dress he laid out for her without making a comment about the lack of underwear he provided.

Tim had an attitude that she'd always admired, but now he'd matured, and there was so much more to him. More layers, more depth.

Had she changed as much in the years they'd been apart? She wanted to ask him that, but part of her was afraid that she'd been slacking off. Hiding from the things that she should have faced head-on.

Every step of their time together had her closer to the point of acknowledging that she *had* run so many years ago, and that maybe her reaction had been wrong.

They stepped into the dining room and she jerked to a stop. The room had been transformed into a glittering spectacle of lights and shiny baubles.

All of it only two feet off the floor.

Matt rose from where he'd been seated on the floor and greeted them, kissing her knuckles and leading her to a large, low cushion.

Tim looked extraordinarily pleased. "Wow. Food *and* ambience. Did I pick the right catering company, or what?"

"There was a group of four that rushed in here to make things over. Who was I to argue?" Matt said.

"Japanese?" Erin asked. "Oh, wow, this looks fantastic." She leaned forward to examine the offerings on the tabletop. "I love sushi, and I love sake and—"

"Then let's start there," Tim said.

He settled on one side of her, Matt on the other. Erin stilled as their warmth surrounded her.

Matt ignored her pause, pouring from the teeny heated carafe. "Body temperature," he explained. "I got the lecture before they left."

Tim lifted his glass for Matt to fill, then waited until they all had their glasses in the air. "May there always be mountains in our lives to leap from."

"And soft objects to cushion the landings," Matt added.

Three glasses clinked together. Erin allowed the first touch of liquor to rest on her palate for a moment before swallowing. The slightly sweet sting made her mouth water, and she turned eagerly to see what Tim thought.

He was staring again, eyes fixed on her. Then he took another sip and leaned closer, his kiss filled with the taste and scent of the alcohol.

Temptation trickled up her spine.

Matt cleared his throat. "Try this first."

He held a small piece of sashimi in his fingers, lifting it to her lips, and Erin opened her mouth automatically to accept it.

The salty tips of his fingers registered even more than the dainty morsel of food. Erin lowered her eyes for a moment so she could concentrate on chewing and swallowing without choking.

There was something going on, and she liked it very much. Her senses that had begun to buzz during the massage were now trembling on the edge of breathlessness.

Tim laid one hand on her thigh and ate with his other, using his chopsticks expertly. He and Matt continued to talk, reminiscing about their past trip down the St. Lawrence River, or something.

Erin lost track of everything outside her immediate sight and touch. The food was delicious, but all she could focus on was the constant circling of Tim's fingers on her thigh. Higher now, then lower.

She debated changing position to make it easier for him to reach more, when Matt bumped her shoulder.

"You're quiet tonight."

She turned her smile on him. "Just lazy. Getting back into the holiday mood."

"I think we all are."

An edgy anticipation hovered around them. Unwilling to break the spell, Erin obediently nibbled on food as it was offered to her, but she found it difficult to concentrate. When would the touch on her thigh change from light and teasing to something more intimate? Was Matt going to watch again? This time from right in the room?

Or was even more on the line?

"You're distracted," Tim noted. "Not hungry?"

She'd eaten enough to take the edge off, but she doubted that any more food was going down tonight. "It's all delicious, but . . ."

He slipped his hand around her waist and tugged her closer, fingers magically slipping under the edge of her dress. His warm palm met her skin and skimmed lightly to her back.

Erin waited, her heart pulsing in her throat.

Tim put his nails to her skin and scratched lightly as he pulled forward. A heavy sigh escaped her as pleasure wrapped her in its embrace.

"Rest." He shifted position. "Come, lean on me if you're tired. Matt and I will finish our meal while you relax."

She turned slightly and reclined against him, easing as close as possible. Her hips were nestled tight to his groin. He was hard, the thick length of his cock pressing her.

The men continued to eat. Matt offered her tiny tidbits that she couldn't refuse, not when each was offered with such heated devotion. The crossed front of her dress opened slightly, and his gaze dipped lower, stroking the curves of her breasts.

Tim nuzzled her neck. "You warm enough?"

"Yes." Because there was no other answer. Announcing she was on fire didn't seem appropriate.

Then his hands were at the front of her dress, pulling the fabric apart and slipping it from her shoulders, and *appropriate* went out the window.

If Matt had stared before, he was now mesmerized, fixated as her chest moved with her rapidly increasing breaths.

She was naked from the waist up. Tim eased a hand around
her waist and settled her against him again, only now the
stakes were that much higher.

Light touches of his fingers over her stomach increased
the ache between her legs. Her nipples had pulled tight, and
Matt hesitated. He took a long drink, then interrupted the
discussion between him and Tim.

"May I?"

Tim tilted her head back, smiling down on her. "If you've
had enough to eat, we can move to the next portion of the
evening."

"Yes," she whispered.

He touched his lips to hers. A tender kiss. Light and barely
there, but the forceful hand he slipped into her hair meant she
was instantly trapped. She didn't mind, just enjoyed his kiss
as he increased the pressure and took possession, hungrily
tasting her mouth as she grew dizzy with passion.

Heated moisture wrapped around her nipple, and she
gasped. Tim tightened his grasp, stopping her from jerking
away.

Only a second later she understood what was going on.
Matt had leaned over and was licking her nipples. Gentle
brushes at first, then bolder. Tim continued to kiss her, but
now there was a distracting tug threading through her body
as Matt closed his lips around one aching tip and sucked.

"Oh God, *yes*." She spoke against Tim's lips, staying as
still as possible as Matt switched sides and gave the same
tender attention to her other breast.

Tim pulled away but didn't let her go. His blue eyes
burned her as he gazed down to watch Matt in motion. "You
enjoy that? Enjoy what he's doing to you?" he asked.

"Yes."

He held her tight but eased the hand he had on her belly
upward until he could cup the underside of one breast. Matt
moved instantly to that side, taking advantage of the gift,
pulling harder as he sucked.

"Use your teeth a little," Tim ordered.

Pleasure shot through her like an electrical zap, not only in response to Tim's words, but to the edge of pain as Matt instantly obeyed. Erin wiggled, unable to keep still.

This was nothing extraordinary—a man taking and giving pleasure at her breasts—but it was so far out of her experience because it was Matt touching her and Tim who held her. "Ahh, that's *good*."

Tim laughed. "You're easy to please."

"Small things." She gasped as Matt bit again.

Then she was on her feet, the dress falling away to leave her naked between them. The suddenness of it took her breath away, as did the kiss Tim pulled her into once again. As if he were claiming her first.

There was another set of hands on her hips, sliding in slow exploratory strokes, but it was the set at her neck and lower back that counted. Tim holding her to him. The rough scratch of their clothing on her sensitive skin. Heated palms and edgy drag of nails—all of it priming her and making her ache.

Tim pulled the hand at her neck forward to cup her cheek. "Ready for more?"

She nodded.

As if they'd practiced beforehand, both men stepped away, and she had to regain her balance. The loss of their heat sent a shiver racing, but she accepted the hand Tim offered and followed him.

Matt walked with them, a short distance behind.

"Where are we off to?"

"To wash up," Matt offered. "Sushi fingers aren't good for what we have in mind."

Oh really? She glanced over her shoulder. "That sounds—"

"Dirty?" Matt grinned, his gaze running over her hungrily. "Just wait."

There was no slow heated watching involved. Tim opened a side door, gesturing her into a small washroom.

He blocked the doorway with his body as Matt continued down the hall and vanished through another door.

Tim stroked her cheek again. "Get yourself ready, then join us."

"Ready for . . . ?" She took a deep breath and tried again, this time forcing out the question. Making herself accept what she'd known all along. "I'll be there in a minute."

He smiled. "You'll have fun. I promise."

He closed the door, and she moved through the room in a sexual daze, the rush of rising endorphins making her mind skip. Normal habits were the only thing that saved her. She used the new toothbrush on the counter. Washed her hands. Washed everywhere else, the washcloth only intensifying the sensation on aching parts.

She was past ready for sex, and the night had only begun.

Walking naked down the hall took a new kind of courage for her. There was no one else in the house who could walk in on her, but the challenge was still there. She had to place her hand on the doorknob and deliberately turn it. Make the choice to step into a world of fantasy for the evening.

Erin pulled the heavy door toward her, and stepped into the room.

CHAPTER 23

,,,,,,,,,,,,,,,,,,,,,,,,,,,,,,,,,,

They stood across the room from her, another bedroom with a leather couch against the opposite wall. Tim and Matt were side by side talking quietly as she entered, both of them falling silent at her arrival.

She waited. Wondered.

Tim answered her unspoken question by calling her forward. "Come here, kitten."

Matt's eyes burned as she strolled in slowly, the short distance seeming to stretch into miles. Tim tossed a pillow to the ground, and her pulse picked up. When he caught her and took her to her knees, she went willingly.

Tim pulled out his erect cock and pumped it a couple of times, the full, heavy length level with her mouth. She caught hold of his thighs, bracing herself, and when he pressed the crown to her lips, she was ready.

She'd given him blowjobs plenty of times before, some rougher, some playful and gentle, but never with another man standing beside them. Every time Tim thrust forward it seemed more raw, yet more intimate because Matt was right there.

Tim pulled back slowly. "Use your tongue to get me wet," he ordered.

Erin eagerly followed his instructions. Licked the heavy vein on the underside of his cock. Paused to suck his balls into her mouth one after the other before turning her attention back on the head. His moans of approval were like tender strokes against her skin.

He pulsed forward a few times. Slowly. Deep, as if unwilling to leave her before coming to a stop. He rested the head of his cock on her lower lip briefly before pulling free.

He lifted her to her feet and guided her to the couch where Matt waited. "Take care of Matt. Use only your hands until he tells you."

She paused, admiring Matt as she slipped back to the floor. His bold smile lit his honest face, and she reached for his waist button eagerly. Opened his zipper and pulled his cock free.

The heavy length felt strange in her fingers as she stroked him. Lightly at first then with increased pressure as he laid his fingers over hers and directed her. "Like that. Yes. That's it, Erin. Play with the head more. Fuck, yeah."

When he pushed away her hands and tugged her head toward his groin, she went quickly, eager for the next thing.

"Suck him, but don't suck him off." Matt protested Tim's command for a second, but Tim only laughed. "Don't look so disappointed, you don't get to come in her mouth yet. We have other plans."

Erin distracted him by covering his cock with her mouth and sucking hard. His gasp of pleasure rang in her ears, and she did it again happily.

Using her tongue to wet his length, she worked him over, dipping lower and letting his cock stretch her lips. What was Tim doing? Was he watching her, wanting it to be his cock she was playing with?

Then her question was answered as a cock nudged her from behind, slipping easily through her folds as Tim pressed forward in one smooth rush.

God, she was pinned between them. Pressure rose inside as she enjoyed working Matt's shaft while the steady rhythm of Tim fucking her continued.

Decadent? Oh yes, and debauched and depraved, and so incredibly hot she was going to melt to the floor.

He pulled out far too soon, and she wiggled her hips in protest, reaching back to find him.

"So eager. I like that, kitten. But just wait, you'll get more."

Only it wasn't his cock that she felt next, but his tongue, and her vision blurred.

Matt threaded his fingers into her hair and pushed her down his length. "Don't stop what you're doing," he scolded.

She braced her hands on his thighs and worked him, but the decadent things Tim was doing made it tougher. He alternated between having his tongue buried deep, then pulsing it against her clit.

With Matt's cock in her mouth, working carefully to keep her teeth away from him, she couldn't afford to be distracted. But there was no ignoring Tim. He slipped his fingers into her. Two, or maybe three, and an edgy burn raced up her spine.

She attempted to wiggle away, but he caught her hips and pinned her in place as he returned to his position behind her. "I'm going to fuck you, Erin. Fuck you hard the way you like it."

Before she could give approval, he'd shoved forward. All the way in until his groin met her butt. Oh *God*, the thick length of his cock stretched her, sending pleasure shooting through her in waves as he moved. Erin caught herself rocking her hips toward him, this time to increase the bite of pain.

Tim thrust, pushing her onto Matt's cock, and she gagged

for a moment. Then she found a balance point, clinging to Matt's thighs as she bobbed her head over him while Tim worked behind her.

Pleasure increased rapidly. Endorphins filled her blood as Tim drove into her. Deep jabs that only stoked the desire for more.

It was more than the physical, though. It was knowing that Tim held her, and another man was there because of Tim—mind-blowing. The rush she got from that matched the physical pleasure as her body pounded into overdrive. Passion rising, her body and senses being seduced into submission.

When Tim pulled out all the way, she complained around Matt's cock. When Matt pulled free, she could give voice to her complaints. "No, no, no, don't stop."

Tim laughed, lifting her easily and resetting her on the bed on all fours. He tossed Matt a condom, then pulled off his own. "Don't worry. We're just getting started."

Then he locked his fingers in her hair, put his cock to her lips, and thrust in.

When Matt knelt on the bed behind her, she wasn't surprised. And suddenly she was pinned between the two of them, hard hot cocks driving into her body. Matt thrust into her sex with a sigh of satisfaction. She was happy, too, wanting the feverish pitch Tim had begun to be satisfied. She squeezed her inner muscles, and Matt groaned in appreciation.

Tim tugged her hair to get her to angle her head back. "You look beautiful spread between us." He fed her his cock slowly, gaze pinned to the point where he disappeared into her mouth. Erin closed her eyes and soaked in the unique pleasure of it all.

"God, if you could see what I see." Tim's voice broke, shaky with raw lust. "Stretched out, and so giving. Our cocks filling you up. You're trembling, Erin. Looking for more, but you can only have what I give you. What you need."

Yes.

"It's everything I want for you. Every part of you craving our touch—but it's all me, kitten. No matter who touches you, it's me giving you pleasure. Taking my own."

Matt held her hips tightly, but Tim was right—those hands were an extension of his own. The pleasure all given by Tim, and she was riding on the edge of coming, but it wasn't enough. Not yet.

They withdrew and switched positions, Matt tearing off his condom to drive into her mouth while Tim . . .

Tim put his cock to her sex and paused. Lingering—stretching out the anticipation until her arms trembled.

Between one moment and the next, she was taken. His cock drove into her. She had nowhere to go. Nothing to do but accept his possession. Oh *God*, he wasn't gentle, either, grabbing her ass cheeks and shoving himself forward, bending over her and fucking into her hard as Matt fucked her mouth.

She was going to explode. She needed one more thing to tip her over, and she would be the one racing off the cliff, spinning through the air before bursting into flames like a phoenix.

The hands on her hips tightened, Tim's nails digging into her skin. Matt caught her hair in his fingers and fisted, and she whimpered lightly at the sharp pain, loving it harder than she'd have thought possible.

And as Tim dragged his nails over her ass, she melted.

Her body rocked in place, while her sex squeezed down, hard rhythmic pulses blasting through her.

Tim roared. "That's it. Come on my cock, kitten. Feel me fucking you so deep you can't escape." He pounded harder, working through her orgasm, driving her higher yet as her body convulsed helplessly. Then he shouted as he came, his heated release deep inside her. Filling her up even as he pushed again and again on nerves gone ragged, pleasure being torn from her in waves.

Matt pulled from her mouth and took himself in hand, pumping fiercely. Tim jerked her upright, his cock pressing into her as he changed their position. Matt came, the spurts of semen flying out to land on her chest, ribbons trailing down her torso in sticky lines. He panted, his face creased into a grimace of pleasure as he shook with the final moments of release.

But Tim was the one who held her, who remained inside her. The heat of his body protecting her like a cocoon. When he pulled his cock out she felt the loss, as well as the ache of tender skin.

"I'm not going to be able to sit for a day," she muttered.

Matt laughed, leaning over and running a finger down her chest, spreading his seed lightly as his nail grazed her nipple. "I can find you a hammock."

Tim turned her from Matt, who winked quickly before there was nothing to see but her lover's smiling face. "Sitting is overrated," he offered.

He scooped her up, striding through the hallways with her arms around his neck. Uncaring of their nudity, he paced to their room, took her to the shower, and proceeded to wash her carefully from top to bottom.

"I can wash myself," she protested.

He squeezed the sponge over her breast before circling it slowly, tormenting the already oversensitive tip. "But where would the fun be in that?"

Erin leaned her head back on the shower tiles and let him take care of her. Let the sensation of being cozened and coveted spill through her like fine wine until she was heady with it.

Even through the buzz of satisfaction a faint chord of fear snaked across her nerves. She pushed the emotion down, shoved it into a corner, because it wasn't something that she wanted to deal with here and now.

But soon? They had to talk about what had really torn them apart so long ago. And no matter that they were years older and wiser now, she still wasn't sure she was ready.

He kept the rest of the evening low-key. A shower, a short soak in the hot tub with storytelling on Matt's side of some harebrained adventure he'd taken part in down in South America the previous year.

Tim observed them carefully—both Erin and Matt. He wouldn't allow anything to hurt Erin, but his friend was special as well. The man had come racing back from death's door eager to live to the fullest, and that meant in this situation being involved in something Tim was very responsible for.

It was a fine line to walk, but he was good at it—caring for others. Making sure they had what they needed. He'd worked damn hard to come to this point after Erin had vanished so long ago.

He tucked Erin into bed, curling around her like a protective blanket as she faded rapidly into sleep.

It took a lot longer for him to find rest. Wondering if he'd finally found his redemption after so many years.

When he woke, it was to a room slowly filling with light as dawn broke. Across from him on the next pillow a silent woman stared intently, her dark eyes glittering as she examined him.

"You're looking awfully thoughtful." He reached under the blankets and pulled her against him, partly draping her over his body.

"I woke a while ago. I've been thinking." Erin stroked his chest, trailing a finger over his skin in intricate designs. "You remember that private party we went to shortly before I left?"

His stomach fell out the bottom. It was the one event he

couldn't forget no matter how much he'd tried. "When I made an ass of myself?"

"That wasn't what I wanted to talk about." She paused. "I wasn't sure what I'd expected that night. I mean, we'd been playing around with all kinds of things, and the thought of the place excited me."

"Me, too. Only I was too young to see what could go wrong. I'm sorry." Tim held her cautiously. "We talked about this when it happened. Or I thought we had."

She nodded. "We talked about the fact that you made a mistake, and I was pissed at you for seeming to choose impressing the guys over sticking with what we'd decided beforehand. We were young, and uncertain, and trying our damnedest to pretend we knew everything there was to know. You made an assumption, I did the same—our two mistakes added up to something that was wrong, and we both knew it. And you did apologize." Erin stared off into space. "It's . . . not that. I forgave you for that, because it wasn't just your fault. I could have stopped the situation at any time myself, and I chose not to. So I was upset with you, but I was madder still at myself."

Tim stroked her cheek carefully. "We were a couple of dumb kids in some ways. I'd like to think that we're beyond stupid mistakes that can be solved by talking them through like adults."

"It wasn't something I could talk about because for a few days I didn't know what was bothering me. And the discomfort grew and grew, and when it did make sense, there was no way to explain it to you."

"So you left."

She nodded.

He'd spent years wondering what he could have done differently. "I always wished I could take back that night. Turn the world to before I'd chosen to act so mindlessly." He ran his fingers through her hair, holding his breath that she was going to finally come out with the truth. "Not to mention when I did try to track you down you were rather . . . derogatory toward me."

"It wasn't one of our finer moments on either of our parts—you got very vindictive at that point as well."

Tim had to agree with that. "I was a jerk, and I can't even say it was all in self-defense. I wanted to hurt you like you'd hurt me. It made it easier to simply try to pretend I wasn't longing to be with you. Even though deep down, I always hoped that there would be a way to someday get us back together."

Erin levered herself to a sitting position. "It wasn't you I was running from, it was me. Even Erin the Scary Bitch afterward, when you tried to reconnect? That was me keeping away from you. Driving you off."

"That makes no sense."

She looked sad and scared all at the same time. "The night we got our signals crossed there were a lot of people there. Some curious like us, some full time into the lifestyle. You remember any of that?"

"Vaguely." Most of his memories were caught up in being worried sick about her, and embarrassed to death that he'd fucked up so badly.

"I watched them when we came in, and in some ways what those couples had was intriguing. They were so into each other, it was as if we didn't exist. The world was all about them and what pleased them. They didn't care if they were naked in front of a crowd, or giving a blowjob, or being flogged."

Tim waited, hoping that she'd be able to explain. To take him to the next stage of understanding without his soul burning in hell even hotter if it had been something he'd done that had torn them in two.

She lifted her eyes to meet his. "I saw them and I was amazed. Wondered if that was something that we'd ever have. If we were going in that direction."

"You as a full-time sub?" There was no hiding his shock.

"You hadn't asked that of me." Erin hurried onward. "It wasn't you, but when things fell apart that night and I didn't tell you to stop, it was like this giant cog slipped out of line and everything fell apart."

"We talked about what went wrong," Tim insisted. "You and I dealt with it."

"But we couldn't deal with the fact that in spite of what I'd planned going in, when the moment came for me to call it off, I gave up all my power. It wasn't about you, Tim. The incident itself didn't matter, and it *wasn't* your fault. It was mine because I made a wrong choice, and that scared the hell out of me." Her volume increased, and she rocked in frustration.

"You left because you were scared?" This wasn't making any sense.

"Yes."

God. "Scared of me?"

"Of course not of you." She shook her head. "Scared that I was so ready to give up my will. Scared that the intensity of what we felt for each other wasn't going to just mean that I did everything you asked in the bedroom, but outside as well. And there were no reassurances you could give, nothing that you could do differently to make sure that I didn't do it again."

Tim pushed himself off the bed, needing to pace. Needing to move to escape his rapidly rising frustration. "Why would you think I'd want you to give up everything you are in the outside world? I fell in love with the woman who kicked ass and took names, and the bonus that in bed you could turn all that power over for me to control only made the situation that much hotter."

Her expression tightened. "And if I'd offered to obey you outside the bedroom?"

"I would have asked if you'd gone out of your goddamn mind." Tim shook his head, his anger growing. He paced to the bathroom, then back to the edge of the bed. Opened his mouth, then slammed it shut.

He wasn't sure what he'd say would be a good addition to the conversation. This wasn't at all what he'd expected this morning. Wasn't what he'd ever dreamed had pushed them apart.

"Timothy?"

"Don't," he snapped. "I'm . . ."

She shifted uncomfortably. "Say something."

"I'm going for a walk." He jerked on clothing, then took himself and his anger out of range before he said something he'd regret.

CHAPTER 24

Erin stared out the living room window at the fresh-fallen snow. A single line of footprints headed out into the maze that was laid out below them.

Well, that had gone even worse than she'd expected.

She rested her forehead on the window and sighed, her breath steaming up the glass.

"That's a sad sound for this early in the day."

Matt must have entered sometime after Erin had made her way down to the living room in the hopes of intercepting Tim. She debated for all of two seconds before letting her hopelessness spill out. "I just fucked things up royally."

"With Tim?" Matt hummed. "He's gone outside, has he?"

"Said he needed a walk."

"Ahh. Cooling off. You got him pissed, did you? Announced you were leaving him for me?"

Erin turned, crossing her arms over her chest and leaning on the glass. The icy temperatures burned her through the thin material of her sleep shirt. "Probably not good to joke about me leaving Tim at the moment."

Matt lost his grin, his boyish charm switching to dead serious. "Oh damn. This isn't because of what we did last night, is it? I swear, I never would have touched you if—"

"No," she interrupted. "It wasn't you. It was me, thoughtlessly throwing us back in time."

Her host nodded slowly before tilting his head to one side and motioning her toward the door. "Come on. Let's find some coffee and a place to talk. If you'd like an ear."

She glanced down at her pajama pants and decided what the hell. "Coffee would be great."

The kitchen was quiet. A coffeemaker waited on the sideboard, and Matt moved smoothly to deal with loading it. Erin sat silently, aching inside for what she'd done. The noise of the machine filled the air, twisting together with her mixed-up thoughts.

Her world had been thrust into chaos, but unlike solving a problem in flying, she couldn't see a safe passage through this one.

Matt poured her a cup and headed to the high counter, settling on a stool and waiting for her to start.

Talking with a near-stranger who was no longer a stranger. She wasn't sure if this was wrong, but she needed help, and after all they'd shared over the previous days, Matt was a far better choice than most.

"Tim and I knew each other years ago. I left him, pushed him away, in fact. In December he came to Banff, found a job with Lifeline, and we've been together since then."

"And there was something that happened before you left that set him off this morning?" Matt asked.

How to explain? How much to explain?

There was no place to start but at the beginning. "When we were younger, we were into experimenting with our sexual limits. Nothing too crazy, just stretching our boundaries and seeing what things we liked. Some ropes, a little bit of physical control. I liked it when Tim took charge, and he enjoyed it as well."

Matt took a drink of his coffee, his expression remaining nonjudgmental. "I could see that working well for you."

She sighed. "We got an invitation to join a private party. A bit more organized, a bit more extreme—people who knew what they were doing. We went in as part of our whole *checking it out* attitude. Not *serious* serious, just looking for more of what turned us on. Before we went, we agreed that all we would do was observe. We were young enough that we pretended to be more sophisticated and knowledgeable than we were." A bitter laugh escaped. "I'm sure they saw us coming a mile away, but we were cocky enough to try anyway."

"Oh hell, I can see trouble already."

"Yeah." Erin rubbed a finger along the top of her coffee cup, pushing away the images that still rushed back after all this time. "He'd had the idea of me going in wearing a collar—you know, Google can get you enough information to get into big trouble, real fast. I was his submissive, ready and willing to kneel at his feet, especially when surrounded by other couples who were full time into the lifestyle. It was hot at first—looking around, being a part of something that was edgy. Then Tim got asked by one of the guys if we wanted to be involved in a demonstration, and he agreed."

"After you'd said you weren't going to be involved in anything that night?"

She nodded.

"Shit."

There was so much to the story—so many layers. "I don't blame the Dom. He did everything he was supposed to. In fact, looking back I think he was trying to teach Tim something that we were obviously ignorant about. And even though I was uncomfortable, I didn't want to call him out."

Erin lifted her gaze to Matt's. "So here's the thing. Tim went through all the right steps with the Dom's guidance. They negotiated limits—I was still partially clothed. There

was no sexual contact with anyone else. All of it they did
properly, and in the end, I took part in a flogging demonstration."

She lowered her voice, fighting to continue, because here
was where her downfall had come. "And I enjoyed it—but
that enjoyment ultimately made me feel even worse. We
talked about the night afterward, Tim and I. He apologized
for making a stupid move and allowing it to happen after
we'd agreed not to get involved that first time. I gave him
hell, then we kissed and made up, and he thought we were
okay. Only I ended up packing my things about a week later,
and I left."

"Because you didn't trust him anymore."

"It wasn't because of the flogging." A long pause before
she forced out the truth. "I told Tim this as well. I was just
as capable of saying no as he was. I had a safe word, I knew
I could say no at any time. Only the fact that I chose not to
proved I was weaker than I'd thought. I was willing to give
up *everything*, and that scared me enough that I ran. I picked
a fight with Tim when he tried to track me down, and I told
him we were done. Gave some bullshit excuse about moving
on with my life, and that while he'd been fun, he wasn't a
keeper. I never wanted to see him again."

Matt cringed. "Ouch. That must have hurt."

Erin sighed. "He retaliated by getting me fired, so yeah,
we both played dirty."

"Shit, really?"

"I was on contract with the company that provided helicopter service to Tim's area. Tim found another company
that was willing to offer a better deal, and we lost the contract, putting me not only out of his apartment, but out of a
job. In some ways I was more pissed about that than anything else because it was a slap in the face to my career."

"Remind me never to get you two mad at me." Matt
leaned back on the counter. Paused. "So, why did you bring

this up now? Why the conversation regarding what made you leave?"

And now came the confusing part of her confession. "I don't know."

"Bullshit."

Erin tightened in shock at his blunt response. "What?"

"I think you knew what you were doing." Matt shook his head. "Trust me on this. I've been there, and I've done the same thing. You deliberately brought up something from your past because you felt the same thing happening all over again. Tim mentioned you gave him control this weekend. Suddenly you're wondering if you've made the same mistake you did back years ago."

"But I trust Tim. We're not the same people we were. We're older, and wiser, and I wouldn't have given him control if I didn't know he'd do what was right for me in the bedroom."

Matt's expression changed as he reached across and squeezed her hand gently. "And there's the root of your problem."

Erin tempered her frustration, waiting for the revelation he seemed to have arrived at.

He leaned back. "Seems to me for all your talk about trust, you're forgetting it's not something you turn off and on. Doesn't matter if you're playing freaky games in the bedroom and you know one hundred percent that he's got your back there, if you don't also believe that's true right here in the living room. Or in the chopper, or on the street corner—and hell, giving it a location isn't even going to work because you could end up having sex any of these places, and it would turn into Tim being in charge.

"But if you don't trust him not to boss you around when you're dealing with life, then you don't trust him. Period. It's as simple as that."

"It's me I don't trust," Erin protested.

"Crock of bull, darling. Trust is trust." Matt pushed his

coffee cup away. "Look, I've known you for less than a week, but I already picked up something about your personality and your character. I know Tim. Why would you assume that he would want to change anything about the way you are? You're passionate, exciting, and wicked smart. That doesn't go away just because you're on your knees sucking someone's cock, or you're getting flogged, or you're hauling the search-and-rescue team into remote situations, or you're saving our collective asses from some crazed kidnappers. How could you doubt your strength? You're a woman any man would be honoured to be with at any time, in any place."

His words rushed her like a cooling balm, stilling some of her fears for a brief moment before doubt rushed in again. The memory of Tim's face before he'd left the room that morning was tearing her heart in two.

What if he decided he didn't want to be with her anymore? That her confusion wasn't worth it to him? It would be her own damn fault for having stirred the pot now.

But maybe it was better now than letting things go on longer . . .

Fuck it, she didn't know which way to turn.

"Thanks for the compliments, Matt. And you've helped, really you have. It's as if I'm on the edge of understanding, but it's still frightening. I . . ." She pushed off her chair and paced the room. "Now I get why Tim went for a walk. I've got so much energy inside I'm about to explode, and I can't think straight."

Matt nodded. "You want a treadmill? Work off a little steam and see if it helps settle your brain?"

Perfect. "You're brilliant. That would be wonderful."

He nodded, then surprised her by opening his arms wide and standing motionless. She stepped into his embrace and accepted the comfort of his hug. Nonsexual, just a good friend who wanted the best for her. "You'll figure it out, you and Tim. I know you will."

She squeezed him hard before stepping away. "How did you get so smart?"

"Staring into your own death before you turn forty makes you think a lot about your life. The mistakes you've made, the people you should have trusted. I meant it—I've been where you are, and I would give anything to be able to go back in time and trust more thoroughly." Matt pulled a face. "I want you and Tim to have the chance that I don't have anymore."

Then he set her up on the treadmill, and she lost herself in the mindlessness of physical distraction for an hour.

She would find a way to make this work. Somehow. She had to.

It took him until he'd hit the end of the trail to burn off his initial *what the fuck* attitude that had rolled in as he'd listened to Erin's confession. The second trip around the loop let Tim work through his anger that they'd spent so many wasted years over what still came down, in his opinion, to a bloody misunderstanding.

Though in fact, maybe the years apart were what made it easier to rid himself of his frustration quicker than otherwise possible. He'd already suffered doubt, and embarrassment. Loneliness and regret—all the fucking stages of grief had passed through his life, consuming time and energy to deal with.

It meant his perspective right now was far from what it would have been earlier. He was mature enough to admit that if she'd shared this directly after their incident had happened, he probably wouldn't have understood. It would have been the end of them.

Now? It was the beginning.

Now he was going to fight for what he wanted, and that meant dealing with what Erin had shared, and not just staying pissed off like a child. Somehow he had to make it clear that while he respected her fears, running away wasn't an acceptable solution.

He was on his way back to the house when his phone rang. It wasn't Erin like he'd hoped, though, but his boss.

"Marcus? What's up?"

Marcus spoke without preamble. "When you stopped by Lifeline yesterday morning, was anything out of place?"

Tim thought quickly. "No. We put away the gear from the chopper, and everything looked normal. Is there a problem?"

He didn't want to go back yet, not until he'd had a chance to talk to Erin, but if they had to . . .

"Alarm went off early this morning," Marcus shared. "By the time the RCMP and I made it down, though, there was no one around. The door had definitely been tampered with. How full was your medical supply cupboard?"

"Not very. I took a lot with me on the call-out, and obviously never restocked yet."

Marcus sighed. "That's probably what they were after, and why they left so quick. Okay—not to worry. Just had to touch base."

"You need us back?" Tim asked.

"Nope. I'll deal with the RCMP. Only when you're on duty again? Make a note to check the narcotics."

"Done." Tim breathed a little easier. "Lock up tight, and we'll be back in a few days."

Dealing with Marcus's questions had been good for him, even though he wondered at the rash of break-ins Banff was experiencing. Between the call and the fresh air, his mood had turned, and he'd lost more of his bottled frustration.

He let himself back in the house and made his way upstairs, somehow unsurprised to discover Matt waiting for him in the living room. His friend's appearance was too timely to be coincidental.

Tim slowed to a stop at Matt's deliberate throat clearing. "What?"

Matt dropped the paper he was hiding behind, folding it carefully and placing it to one side. "That woman is in love with you."

Tim laughed, unable to remain annoyed at his friend for his obvious upcoming interference. "You're a relationship expert now?"

His friend shrugged. "She's got all the signs of it, in case you're too close to notice. She told me everything, by the way. Everything that happened back in the old days, and what she did this morning. She's in the gym working out the advice I gave her."

"Which was?"

"That she needs to trust you all the time." Matt rose to his feet and paced toward him. "Tim, I've been your friend for years. We've done some crazy things together, and I don't trust you just because you saved my life. You're an amazing man in so many ways. I don't think she understands how much thought and caring you put into being in charge."

Sudden clarity struck, and Tim felt damn near lightheaded with the rush of inspiration. *Holy fucking shit.* "Matt, you're a genius."

His intense approval made Matt pause. "Well, thanks, but—"

"No, I'm serious. Damn. *Damn.*" After all his concern regarding how he was going to move them forward, the idea triggered by Matt's casual comment was like having an impossible algebra equation magically unfold before him. "You know how I asked if you'd help me give Erin a fantasy? Would you be willing to also help straighten out this mess?"

A crease formed between Matt's brows. "I don't know what more I can do than offer advice. I mean, I'm willing, but what do you have in mind?"

Tim paused, ideas rushing him, but the specifics still falling into place. "Give me a bit to work out the details, but your point is valid. She *doesn't* know everything I think about heading into a situation, sexual or otherwise. Maybe that needs to change. Maybe what Erin needs is a hands-on dose of being completely in charge, not just the bit of holding back I was doing over the last couple of months. It might be the eye-opener we both need."

Matt clasped him by the shoulder, his smile growing firmer as he nodded. "Whatever I can do to help, I'm your man."

Tim slapped his back earnestly, then took off to figure out exactly the right way to make his point.

Erin was going to be his because she would know one hundred percent he was not only what she needed, but what she *wanted*. Heart and soul.

No turning back. Her body, her choice—it had to be for him.

CHAPTER 25

''''''''''''''''''''''''''''''''''

It was one thing to know where they had to go. It was another situation entirely to convince another person to take them both there. Tim changed quickly and headed down to the workout room before Erin could vanish.

She had finished her run and was seated on the floor stretching. Her dark eyes tracked him cautiously as he headed straight across the room into her space. When he squatted and wrapped his fingers around the back of her neck, leaning their foreheads together, tension oozed out of her like a slow leak in a punctured tire.

"It's going to be okay," he whispered. "We'll figure it out." They weren't typical words for a vow, but it was still a promise.

Erin nodded silently, and he ignored the extra moisture welling in her eyes. A bit more space was called for, so he pressed his lips to her forehead, then stepped away.

He headed to the free weights and grabbed a couple of light dumbbells to use for warmup. "Matt's got some business to take care of this morning, so he said for us to help ourselves to breakfast. He'll be free after lunch."

"I thought he was on holidays until Wednesday?"

Tim met her gaze in the mirrors. "He's giving us time to work this out."

"Just like that?" Utter misery in her voice. "We can get rid of years of baggage in a moment?"

"Make a start then. Move forward."

Erin didn't answer.

"Come and spot me while I do bench presses," Tim requested. What he was thinking was *no more running away allowed*.

Erin moved into position, and slowly the awkwardness drifted away. For the next forty-five minutes they fell into a comfortable, familiar routine. Not as Tim and Erin who were friends and lovers, trying to find a way to deal with the past. Not as Tim and Erin who walked a fine line of excitement and needed to find a way into their future.

Just steady co-workers. People who used their bodies to do a job and needed to keep their equipment in peak working condition.

When she laughed out loud at a snarky comment he dropped, Tim smiled. The next time they both had their hands empty, she surprised him by sneaking in and curling herself up close.

"Hug attack. I like it." He stroked her back softly as she relaxed against him, both of them slightly sweaty, but damn if he cared. It was far more important to have her cheek resting on his shoulder, rhythmic puffs of air crossing his neck as her breathing evened.

It was time.

He stole one final brief kiss before adjusting their position so he could look into her eyes. "We need to talk."

Erin made a face. "Can I apologize first for having the worst timing ever? Here we are in the middle of a fantasy-level vacation, and I dumped on it."

"No apologies. If anything, I'm as much to blame because we should have had this conversation back in December when I first arrived in Banff. So instead of figuring out who did what wrong, let's move on."

"Agreed."

He led her to the workout bench and sat her down, dragging a second bench closer so he could sit by her side. "I listened closely to everything you had to say this morning."

"And you were pissed."

"I was, but I'm not anymore. What I am now is confused."

She frowned. "What part didn't make sense?"

Tim hoped like hell this was going to work. "You were afraid you'd be willing to give up all control, inside the bedroom and out. Matt made a comment when I got back that helped me realize something."

"Matt said a lot of things this morning," Erin muttered.

Tim laughed. "He's an opinionated bastard, isn't he?"

Her expression twisted into a wry smile. "Sly bastards. I'm surrounded by them."

Tim caught her fingers in his. "Serious now. Erin, what happens when you give me control in the bedroom? Think it through, and tell me everything."

She paused. "You . . . make me feel good. Take me places I can't go by myself." He nodded for her to continue. Her pupils widened slightly, as if in remembered passion. "You push my boundaries at times, but it always ends up with me trusting that the result will be worth it. Like having sex in front of Matt. I enjoyed that so much, and I can't even explain why."

"I still take my pleasure," he prompted. "It's not just about you."

"It feels like it's all about me."

Tim waited while a soft stream of curses escaped her lips.

"And that comment proves I'm a bigger ass than I thought." She sighed heavily before lifting sad eyes to meet his. "You just seem so damn careful and considerate all the time, but it is about both of us, isn't it?"

"Yes." Tim lowered his volume, his voice barely above a whisper. "I think about you the entire time. I watch. I listen closely. Trying to figure out what you need—*really* need—and what's going to take us both there." He stroked her fingers lightly, needing to touch her. "I'm selfish enough to want the result to be pleasurable for me as well."

She turned her hands over in his and watched as he traced his thumb back and forth over the sensitive inside of her wrist. "I'm pretty sure if it were a choice between my pleasure and yours, you'd pick mine."

"It's not difficult to want the best for you."

Erin cupped his face with one hand and leaned in to kiss him, the moisture clinging to her lashes wetting his skin as she brushed her cheek against his.

He took her offering but didn't let it end there. He couldn't. "You were afraid the next step would be giving up all control to me outside the bedroom."

She nodded.

They hovered on the edge of a knife blade. Could he help her understand? "Think for a moment. Think of what you said I do when it comes to the control you grant in our sex lives. What if, and I'm not asking you to become my full-time sub, but just *think*. What if you did give up control to me in all places, and all times? What do you think I would do with that power?"

Erin pulled back as he spoke, her expression changing rapidly. A second of shock, followed by bewilderment, confusion, then finally frustration. "I . . . Dammit, Tim, I don't know. I want to say one thing, and then images of what I've seen over the years invade, and I lose my mind and can't spit anything coherent out."

He soothed her, stroking her arm carefully. "You've been to clubs, I take it, and . . . what? Read books? Seen full-time subs at their Master's feet, naked and on display during dinner parties?"

"Collared and controlled," she offered in a whisper. "The thought gives me shivers for all of three seconds before it nauseates me. I don't want that, I *don't*. And yet . . . I do."

"Oh, love. You've got the right idea headed in the wrong direction." He pulled her across the short distance separating them to give her the hug she so clearly needed.

She clung to him, curling her legs up and nestling in like she was craving the contact.

They sat in silence for a good five minutes. Her breathing remained rapid, and she twitched at times while he stroked her back and caressed her softly. Their positioning wasn't sexual, but in many ways the contact was intimacy of a far greater nature than full-out sex.

His hopes rose.

"Explain. What wrong direction am I headed?" Erin asked, firmness reentering her voice.

"Your admiration for the Doms and their subs—it's the depth of the relationship that you're craving. The commitment to caring, the complete connection. However, you've also got a bit of an exhibitionist streak, if you're willing to confess to it."

She snorted. "Fine. I like to be watched."

"When you see subs on display, you like what that represents, but, Erin"—he tilted her head back to stare into her eyes—"you're right—you don't want that all the time. You have other needs that rise stronger when you're in public. If you were twenty-four-seven with a Dom who really paid attention, you would still not end up like those subs. That's not your fantasy—and a relationship that intensely controlled isn't right for many people. In fact, there are as many different variations as there are couples."

"So you're saying I don't have to worry about losing my will by being involved with you?"

"I'm saying you'd never make a full-time sub of the naked

variety, even though you do like to be watched. It would
make it damn near impossible to pilot the chopper on rescues. You'd distract everyone."

"Smart-ass."

The tension was there still, but she was smiling again.

Tim went for broke. "I have a proposition. I think it will
make things clearer for you."

"Go on."

He twisted her to face him. "I suggest that for the rest of
the day, you be in charge."

An adorable frown creased her face. "Of sex?"

"Of everything. Unless you intend to spend fourteen
hours fooling around, which . . . okay."

Erin hesitated. "Me being in charge in the bedroom
doesn't do it for us. If I'm being honest. We did that for the
past few months, remember?"

"Well, it didn't suck *that* bad."

She smiled.

Tim went on. "I know what you're saying, but the experience could still be educational, if we approach it from a new
angle. Don't think about the kink, consider the mind-set."

A momentary flash of delight broke free. "I get to order
you around for the entire day?"

"I'll be putty in your hands. Everything you desire from
me. I'll be your magical genie, and your wish will be my
command." He waited, absolutely sure she would get the
full picture without him prompting her.

The truth of what being in charge actually meant.

When her amusement rapidly faded, Tim waited to see
what she'd do.

It was either the smartest thing he'd ever done, or the
stupidest. The next few hours would tell.

Her head felt full of stuffing. Tim's suggestion that she take
charge had been unexpected and, in a way, unwanted. Until

she realized it was a serious, well-considered proposition, like everything he did.

There were far more reasons to accept the task than to turn it down.

The most important was that working through this day might somehow help them take steps to make their relationship work. She hadn't brought up old wounds for fun, or even as Matt had hinted, in a twisted attempt to tear her and Tim apart.

After last night she *wanted* them to work, but the fear that remained was too much to conquer on her own.

So she pulled herself together and took a deep breath. Refocused on what needed to happen next, as she would in a rescue situation.

She was in control? This wasn't the first time, and it wouldn't be the last. She knew how to deal with it.

Erin found her feet, putting herself into position over him. "Challenge accepted."

Tim leaned back. "Good for you."

Then he sat there.

Waiting.

She laughed. He was going to take this to the extreme, was he? Put her in charge of absolutely everything? "I hope you don't expect me to tell you when you're allowed to take a piss, because you're on your own for that one."

Amusement bloomed over his face as he pushed back his dark hair. "Acknowledged. I'm in charge of my own pissing."

They grinned at each other for a moment, and then she stepped forward and laid a hand on his shoulder, stroking the firm muscles under her fingers. "You done with your workout?"

"Enough for today."

She stroked him with her words now, as well as her fingers. "You want a shower?"

Tim's eyes lit up. "I thought you'd never ask."

They linked fingers and headed off through the maze of

the rental house. "I still can't believe you have random billionaires on speed dial."

"I know lots of interesting people. Wait until we get front-row invites to a couple of rock concerts."

She wasn't sure what to make of that comment, so she concentrated on their target instead. Considered their *plans*, since she had to make the decisions. Shower, then breakfast. Then another day in paradise . . .

Her feet stalled, and she jerked to a halt. "What about Matt?"

Tim stepped around her, pacing backward down the hall. "You need to double-check, but he said this morning that he was good with whatever we had going down."

Of *course* he had. Great. Wonderful. Fucking *marvelous*. This changed things . . . and yet, not.

Screw it. Erin powered forward. She'd been flying missions for years. Done what needed to be done in scary, hairy circumstances. This was simply one more day, and she wasn't going to be frightened off by the fact that she now had two grown men at her beck and call.

Two men who'd fucked her senseless the night before.

She slapped down her brain before it could head further into stupid territory. Instead, she turned the stress around, and as they entered their suite she summoned up all the rules she'd used for so many years in her life.

Gather information. Make observations. Set in motion what needed to happen.

Getting in the decadent two-person shower didn't take any huge powers of persuasion. Tim wasn't pushing too far in terms of making her tell him *everything* to do, which she appreciated.

Stepping into his personal space and tilting her head for a kiss was like any other time—with an instantaneous and enthusiastic response on his part.

Even as their bodies came into contact, though, she was thinking about what they were going to do. Not in an "I

wonder what comes next?" kind of way. Not even in the "do
we have time for sex before breakfast?" mind-set, watching
the clock and working the odds. She'd already figured out
there was plenty of time for whatever they wanted to do—
so . . . what did they want to do?

Or more importantly, what would make Tim the happiest
right now?

Far too many options instantly flashed to mind.

He stilled, smiling against her lips. "And you're chuckling while we're kissing. Way to make my ego swell."

"Sorry. Mentally running through different scenarios
and considering what kind of sex you'd enjoy is pretty entertaining."

He settled his hands on her hips, sliding their bodies back
and forth slightly. The water had slicked up their skin so
they rubbed in the most interesting way, the dusting of hair
on his chest and thighs a sensual tactile contrast to her
smoothness. "Entertaining sex is what I do best."

"You are easy to please." She draped her arms around
his neck, twirling her fingers in his hair. "No sex right now.
Turn around. Let me take care of you."

He moved to follow her order while she grabbed the soap
and lathered up her hands.

Last night had been amazing. This morning—not so much,
and this shower was as much a symbolic act as a necessary
one after their workout. She worked the soap over his torso,
hands moving quickly, not as a tease, but as a renewal. Fresh-
ness coming into their relationship. A new start.

"May I wash you as well?" Tim asked after she'd worked
her way around him, fingers lingering on his chest. Admiring the contrast between their skin tones, and the other
physical differences—mass of muscles, overall size.

"Would you like to wash me?" she asked. "I thought
you'd be hungry by now."

His eyes flashed with desire. "I'm always hungry."

It was inevitable, she supposed, that one thing led to

another, and she ended up pinned to the tile wall, one leg lifted high as he supported her under her knee and fucked her silly.

In the shuddering aftermath of their orgasms, his cock slipped from her, and they stood under the twin showerheads and held each other as the water poured over them. Breathing slowly returning to normal.

Erin rested her cheek on his chest. "So much for being in charge."

"Trust me, that was completely your idea," Tim insisted. "I'm starving, but since you ordered me to do all kinds of dirty things to you, there was nothing I could do but obey—*oww.*"

He rubbed his chest where she'd leaned in and playfully bitten him.

She tossed him a smirk. "Fine, it was my idea. So now let's get dressed and find some food before you keel over from hunger."

"Yes, Mistress." He backed off quickly, hands held out front to guard himself as she bared her teeth in warning. "What big teeth you have, kitten. And what sharp claws."

"You'll feel them both if you don't haul ass." She grabbed a towel and twirled it for a second before snapping the end at his bare butt. A sharp crack rang through the air, followed instantly by his shout.

Dressing took longer than expected as an *every man for themselves* towel war broke out and they chased each other around the bedroom.

By the time they made it to the kitchen, Erin was hungry enough to eat just about anything. Tim had to be starving. She was happy to discover an assortment of food waiting for them in the fridge—more than enough variety of baked goods and fruit to satisfy even their appetites.

She couldn't stop smiling as they found a spot at the long breakfast bar. Outside the day had brightened, sunshine now pouring in on another cloudless Alberta winter day. Erin grabbed them cups of coffee and settled at Tim's side with a contented sigh.

"You're looking far happier than you did first thing this morning. I'm glad." Tim lifted his coffee mug to click with hers.

"Amazing sex will do that to a girl." Erin lowered her cup, keeping eye contact with him. "It's not only the sex, though. Thank you for not dismissing my fears. I'm still not sure what we're going to figure out today, but it's been a whole lot of fun so far."

He winked. "The day doesn't have to be big and scary. But you're right. We've just begun to figure things out. Enjoy yourself." He speared another forkful of bacon he'd found and hummed happily. "I always enjoy my time while calling the shots."

"Always?"

Tim paused. Considered. "Honestly, yes. Because even when there are tough decisions to make? There's a pleasure in it for me that . . . Damn, I don't know that I can explain it. It's a kind of excitement bordering on a thrill. Like heading out skydiving, but more powerful because it's right here in real life."

That made more sense than she'd expected, and Erin nodded. "I get that sensation in the middle of a rescue. When things are going well, or even when they go to hell. Being pushed to react instantly, to make the right decisions—ones that could make a difference in saving someone's life . . ."

She did know what he was referring to, only she'd associated that kind of pleasure with her work. With her lifestyle outside the job, things were different. Even her decision to go to The Wild and only hang out in the bar area with Phillip—exercising a level of control that meant she had a safe haven around her, but the edge still gave her a kick.

Maybe not to the same degree as if she were being tied up and restrained, or being watched on the sly. The rush from that was a different kind of exhilarating.

Gentle contact with the back of her hand pulled her from her ponderings. Tim stroked a second time lightly with his fingers. "You get this. It's powerful to be in charge, isn't it?"

"High-test adrenaline shot straight-up into a vein." Erin grinned. "Okay, I'm ready for the next challenge. One sunny day—what shall we do with it? And don't suggest cliff jumping because you already did that at Matt's."

"Spoilsport." Tim filled his plate a second time, then started spouting off the wildest and most insane suggestions. Everything from spearfishing to building a massive labyrinth in the *outdoor entertainment area* and setting up a paintball fight.

Erin bantered with him and enjoyed every minute, right up until reality kicked in again.

This exercise was supposed to show her why she could trust Tim all the time, in all the places. And even though they were having fun, she still wasn't sure where their worlds overlapped. How to take the trust she had for him into the real world and move it into this other place.

What they had still seemed more suited to a fantasy realm out of normal time and space. Somewhere her sexual desires and urges toward submission didn't seem so contradictory to everything she admired in the women she worked with. Everything she'd fought for over so many years in becoming a pilot. In dealing with the naysayers who didn't like her sex. Who didn't like her skin colour. Hell, who didn't like the friends she kept.

She liked who she was, and no matter how much fun it was, and how much she . . . *cared* for Tim, this couldn't become a forever thing if she had to give up everything that made her tick. Hopefully this exercise would be the final proof that would let her move forward with confidence.

Because her independence and strength were too important to be abandoned even for out-of-this-world sex. Even for a man with whom she was beginning to think she was falling in love.

CHAPTER 26

She was holding back. It was subtle, but it was there, and Tim fought to keep his damn mouth shut. If this exercise was going to work, she had to figure this out by herself.

If it didn't work? It was probably for the best. He wanted her, but he wanted her fully onboard, and if he couldn't have *that*, he'd have to let her go.

Like. Fucking. Hell.

He chuckled at his own internal dialogue. He wasn't going to give up, but it would be so much simpler if Erin got the message now than down the road, because he had no intention of going anywhere.

She was stuck with him. Let *that* truth soak in.

They'd spent the last hour tromping through the beautiful winter scenery, snowshoes strapped to their feet. They'd traveled a fair bit already and had reached the giddy-with-fresh-air stage of the afternoon.

Matt laughed as he ducked to avoid the snowball Erin beaned at his head.

Then they both turned their attention in his direction, and he swore, racing for the protection of the trees as Erin and Matt ganged up on him. A flurry of snowballs flew around him.

"Cheaters," he shouted over his shoulder.

"All's fair in love and war," Matt retorted, a hard-packed snowball accompanying his words, smacking Tim in the back of the head.

"Oh, nice one," Erin said.

Her encouragement turned to a scream, and Tim whirled to discover Matt had tripped her, following her to the ground and pinning her under him in the snow.

They rolled a few times as Erin struggled to get away, laughing far too hard as their bulky snowshoes interfered with a normal romp. Matt paused, staring down at her, and for a moment Tim held his breath.

The violent urge to knock off Matt's head wasn't there. It wasn't that jealousy had no place in his life, but with both Erin and Matt, there were issues he'd already taken into account.

Instead of the green-eyed monster sweeping in, the ideas buzzing through his brain were far different. He hoped she'd have seen what he'd seen. That she'd have the courage to take one more step . . .

She reached up with gloved hands and caught Matt around the neck, pulling him down for a passionate kiss. Tim paced back, watching closely as flashes of tongue and clouds of heated breath fogged the air around them. Matt eased his elbows to the snow on either side of her head, stretched over her while their snowshoes tangled together awkwardly.

They broke apart when Tim stopped beside them, Matt rolling off and grinning happily skyward. No guilt there, either—which was good. Tim offered his hands to them both, and had two hard clasps wrap around his wrists a second later.

Oh shit, he hadn't thought *this* situation through very well.

An instant later he, too, was in the snow, Erin chuckling madly as she scrambled on top to pin him down in the field of icy white.

Matt's bold laughter echoed off the trees. "I can't believe you fell for that," he taunted.

Erin tilted her head to the side, smiling contentedly. "I'm glad he did."

Then she leaned over and kissed him as well. Tim wrapped his arms around her and hung on tight, keeping her close and savouring her touch. She lifted off him, just a bare inch, and stared earnestly into his eyes. "Did I read your signals right? Was that okay?" she whispered.

"Nothing wrong from where I stand. Lie. Whatever."

Erin kissed him again, her tongue sliding smoothly along his as they found a place between anticipation and acceptance. Not quite at the *ravish each other* point, but far beyond a casual kiss.

Tim thrilled at her question, though. She'd been watching closely, had she? It was still a sexual kind of situation, but to take the chance to flirt and kiss with Matt right out in the open gave Tim hope she was getting the point.

The whole way back as the three of them bantered and eyed one another, he wondered what else she'd be brave enough to arrange.

Was it working? *God, let her get this.*

They dumped their gear in the storage room, and Erin lifted her chin as she checked them over. "Either of you starving?"

They shook their heads.

A greedy grin blossomed that turned her expression into pure, molten gold with a dusting of lust. "Then it's time for a lazy afternoon by the pool. Tim, could we convince your magical food delivery crew to drop off appetizers later, so we can just hang out and not go anywhere?"

"Brilliant woman." Tim pulled out his cell phone and passed it over. "Here, it should be one of the last numbers

I dialed. Go ahead, and Matt and I will wait for you by the pool."

Erin accepted the phone, curling her fingers around it and squeezing tighter than necessary, the explanation for her tension clear only a second later. "No swimsuits, by the way," she ordered.

She was working with the power she'd been given, even though it made her uncomfortable. Tim wanted to give her a high five for pushing through.

"Not a problem," he confirmed, not bothering to hide his smirk as he realized something. "I look forward to seeing the caterer's face when he delivers our appetizers."

Matt smacked him in the chest, and Tim groaned in mock pain. "You're such an asshole at times," Matt deadpanned.

"You got a problem being naked in front of strangers? I don't. Hell, call back the masseur—the man is welcome to torment my ass some more if he'd like."

"Freak. Get your ass out of here before I change my mind and make you my slaves for the afternoon." When he and Matt both paused to exchange dirty grins, Erin rolled her eyes. "Double freaks. That was a threat, not a promise."

"Hard to tell," Matt pointed out. "As if being your slave would be punishment."

Tim spotted the telltale signs of her excitement. He tapped Matt on the shoulder and motioned to the door. "We'll work on our definitions later. Let's go before she orders liver paté or some rotten vegetarian crap in retaliation."

His friend was quiet as they headed down the hall, Erin slowing behind them as she made contact with the caterers.

Tim spoke softly so as to not interrupt her conversation. "You really do have an enviable lifestyle, Matt. I take it things are going well businesswise even now that you've stepped back from micromanaging the entire show?"

"Business is fine. More than fine. Consider this your

open-ended invitation to join me in Spain when you can this coming summer—I'm thinking about renting a villa for a month or two."

"You deserve it. I'm glad to know things are good for you."

Matt glanced over his shoulder. "You've got a pretty good lifestyle as well. Things get squared away okay with Erin?"

"We're working on it." Tim held the pool door open for Matt to enter first. They'd lost Erin around one of the corners, and he took advantage of the moment. "Thanks for being willing to help. You've been more than giving—I can't imagine throwing this much chaos at anyone else and having them still welcome us with open arms."

"We're friends," Matt insisted. "And like I said to you this morning, Erin's an amazing woman. Anything I can do to help, I'm willing."

Tim patted him on the back. "You'll probably get your chance. I have no idea what she's got in mind, but let's give her the reins."

"No problem, if it's half as much fun as last night."

Tim eyed the indoor pool gracing the length of the lower walk-out portion of the house, a steaming hot tub visible on the deck outside the solid wall of floor-to-ceiling glass.

Casual wealth would never cease to astound him.

He reached over his head and grabbed his T-shirt at the back collar, pulling it forward and off, tossing it onto one of the deck chairs. He stripped off his pants and underwear all at one go. "I need a quick rinse before I hit the pool."

Matt paused in the middle of getting undressed to point along the sidewall. Tim ditched the rest of his clothes on the chair before striding across the deck and flipping on the water.

"Do we have any plans for tomorrow?" Matt asked.

"Not yet." Tim stepped under the heated stream. "Maybe we should wait to see how tonight goes."

Matt nodded, standing to the side of the shower and waiting his turn. "No matter what, I'm there for you."

"I appreciate it, more than you know." Tim stepped aside, dashing water from his fingers. "Any time you get the urge for some company, you're welcome to visit me in Banff. I've always got room for you."

A few more nights, a few more *days* to get Erin to acknowledge that what she wanted was the same thing he wanted. He pulled himself back to alert as a fine spray bounced off Matt's head, the other man sliding under the shower head and soaking himself down.

Tim turned to the pool and took a running leap at the water, cutting through the surface in a mass of bubbles as the cool water wrapped around him.

Erin stood outside the massive room that housed the pool, gathering her nerve. She'd ordered food, ordered the guys to the pool, basically ordered them to strip . . .

Now she watched.

They moved around each other with an easy flow. Typical guys, no hangups, no lingering. Tim was naked before she could blink, and then she didn't want to blink because the man was spectacular. He tilted his head back under the shower and rubbed his hair, and the muscles flexing in his upper body and shoulders made her mouth water.

Then Matt was there as well, and she could only hope that by the time she was in her midforties she'd have the courage to strip down and wander the pool deck as easily.

The two of them paused under the shower briefly before Tim took off, diving into the pool with a splash that sent water rippling over the gutters onto the deck.

While Tim began an easy freestyle stroke down the length, Matt remained in the shower, turning slowly under the water, adjusting the taps. He stared at the pool and the rhythmic turnover as Tim raised his arms over the water's surface again and again before flipping at the end of the length and making his way back.

She was hiding in the hallway, and she knew it. When Matt glanced in her direction, there was no more time to delay. She stepped in to face them.

Matt grabbed a towel and wrapped it around his waist before crossing the deck to meet her. "Everything good?"

"All done." She glanced at the pool. Waited.

Matt cleared his throat. "If you don't want me here, I can leave. Whatever you're comfortable with."

Erin took a deep breath. "I think being uncomfortable is part of the point. If you're willing to stay, please stay." She met his serious gaze. "Thank you for this morning. Your words of wisdom about trusting. That's what this is about right now—figuring out what trust means in different situations. If I can . . . just get past this mental block I have, I might understand."

"As long as you're sure." He tweaked her nose. "I'm not at all upset being involved as long as it's what you want."

She leaned in and kissed his cheek, enjoying how easy it was to be around him. "You're a very special guy, Matt. And I want you here."

The mental debate took all of three seconds, but she did think it through before grabbing his towel, fingers slipping under the edge and brushing his abdomen.

He coughed lightly. "No swimsuits, right?"

"Right. Only I understood the towel. It's difficult to have a serious conversation while all your good bits are out there in the open air."

Matt chuckled. "Talented, beautiful, and wise."

"You want to get in the pool?" Erin motioned, not hiding her grin. "I'll be there in a minute."

He covered her hands with his own, squeezing so she had to take hold of the fabric before he loosened one edge and stepped away. Bare-ass naked, butt flexing smoothly as he paced toward the pool and left her holding his towel.

Oh boy.

Tim pulled up to the end of the length about the same

time Matt leapt in, the wave catching him and slapping him in the face. Tim gazed expectantly at Erin.

She stepped over, enjoying the position of looming over him, even if the illusion of power was just that, an illusion. "You having fun?" she asked.

"Terrible time until about two seconds ago. Now my heart's arrived, and I can breathe again."

The resulting flutter in her belly shouldn't have come so easily. He was nothing if not a charmer. "You've got the silver tongue of your Irish forebears, that's for sure."

"It's good for more than pretty compliments, if you need any ideas." Tim winked as he leaned up on his elbows, Matt at his side.

The game changed. She examined them carefully as she'd done outdoors, the way she would if this were a rescue situation and she were in charge.

There *were* small clues when she really looked. Tim's gaze remained on her face ninety percent of the time, but when it slipped away, it lingered on her breasts. Matt full-out stared when he forgot—

What did they want? It was fairly easy to know right now, so what the hell. Erin wrapped her fingers around the bottom edge of her T-shirt and shimmied it up a couple inches.

Tim leaned forward. Matt gave up pretending he was looking anywhere but at her chest.

The naked gap shifted higher, fabric caressing her breasts. "How's the water?" she asked.

"Getting hotter," Tim quipped.

She paused, changed her mind, and dropped her hands to her waistband.

The sheer disappointment pouring off the guys grew tangible. "Don't stop on my account," Matt muttered.

"This will work even better," she promised. Erin slipped the fabric off her hips, going down to her panties as she stepped out of her pants and left them puddled on the deck.

She definitely had their attention.

The T-shirt hung to midthigh, covering her bra and panties. "Decision time," she announced.

Tim reluctantly dragged his gaze off her legs and back to her face. "Are you deciding which of us to fuck first? Because I don't care, as long as fucking is involved."

"So impatient. I'm still dressed." She moved to the very edge of the pool and stroked his forearm with a foot, delicately balanced on one leg. "I'm wearing three pieces of clothing. You get to choose one for me to take off, and Matt chooses one. Whatever you don't pick, stays on."

"Choose well, my young apprentice," Matt intoned, and the rising sexual tension broke into laughter.

Tim raised a brow. "You're creative, I'll say that much."

"You'll need to be creative as well, depending on what you decide to leave behind."

He watched her face, and there was a question in his eyes, but his amusement went far deeper than the frustration she'd seen this morning. He was both turned on and having fun, and *she'd* done that. She'd made the decision that brought them here.

Tim held out his hand. "Panties. I can fuck you around them, but there's too many things to do where they'll get in the way."

Matt snorted. "I was going to say the same thing, but I have another idea." He smiled up at her. "Bra. Let's see you take it off without removing your shirt as well."

"Smart man," Tim commented with approval.

She was already moving, reaching under her shirt and undoing hooks. She slipped a hand into her sleeve and tugged one strap over her elbow, repeating the other side and pulling the bra off through the sleeve. It took less than ten seconds.

Their expressions were priceless.

"What? You've never seen a woman take off her bra like that before?"

They both shook their heads, utter disbelief on their

faces. She tossed the fabric aside, then motioned for Tim to come forward.

"You want my panties? Take them off me, then," she ordered.

He was out of the pool in one motion, water streaming off his broad shoulders and down his body. He stalked toward her with animal lust in his eyes. His cock was primed, hard and rising toward his belly. He knelt at her feet and gazed up, a proud smile and the haze of lust mixing into one. "It's not so bad, is it? Being in charge?"

She answered him just as quietly. "Not bad, but yes, you were right. It's a different mind-set."

He ran his hands up her legs, nails scratching lightly on her inner thighs as he hooked his thumbs into the fabric of her panties. "Watch. Listen. People give out clues all the time as to what they want."

"You're doing it to me now, even while I try to read you and make the decisions."

He tugged the material down an inch at a time, teasing her skin with the slowness. "It's not something I can turn off, I guess. But it simply means I want the best for you."

She placed a hand on his shoulder to balance as she stepped out of the flimsy material.

What did he want?

His rising cock made the answer pretty clear.

She glanced at Matt, but he only smiled, easing himself into a comfortable position in the pool. The watcher wanted to watch—and *she* wanted Tim.

Tim planted a kiss on her thigh. "May I?" he asked, teasing his fingers up the inside of her leg.

She hesitated.

"Don't deny yourself something I really want to do," he coaxed.

"You can't turn off the bossy part, can you?" Erin shuffled her shirt higher again, twisting so Matt had an unobstructed view.

"You don't mind," Tim muttered, leaning in and nuzzling her belly. "Jeez, so soft. So perfect. I need to taste you."

He eased his fingers through her curls, and right about then, Erin gave up worrying about who was in charge. This was all about sensation, especially as he found her clit and stroked it gently, leaned in close and applied his tongue.

Erin braced herself the best she could as Tim buried his face against her and thrust his tongue into her pussy. He planted his hands on her ass to hold her in place as he licked greedily, throwing her body to the edge of pleasure far more rapidly than she'd expected.

It wasn't just his touch. It was being watched as well.

Hell, it was everything leading up to now, and Erin confessed, "I liked getting to order you around a little, but I like you in control even better."

The sound of splashing water briefly drew her attention to the side, where Matt was now out of the pool and moving closer.

What was next? What did the situation call for? Did she ask Matt to join them again, or let him simply keep observing? Coaxing her brain to focus while Tim went down on her was nearly impossible, but she tried. She threaded her fingers into his hair and used him as an anchor to stay vertical.

Matt paced around them, one hand wrapped around his cock as he pumped lazily. His gaze dropped over her, falling onto Tim, totally mesmerized as he continued his slow journey.

That was when she noticed it. A gaze that lingered for a second longer than necessary. A little more heat aimed in a direction she hadn't expected. She checked again, but it was real. Matt wasn't just getting off on being there while she and Tim fooled around.

He was watching Tim with something near enthrallment in his eyes.

A ripple went through Erin. A sensation she wasn't used to at all—

Jealousy.

Followed immediately by shock, because Tim seemed unaware that his friend not only liked to watch, he liked to watch *Tim*.

The lack of awareness seemed so out of character—he was the one who always knew exactly where everyone was. What they were doing. What they needed. But he seemed blind to the fact that his good friend was as turned on by being next to him as by her presence.

Did she point it out? Was that the next decision to make? Images leapt to mind of all that powerful male flesh around her connecting intimately, and suddenly it wasn't just Tim's talented tongue flicking in slow circles over her clit that made her moan.

Tim and Matt fooling around? God, part of her would give anything to watch some of that.

A near-paniclike rush hit her, of the responsibility she held. What if the revelation wasn't welcome on Tim's part? He'd said she should never be afraid of sexual attraction, but he'd never mentioned that he was okay with exploring that kind of new territory. Maybe he did know Matt was interested, only had chosen not to act on the attraction for his own reasons.

On the other hand, what if *Matt* had been holding on to this information for years? Perhaps he didn't want to bring a new element into a relationship that had been around for a long time and seemed rock solid in spite of how seldom they got together.

Suddenly there were no scenarios that didn't end in someone being hurt, and the hugeness of the decision became nearly overwhelming. She wanted the best for them, which meant her first impulse of asking Matt to join them and working toward a little guy-on-guy time was not going to happen.

If comprehension built like slowly falling rain, complete understanding hit like a thunderclap. Being in control was about far more than temporary pleasure. It was huge and ominous even while it was exhilarating.

Humbling. Terrifying in terms of not wanting to make a mistake, and deeply humbling to know this was what Tim put into every moment of his time with her.

The entire time she'd debated, the talented man had continued to torment her.

She stroked his hair and fought to keep her feet. He eased his fingers into her, slowly at first as he stretched her. Once they were wet, though, he showed no mercy. Hard, wicked pumps, fingertips curling inside her, driving her to the point of exploding.

Erin's pleasure levels were skyrocketing, but the choice she had to make was clear. This was what Tim needed. What he craved. He'd given her the time with Matt the previous day, but when it came down to it, he wanted her for himself.

His next words confirmed it.

"You like me in charge of your body." Tim tilted his head and caught her gaze, refusing to let her look away. It was the two of them in the room, and no one else. His words rasped like a physical stroke over her skin. "You like it when I push you to the point of pain, easing off just before you lose control. Taking you up again and again until there's nothing left but us. Nothing you want more than me. Fucking you with my fingers. Fucking you with my cock until your legs are shaky, and you're sure you're going to fall over. And I'll fuck you until there's nothing you can do but feel me, everywhere, because you're *mine*."

The unrelenting thrusts mixed with his words—"Oh *God*."

"Say it. You're mine, aren't you?" He pumped slower, adding a third finger and pushing deep inside her, drawing a gasp from her lips. "You're mine, and you love everything I do to you."

"*Yes*. I'm yours."

He put his mouth back on her and sucked her clit hard. The wild pressure combined with his clever mouth and fingers were too much. She clutched his head and shook as she came.

Before the waves were completed he had her over his lap, cock nudging her pussy as he slipped past her folds. He thrust upward, dragging her hips down, and filled her.

Tim paused, Erin continuing to shake around him as the aftershocks of her orgasm squeezed him tight. His head fell back and a low groan escaped. "Sweet fuck, that's good," he moaned.

Through her hazy vision, Erin caught a glimpse of Matt, now seated on a chair to one side. Their eyes met, and a flash of understanding settled as Matt glanced over at Tim, then back to her. He smiled softly, then rose and left the room.

Matt was the one keeping his attraction on the quiet. He was content with it staying secret.

Then she couldn't focus anymore as Tim raised her hips and found his rhythm, thrusting into her with steady, solid pulses. She clung to his shoulders, relinquishing her power. Accepting the gift of his complete attention as he tore her apart physically with another powerful climax, the two of them shouting as they came.

He took control and, in doing so, put the missing piece of her soul back. The part that had been absent since she'd left him so many years ago.

CHAPTER 27

,,,,,,,,,,,,,,,,,,,,,,,,,,,,,,

The rest of their days off passed in a state of lazy relaxation and easy companionship. He and Erin hadn't come right out and talked things through after that explosive session by the pool, but they hadn't had to. Not yet.

Tim had never been more grateful for Matt. For the maturity and strength his friend had shown as he eased back on the sexual overtures, following Tim's lead as promised.

Erin . . .

She continued to observe everyone around her far closer than Tim had ever seen her before. More importantly, though, she softened. Not a diminishing of her bold and sometimes demanding attitude, and she didn't lose her wicked sense of humour, but when he turned his gaze on her, it was if there were no longer any walls between them.

She'd accepted him as he was. Accepted herself, and was willing to move toward accepting *them*.

Somehow in the midst of the casual conversations and board games the three of them shared, the sense of *more* continued to grow. More of them—of Tim and Erin as a couple. The sex didn't stop, the games and the exploring didn't stop, but even the casual activities seemed more intimate.

It wasn't about exploring the limits, not like it had been when they were young. He wasn't in a hurry to do anything else too wild sexually, not for a bit. Watching her tentative but complete surrendering of her trust was enough of an incredible thing. Like stepping into a honeymoon stage of their new relationship, fresh and intoxicating without the need to add additional kink.

Tuesday afternoon they stood at the front door of the rental waiting for Matt's ride to arrive to take him to Calgary. Erin kissed him full on the lips, and he tangled her up for a moment in his arms, enveloping her in a huge bear hug and squeezing tight.

"I'm going to miss you," Erin confessed.

"Door is always open, even if Tim's not with you," Matt promised. "And I will be coming to Banff in the near future. You can count on it."

Tim held out a hand, but when Matt took it, Tim pulled his friend close and gave him another enormous hug, patting him heartily on the back, doing that guy thing. "You're one in a million. Don't be a stranger."

"Are you kidding?" Matt glanced at Erin and winked, a moment passing between them.

Tim kept silent, then waved his friend off, Erin tucked against his side.

The return trip to Banff passed quickly. Erin curled up next to him on the bench seat, her fingers linked with his. "Thank you for introducing me to Matt. He's a good friend."

It was as good a time as any to clear one issue up.

"He'd like to be more than friends." Tim smiled as Erin lifted her head from his shoulder to turn to stare at him. "You figured that out, didn't you?"

"Yes, but . . ." She shifted farther away, disbelief on her

face. "He's attracted to you, yet you seemed completely oblivious."

"Because while there's a physical attraction, that's not what Matt really needs. A lifelong friend is far more important than a temporary lover."

Her gaze shifted out the window, as if processing his comment.

Tim adjusted his hand on the wheel, speaking softly. "It's part of knowing what I want as well. He can't give me what I need long term."

"So you pretend not to even notice the hints he's giving?"

"He doesn't usually give hints anymore," Tim admitted. "That was because you were there. Maybe he felt your presence would distract me, and he was safe to show a little more of what he usually keeps hidden."

"Maybe he was hoping for more," Erin pointed out. She caught his eye. "Is he happy?"

"What do you think?"

She stroked his fingers softly. "Yes. Even though he wishes for more, he knows what he's got is very special."

"And I'll never take that from him." Tim squeezed her hand, turning on the signal to head down the center of town toward her house. "Besides, he knew there was someone I'd been hoping to get back together with. Someone who had a special place in my heart."

"Matt knew about me?"

Tim nodded. "Of course. I'd talked about you often."

"Huh."

He pulled in front of Erin's small bungalow, the tall pine trees that lined the block casting shadows over the snow covering her front lawn. He caught her before she could wiggle away to the other side of the truck. Fingers firmly wrapped around the back of her neck, slowly easing her forward until their lips were only inches apart. "Let's get your things, then head to my place. I have some ideas for the evening."

Her kiss was as eager as his. Total involvement, a melting under his touch that made the hurts and time apart fade into nothing but the here and now. Their past was put aside. The future grew brighter by the moment, and that was what he wanted to concentrate on.

Breaking apart to crawl from the truck took effort when all he wanted to do was sit there and neck like some love-besotted teenager. Erin slipped out his door, her fingers still linked in his as if she couldn't get enough of him, either.

Stupid, crazy emotion like he hadn't experienced in years blasted his brain into near incoherency. He scrambled for something to say other than blurting out *I love you* far too soon and with far too little fanfare.

"Someone's shoveled the walks." Tim stifled his groan at the fake perkiness in his comment, then laughed as Erin sounded just as stilted as she replied.

"Since I never know when I'll be gone, I pay the teen next door to shovel and mow."

They grinned at each other, sheer happiness soaking through as Erin led him up the steps and unlocked the door. "It won't take me long to pack a bag."

"You need me to go through the fridge?" Tim asked.

She tossed her keys on the side table, then headed down the hall. "You can look, but there shouldn't be anything rotting. I only shop for fresh stuff a day or two at a time, and our last call-out happened before my shopping day."

He'd just stepped into the kitchen and pulled open the fridge door when a burst of unexpected sound rang from her room.

"Erin, you okay?"

No answer.

Tim moved quickly down the hall only to jerk to a stop as a familiar, but unwelcome, face reappeared.

Ken held a gun straight in front of him, forcing Tim to back up.

Adrenaline and fear shot through him instantly. "Shit."

"Yeah, shit." Ken waved the gun, continuing to close the distance between them. Erin emerged into the hallway, her arms locked behind her as John manhandled her forward.

"Don't hurt her," Tim snapped, a hand raised before him in caution. Erin's eyes had gone wide, her lips a tight line as Tim backed into the living room and the others crowded around him. "I don't know what you're doing here, but we don't want any trouble."

"You should have thought about that before you took off. Now where is it?" Ken asked.

"Not trying to be a smart-ass, but where is what?" Tim frantically rolled through escape options, discarding them as quickly as they came to mind. If it had been only one person with a gun, he might have risked rushing the man, but two?

Waiting was the only option.

Ken kicked the grey-striped backpack Erin had abandoned to the floor the other day. "There was another one of these in the helicopter. Where is it now?"

Erin shook her head. "I don't know for sure. Either in the back of the truck, or at headquarters. I can't remember if that's one of the bags we dropped off the other day."

"Both of you, drop your cell phones."

Ken waited until they'd reluctantly followed his directions.

"Take her outside to check the truck," Ken ordered John before facing Erin. "Don't try anything. Your boyfriend stays with me as insurance."

Tim cleared his throat. "I need to give her the keys for the canopy. They're in my pocket."

"Slowly," Ken said.

"I'm not stupid," Tim assured him. He pulled out the keys and held them in an open palm. "Get whatever it is you need, and go. We just want to get on with our lives, and you're welcome to get on with yours."

Erin took the keys from him, her eyes haunted. They'd

seen John kill a man—Ken had ordered it. It wasn't going to be that easy to simply walk away a second time. But saying that out loud wasn't going to help anyone.

One second, and the world had turned.

Tim watched the laughter and hope in Erin's expression fade to misery. Fear. Tim did the only thing he could. He lied like an ace.

"Do what John tells you. We'll be okay."

The woman he loved stepped outside and took all the warmth with her, leaving him alone with a gun pointed at him, and a horrifying fear that this was one situation he wasn't going to be able to talk his way out of.

Erin moved slowly toward the car, desperately taking in everything around them as John silently escorted her, his grip on her arm steady. She wasn't aware enough of who drove what in her neighborhood to identify an unexpected vehicle, but they had to have gotten from the ranch to Banff somehow.

The gun had disappeared, but she wasn't positive she could escape his hold easily. Breaking his grip and running was out of the question, not with Tim still in the house.

"Do you want me to open the back?" she asked, the keys dangling from her fingers after undoing the two side locks holding down the back canopy window.

"I don't see the pack in there," John snarled, leaning against the truck and glancing in a side window. "Yeah, open it."

She lifted the canopy and dropped the tailgate, but the only things in the back were the two small gym bags they'd had with them on their holiday. "We must have dropped it at headquarters with the rest of the gear from the chopper, but I'm not sure." Desperate to make sure there was a reason for them to stay alive.

John growled his frustration. "Get in the back," he ordered, jerking the keys from her fingers.

Shit. Erin moved slowly, but followed his directions, bruising her knees on the hard metal, bare fingers cold on the chilled truck bed. He put his hand on her hip and shoved, toppling her off balance. By the time she'd made it upright, he'd flicked up the tailgate, dropped the canopy cover, and locked her in. She had plenty of room to move—the canopy cover was as tall as the roof of the truck cab. There were windows on all four sides, but being able to see wasn't reassuring at the moment.

She was still trapped.

"Don't make a fuss. We'll be bringing out your boyfriend, and if we find a group of neighbours gathered, it won't be good for anyone."

John walked back to the house, head pivoting from side to side as he kept an eye on the nearby houses. Erin checked as well, but it was early enough in the day that most of the people in her area were still at work, and there were no children on this section of the block, thank goodness. Last thing she needed was to have kids get involved.

Tim appeared in the doorway, Ken immediately after him. John closed the door, and the three of them headed toward her.

Only Ken split off, taking Tim with him. The two of them got into a second truck parked just down the street, Tim behind the wheel. Erin struggled to see anything that might be helpful—license number, truck model.

Loud banging made her jerk back from the glass.

John scowled in at her. "Stay down. We're going to your headquarters, and if you're telling the truth, we'll be gone in no time. You do anything stupid, I call Ken."

Erin lowered herself into the corner, head below the level of the windows.

John could still see her through the double glass separating the truck cab from the canopy, but she was out of reach. And out of control when he shot forward from the curb with a jolt that rolled her toward the tailgate.

Erin thrust out her arms to brace against the truck sides.

She stayed low, counting corners as John followed Tim. After the first few, though, she got lost when they didn't head in a straight line toward HQ, instead taking smaller residential streets to go through most of town.

There was only so much distance to travel in Banff, though, and they were going to be at the business park end soon enough. What was she going to do?

She crawled on her belly, easing toward the tailgate so she could double-check the canopy locks, but there was no way to disengage them easily from the inside.

The road under the tires switched to gravel, and she knew they were almost there. She checked her watch. Five P.M. There shouldn't be anyone at HQ at this time of day—not with them being on a break.

She risked a peek over the edge as she shuffled to a safer position near the cab, and braced for the brakes to be slammed on.

Alisha's car was in the parking lot, which made sense once their training on the coast registered. There were no signs of anyone else, and Erin's heartbeat slowed one notch. At least more of her friends wouldn't be unnecessarily involved with these crazy people.

John parked, the second vehicle pulling in beside them.

She sat up, hands pressed to the glass. John ignored her as he stepped past, joining with Ken as he led Tim to the front door of the building.

Tim punched in the security code, then glanced over his shoulder a bare second before he was pushed into the building. The three of them vanished from sight, and Erin swore violently.

This was one of those moments when there was no way she could sit and wait. Whatever it was that Ken and John were looking for, they had no reason to worry about keeping Tim safe once they'd found it.

She had to help him.

Erin changed position and put her feet on the canopy cover over the tailgate. Raising both feet at the same time, she slammed her heels into the glass. The entire flap shuddered.

She did it again, harder this time, carefully aiming at the extreme corner where the small turned lock was the only thing holding the lid down.

With a horrid noise, the lock broke and the glass twisted. She was still trapped, but there was a small space open between the two closures.

Erin scrambled forward, put her shoulder to the glass, and with it wedged open, snuck her hand out to undo the tailgate. The metal slammed downward loudly, and she rolled out as quickly as possible. It might be wasted energy to hide that she was free, but she closed the tailgate before twisting her way to the side of the truck and staying out of sight from any casual glance out the HQ windows.

Half the battle. She was free. Now she had to get into HQ and find a way to save Tim.

Only that.

She ran for the side of the building, her feet sinking into the snow on every step. There were plenty of tracks, though, and she followed a set as the snow got deeper. Not until she was safely out of sight up against the side of the large industrially built structure did she stop to make some plans.

There was more than one way to get into the building, including doors that would set off the silent alarm Marcus had installed. Tim had shut off the main-door alarm, but she'd bet anything that was the only one he'd turned off. The snow complicated matters, but it was more her concern of wanting to go quickly that made her breathing hitch and her heart race.

How long before they found the backpack and whatever they were looking for? How long before Tim became a burden to deal with?

Erin slipped to the hangar door, pausing before she reached the spot when the motion-sensor light would be triggered. Instead, she carefully climbed on the storage units stacked outside the door, moving upward as close to the building as possible until she could reach out and unscrew the bulb.

Down on the ground again, she struggled to open the storage combination lock in the dark, fumbling as she squinted at the tiny, faint numbers. She got the door open and rushed in, tapping her fingers on the shelves until she'd found the flashlight stored there.

Her other prize? The spare key for the door off the training-yard side.

Silence lay thick over the industrial area with only the rare car driving through other buildings, their tires muffled by the snow on the road. The noise of the Trans-Canada Highway was far enough away to be nothing more than a faint hum.

The sense of being alone was nearly overwhelming.

You're never alone. You're in my heart.

Tim's voice whispered inside her head, and it was more than enough to drive the courage she needed to the forefront again. Erin climbed over the chain-link fence defining the training area and made her way to the door. Once she got inside, ideas of how to help Tim were still foggy, but she was going to do the one thing she knew would help—set off the alarm—and the rest she'd make up as she went along.

Slowly, silently, she turned the key. The door opened an inch at a time as she pushed it, careful to slip inside before the wind could pick up and announce her presence.

On the wall beside her, the small green light that shone when the alarm was armed had turned to a faintly blinking red.

Erin closed the door behind her and stepped into the dark unknown.

CHAPTER 28

‚‚‚‚‚‚‚‚‚‚‚‚‚‚‚‚‚‚‚‚‚‚‚‚‚‚‚‚‚‚‚‚‚

Tim moved as slowly as he could without prompting a shove between the shoulder blades that would send him to the ground a second time.

He'd fallen to his knees in the moments after entering Lifeline, Ken and John looming over him. The temptation to lash out with a leg sweep was strong, and if it had only been him to worry about, he'd have taken the risk. But with Erin supposedly trapped in the back of the truck, he exercised a little caution, until he'd given her enough time to get out and go for help.

Right now it was a waiting game. He'd gotten stuck in the back of a truck once by drunken friends who thought it was a hilarious joke. Even with his blood alcohol running on high, it hadn't taken much to figure out a way past the locks. Erin should be out in no time.

Once she was free, he calculated it would take another five minutes to run to the highway and flag someone down. Use their cell phone and get the police on the way. If he could stall for a good fifteen minutes, the two assholes tormenting him would be out of his and Erin's life for a long time.

"Find the damn backpack," Ken demanded again.

Only the hall lights lit their path. "If I could turn on more lights—"

"Nice try, but no. We don't need anyone spotting the place lit up."

"It's not that strange," Tim insisted. "My truck is outside, and this is a search-and-rescue base. People come and go at all hours around here."

"Just find the bag."

John stepped past him into the staff area and started going through lockers, jerking contents to the floor. Heavy coats, personal storage bags, all of it a mess underfoot.

"That first storage area you checked—is it the only one in the building?" Ken asked.

"No, I'm working my way through them logically. It's how we do a search—"

He bit back his grunt of pain as Ken hit him in the back of the head with a fist. "I'm not interested in the lessons, flyboy. Think. Where would they have put that pack?"

"Do you know what was in it? I mean other than what you're looking for?" Tim moved toward the second storage center. "Ropes? First-aid supplies? That makes a difference where someone would unpack it for storage."

Meanwhile his brain was ticking down an imaginary timer. *Erin should be free by now. She should be nearly at the road by now . . .*

Ken paused. "Plastic bags filled with gel. Water bottles," he offered reluctantly.

Shit. Tim nodded slowly as if deliberating hard, careful to keep his expression neutral. This one was too easy if the ass used his brain instead of the damn gun. "Definitely storage area," he lied. "That's where the extra medical supplies like that are kept."

He opened the door to the oversized room and stepped

forward, jerking to a halt as he spotted an arm disappearing around the shelving stack in the right corner.

My *God*, that was Erin. His heart raced again. What the *fuck* was she doing here instead of getting help? He paused as if trying to figure out the right direction to go, but his brain was spinning. This changed everything.

Keeping his cool in stressful situations wasn't usually an issue. Not losing his shit over the woman he loved being back in danger? That was tougher.

Academy Award–quality acting time. He pointed to the left. "Best guess is over here."

Ken motioned him toward the large set of storage lockers, and Tim went willingly. He opened one set of doors at a time, pushing aside the front items. Taking things down carefully and putting them back into place.

John was still missing, and from the sounds in the background, he was still in the staff room causing chaos.

"There. What's that?" Ken asked as Tim swung open the doors on the transport bag cabinet.

"This is where the large bags are kept," Tim explained. "It might have been misplaced in here." It was also the location for his medical bag. One step forward, and he pulled aside the front couple of bags, a huge sense of relief sweeping in as the brilliant red of the cross on the label shone at him—

Then vanished as the room flashed into darkness.

Tim ignored the shouts behind him and focused on dragging open the zippered compartment under his fingers.

Erin slipped her hands off the master power switch, turning without a pause toward the main area of HQ.

She'd seen Tim and Ken in storage, leaving John as the one now fumbling in the dark in the staff area. With the set of night vision goggles she'd pulled off the shelf, she had a definite advantage, adding to her knowledge of the building layout.

Before Ken's shout of dismay had faded, she was at the staff room door, the glowing green form of a body shuffling toward her with his arms extended to the sides.

Erin gave in to her frustrations and lashed out with a rapid kick to his chest. With no advance warning to brace himself, John went flying backward, a loud crash sounding as he hit the floor.

She grabbed the door and slammed it shut, engaging the lock. Two steps put her at the side of the tall metal filing cabinet.

With mental apologies to Marcus for making a mess, she put her shoulder to the top. It took two rocks to set the heavy object in motion, but once it started, it didn't stop until it, too, hit the floor with an enormous clang that echoed off the walls.

"Don't move," Ken ordered, his shout ringing in the storage area.

Bullshit on that. Her heart might be about to pound out of her chest, but she wasn't done.

Erin grabbed a spray can from the shelf as she stepped carefully down the hall. The open door to the storage area was up ahead on the right. She walked with her arm extended in front of her, finger on the top of the plastic plunger. Her hand was steady, and she forced herself to breathe slowly, calming herself as she took the final steps forward.

The ghostly images of two bodies appeared, one close to her, one by the shelves. All three of them silent, only the pounding of John's fists on the staff door drifting down to them.

Staccato. Harsh.

Ken adjusted his hand to the side, as if trying to track Tim in the dark.

Tim remained silent. The glow of his outline decreased in size as he got down on the floor. Smart man—smaller target for Ken if he did take a shot.

Only Ken was backing up, one hand running along the

wall. Was he looking for the exit? Trying to escape? Erin pressed herself back against the hall, waiting until the moment was right . . .

The keys stored on the wall jingled under Ken's fingers. Tim was on his feet, body doubling in size, arm rising.

As if observing a slow-motion video, Erin spotted her mistake. With her move forward, and Tim's adjustment along the floor, it wasn't only Ken who stood in the potential line of fire. If that was a gun in Tim's hand, she was hooped. She had only an instant to react. She shouted the first thing that came to mind.

"Spider."

Layered on top of each other came the responses.

Ken whirled toward her. A shot rang out. Erin pressed the top of the can.

Chaos broke.

CHAPTER 29

''''''''''''''''''''''''''''''''

Tim had been in soul-shredding spots before. He'd leapt off cliffs, for fun and for work. He'd made the occasional wrong decision that had left him seconds from potential death. None of those situations compared to the nightmare unfolding in the darkness before him.

High-pitched screams sounded, one after the other. A tortured, skin-crawling sound that had his heart in his throat as he lowered his unfired weapon to his hip.

Erin.

Another clatter, metal on concrete, and everything that could have gone wrong flashed like a whip across his nerves.

"Tim, are you okay?" Erin called over the persistent cries.

Thank God. Tim finally took a breath.

And tasted pepper.

"Shit, Erin." Tim squeezed his eyes shut as he inched toward where the exit was. There was nothing to see in the pitch black anyway. "I'm fine. You got Ken contained?"

"I got his gun. John's locked up. Police are on the way." She sneezed violently.

Tim wrapped his fingers around the doorknob. "Watch your eyes, I'm opening the door."

"Roger."

Fresh air pushed the pepper scent away from him and farther into HQ. A narrow beam of light snuck in the door off the distant climbing tower beacon, like the curtain going up at the theater to dramatically reveal the current setting. Ken on his knees, his fists pressed hard to his eyes as he rocked and wailed. In the distance John had found something metal and was smashing it into the door again and again.

Walking toward him, Erin held Ken's gun in her left hand, a can of bear spray in her right. Her forehead was hidden under a set of night vision goggles, the viewing scopes currently tilted toward the ceiling. The cocky smile gracing her lips was one hundred percent Erin.

If he hadn't already been there, he would have fallen head over heels in love. "You're so fucking beautiful."

She laughed, a bright sound that smashed away the last of the fear in his soul. The gun was carefully put aside before she threw herself into his arms and kissed him, cold fresh air whirling around them as Ken continued to serenade them with his crying.

The life-and-death adrenaline that had filled Tim's veins for the last thirty minutes transformed into heat of another kind. He wrapped his arms around her and took what she freely offered.

When she pulled back, he stroked a finger over her cheek. "Smart-ass. *Spider?*"

"I wanted you to stop what you were doing, but thought it might confuse Ken a little more than simply shouting *stop.*"

He shuddered involuntarily again. "Darkness, a gun in my hand, and you bring up spiders. Damn it, woman . . ."

Blue-and-red lights flashed in his peripheral vision, interrupting her soothing, yet teasing apology. Their backup had arrived, running on silent mode.

"The police. I'll go let them in," Erin offered, holding out the goggles.

Tim glanced at Ken, but the man wasn't even attempting to get off the floor. "I'll turn the main power back on and meet you at the front door."

By the time he'd set the panel back to rights, two full teams stood in the Lifeline gathering room, waiting for orders. Their main contact within the RCMP looked up as Tim stepped forward, Erin already explaining what had happened. Marcus stepped through the doors and joined them.

James nodded, motioning to his teams. "Get the man in the staff room first. Once he's secured, move the man in the back, and take them to the station."

"Yes, sir."

With things under control, Tim headed in a new direction, his fingers linked with Erin's. He wasn't letting her go any time soon, but he was curious.

"Where are you going?" James asked.

"For a snack." Tim squeezed her fingers lightly.

Erin raised a brow. "Come again?"

"The bag they wanted. We should make sure James gets it, right?"

"You knew where it was all along?"

"No." Tim slipped into the staff kitchen, glancing around. "Not until Ken told me the bag held some water bottles and plastic bags filled with gel. Could have been first-aid supplies, but more likely if it was a grey-striped bag about the size of your clothes bag—"

Another burst of laughter broke free. "Our lunch sack? They wanted that?"

Marcus and James followed on their heels. "These are the guys you rescued off the mountain?" Marcus asked.

"And they came back for something we accidentally took,

yes." Tim pulled open drawers. "A backpack. They must have shoved whatever they were transporting that was important enough to kill for into the bag while Erin was refueling the chopper at the cabin airstrip."

A far more somber Erin joined him in his search. "And then when we took off in the middle of the night, we took the bag with us."

"Bad planning on their part," James noted. "Is that it?"

Tim turned as Erin pulled the bag out of the side cupboard. "That's it. Open it up."

She laid it on the table and unzipped every compartment. Nothing.

A frown creased her forehead as she looked across the table at him. "We dropped off the bag. Someone went through and emptied it, putting everything back where it belonged, including the bag, which means they should have found whatever was in here . . ."

"It makes no sense," James pulled the bag closer, running his fingers through all the pockets, pressing on the seams. "It doesn't seem likely that they'd have sewn anything right onto the bag."

"They didn't have time for that," Erin agreed.

"Or written something?" Tim asked. "But what would be that valuable . . . ?"

He was looking into Erin's eyes when the idea struck. She must have thought of something as well, as her eyes widening. "We guessed the flight originated from somewhere in the Northwest Territories?"

She was going the same direction he was. "Red said he was hired to transport a bag, nothing else."

They both looked at the fridge. "You think?" Tim asked.

"It's the only thing that makes sense." Erin opened the door and peeked inside. "Jackpot."

She pulled out two oversized water bottles.

Tim went for a drawer, bringing out the largest pot they had in the place and placing it on the table. "Open one."

He stuck his hand into the pot, palm up, and waited as Erin poured the water over his fingers, the steady *glug, glug* of the bottle emptying the only sound.

Something hit his palm, and he swore softly.

"What's that?" Marcus asked.

Erin tipped the final water out, splashing a little on the table as she put the empty bottle aside and leaned over to examine Tim's hand. "The one thing easily carried out of the north worth killing someone over."

Tim lifted his hand to display a glistening pile of rough-cut diamonds.

CHAPTER 30

,,,,,,,,,,,,,,,,,,,,,,,,,,,,,,,,

They still had their fingers twined together when James gave the go-ahead to leave the RCMP station.

Marcus exited the building with them, shaking his head. "You two just about done with the excitement?" he asked.

"You want to give us more vacation time, we're game," Erin teased.

Their boss gave Tim a slap on the back. "I gave you a vacation, and you got involved with diamond smugglers. How about you just stay put for a while. Might be safer."

"Deal."

Erin tucked up against Tim's side as they got into his truck, the position as natural as breathing. He kissed her temple, but other than that he didn't say anything. Her brain had reached the point of overload, so silence suited her nicely while she relaxed and let him figure out where they needed to go.

It didn't matter. If he took her home, she'd pack a bag. If

he took her straight to his place, she'd steal a shirt from his closet and wear that until she found something else.

The one thing she didn't expect was for him to drive them back to Lifeline HQ.

"Tim?"

He put the truck into park and stared ahead, his expression serious enough she didn't want to interrupt. Outside the building more of the ground cover had been trampled by the RCMP, but a fresh layer of snow was slowly covering the tracks that wandered in all directions.

A fresh, clean start.

It was pitch-black out, the falling snow visible in the lights shining like spotlights. Fluffy flakes landed on her lashes as Tim tugged her from the truck and headed back up the steps, his hand wrapped carefully around her fingers as he guided her forward.

"Don't set off the alarm," she teased.

"Poor overworked RCMP."

"Poor Marcus."

They grinned at each other, slipping into the main area. "You brought us back so we could start cleaning up the mess in the staff room," she guessed.

"Bullshit on that. I plan to shovel it all into a pile and tell Tripp it's a training exercise in searching for small objects."

She poked him in the side. "He'll never fall for that."

"What about Anders? Or maybe Alisha?"

Erin snickered, then fell silent as he led her into the back room where so recently they'd stood under totally different circumstances.

Tim faced her, examining her from top to bottom with a careful thoroughness that she'd come to expect. She let herself indulge in the same satisfying scrutiny. There were cuts on his knuckles that he'd gotten at some point since the second appearance of their kidnappers. A faint darkening on his cheek as a bruise surfaced.

She stroked the spot gently. "Ken hit you."

"He didn't like the suggestions I made regarding what I'd do to his guts if he laid a hand on you again."

"Oh, Tim."

He covered her fingers with his own. "I was perfectly polite, and not a bit over the top. But the truth was . . . in the end, you saved me."

"We did what we had to do," Erin insisted.

Tim eased away from her, his hand dropping to his side as he paused beside the storage shelves. "I don't know any other way to tell you this than straight out, and straight up. I love you, kitten. Claws and all."

Erin held her breath. The intense passion in his blue eyes was enough to burn her where she stood.

"Hell, I love your claws most of all." Tim took her hand and kissed her knuckles before flipping her brain offline as he sank to one knee.

"Tim?" The word whispered out through a throat gone tight with emotion at the love shining up at her.

"Whatever it takes to convince you, I'll do it. Whatever promises I need to make, I'll make them." He took a deep breath, his hands growing unsteady. "I sat here in the dark, Erin, and considered a life without you, and I didn't want to have to face that reality. And then you showed up, with all the fire you have inside you. The passion for life and the power you bring to whatever you do, and I knew in here I couldn't live without you another minute."

He put a fist to his chest, knocking solidly.

"You don't have to live without me," Erin promised. "We belong together. Whatever that *together* looks like, we'll figure out the same way we figured everything else out."

"With pepper spray?"

The joke came at the perfect moment to stop her from bursting into unwanted tears. "Do you plan these things in advance, or is perfect comedic timing a God-given gift?"

Tim lifted a hand and tilted it from side to side. "A bit of both. Now take off your clothes."

The change of topic didn't surprise her one bit, which also made her laugh. She pulled her top over her head, folding it carefully and placing it on the shelf beside him. Taunting him as she brushed past him on each trip, stroking his shoulders and arms with naked skin.

He didn't move, except to reach behind him and pull something from the shelf.

Erin turned, stark naked, to see what he'd found.

Tim pulled the packaging from a brand-new rope, his eyes wild with fire as he rose and closed in on her. "I have something for you."

She placed a hand on his hip, slipping her fingers over his groin. "I bet you do."

It was his turn to smile. "No agendas. Nothing but Erin and Tim, and what makes us happy. In work, or in play, we do what we need to. Agreed?"

This she could wholeheartedly agree to. Finally, and without reservation. "Yes."

He pulled her against him, the rough texture of his clothing sending an instant thrill through her system. A head rush like no other, edgy and dangerous as they played right there where they could have lost each other forever. Tim lifted her chin with a single finger so their lips met, and the fire she'd seen in his eyes consumed her all over again.

Possessive, and being possessed. There was nothing more that she could have asked for.

They were both breathless when he let her lips free, her fingers fisted into the fabric of his T-shirt tight enough to threaten the seams. Tim panted for a moment before finding his control.

Deep, dark. The command came out exactly how she wanted to hear it.

"Tell me you love me," Tim ordered, his lips shifting against the tender skin of her neck, as if he couldn't bear to move any farther away. "Tell me you want me all the time, and in all the ways I can take you. I need to know you're mine."

Her response came easily. "I love you."

She scraped her nails down his chest, pushing the boundaries. Pushing him because she could, and because she knew that once he took control?

Hmmmm.

Erin looked him straight in the eye, letting everything she felt inside show on her face. So many years lost, so many doubts that had haunted her, and they'd all fallen aside as the truth shouted louder than anything. She could be strong *and* submissive.

She could be herself.

"I love you, and I'm yours." She caught the rope he still held in his fingers and tugged it lightly. "Now tie me up and fuck me, you bastard."

His slow chuckle rolled over her, making her skin more sensitive in anticipation. He caught her wrists and trapped them behind her back. "I thought you'd never ask."

An Adrenaline Search & Rescue Novel

NEW YORK TIMES BESTSELLING AUTHOR

Vivian Arend

When unexplained accidents begin happening to the Lifeline team, their newfound unity may be their only hope for survival...

LOOK FOR IT IN PAPERBACK

VivianArend.com
facebook.com/VivianArend
penguin.com

M1370T0913